M000289761

LAURA'S QUEST

Penelope Gladwell

ISBN 978-1-63630-124-2 (Paperback)
ISBN 978-1-63630-125-9 (Digital)

Copyright © 2020 Penelope Gladwell
All rights reserved
First Edition

All rights reserved. No part of this publication may be reproduced, distributed, or transmitted in any form or by any means, including photocopying, recording, or other electronic or mechanical methods without the prior written permission of the publisher. For permission requests, solicit the publisher via the address below.

Covenant Books, Inc.
11661 Hwy 707
Murrells Inlet, SC 29576
www.covenantbooks.com

For Jennifer, my gift and my heart

ACKNOWLEDGMENTS

I grew up in South Jersey and our extended family spread through a cluster of communities that were much like the fictional Laurel Hill. It was there that I learned to appreciate the "Quaker ways" of peaceful coexistence and silent waiting, along with other expressions of the Christian faith. Scouting and camping introduced me to the culture and spirituality of the Lenni-Le-nah-pe, part of the Delaware Indian nation living in New Jersey when European settlers first arrived. Our summer weekends were spent as a family in the Pine Barrens, a hauntingly beautiful region with teaberry bushes, exotic wild flowers, and sandy roads leading to spring-fed cedar lakes. Day trips to fish on Long Beach Island or Barnegat Bay were regular occurrences as well. Philadelphia also looms large in my childhood memories, with its department stores, museums, historical sites, sports teams, musical venues, and restaurants. I hope this tale honors all that was good about the places where I grew up and the place that I still think of as "home."

For the works of M. R. Harrington, rich resources for the customs and lore of the Delaware and other native people;

For my fellow writers Lynn Swanson, Cynthia Kehr, and Donna Watson, who keep encouraging me to put my stories down on paper;

For Donna Talbert (1949–2019), whose story connected to mine and reminded me that life is filled with extraordinary experiences;

For Marilys Gilbert for sharing her expertise in medicine and law;

For Kathie Houchens, my gifted sister, who nudged me to explore the ecological plight of Toms River and the gardens of Mt. Holly;

For my husband Dave, who waited patiently for his supper many nights while I finished writing one more paragraph,

I am grateful beyond measure for your gifts to Laura's story and to me.

While I stood there I saw more than I can tell
and I understood more than I saw;
For I was seeing in a sacred manner
the shapes of all things in the spirit,
and the shape of all shapes
as they must live together like one being...
And I saw that it was holy.

—Black Elk

PROLOGUE

It was not yet dawn on the farm, and a shimmery mist lingered over the pond. A tall figure stood on the bank, gazing across dark water toward the meadow on the other side. It was an old man wearing baggy overalls, sturdy boots, and a denim barn jacket. He was leaning on a cane, facing the direction of the rising sun, and slowly reciting a Native American prayer.

> Thanks be to our Mother Earth, who sustains us
> Thanks be to the rivers and streams for our water
> Thanks be for herbs and plants to cure our illnesses
> Thanks be to the moon and stars who give light
> when the sun goes away
> Thanks be to the sun who returns each day to bless us
> Thanks be to the Great Spirit, who is all goodness

Lawrence Gardner had been walking to this spot and speaking into the stillness for the past several months. He was waiting for a word, a thought that would resolve the uneasiness he felt in his soul. *I am running out of time.* But as a good Quaker, he trusted the silence to calm him. His own breath would bring the message of the Great Spirit to him.

On this morning, as the sun climbed above the horizon and its light began to glint through the trees, the watery haze dispersed more quickly than usual. So did the old man's doubts about what he had to do. As he made his way back to the house, the unambiguous instructions came from beyond and settled in his mind. He was to act with courage and go forward with the plan. He was to telephone Laura.

CHAPTER 1

The phone rang at the Marshall family home. It was an early afternoon in August, and Laura was sitting at one end of the deck jotting notes on a legal pad. Her two daughters were seated at a small table having a tea party with a stuffed bear and a rag doll. Seven-year old Noel rushed inside to answer the plaintive ringing. "It's for you, Mommy," she called using her grown-up tone. Then she added, "It's someone with a really shaky voice."

Laura stood and carried the tablet with her into the kitchen.

"Oh, hello!" Laura recognized the quavering speech on the line. "How are you, Uncle Lawrence?"

Laura immediately envisioned the farm in South Jersey where her mother, Christina Andrews, had grown up and where Lawrence Gardner, her mother's uncle, still lived. She pictured the gravel road meandering through an old apple orchard to the three-story brick house which stood in the center of the property. The front porch had been an inviting place, she recalled, with its whitewashed pillars, wicker furniture, and hanging baskets overflowing with trailing geraniums and ivy. Casement windows with tall wooden shutters graced the ground floor, and at the second-story windows, lacy bedroom curtains would always flutter in the breeze. Dormers poked out from a red tin roof, allowing bits of sunlight to slip into what Laura thought was a spacious attic. Stately chimneys graced each end of the main house. It had seemed like a castle to Laura when she had seen it for the first time as a young girl.

So many memories! Picking and eating raspberries from the canes that grew beside the back porch and helping "Uncle Lawrence," as Laura was told to call him, when he weeded the herb bed. She could still recollect the aroma of thyme, oregano, and savory sprigs crushed between her fingers. There had been a vegetable garden too: tomatoes, beets, and leaf lettuce, all planted in neat rows.

This man was someone with whom she rarely spoke, however. They had exchanged greeting cards and sent short written notes through the years, but they had not actually had a conversation for some time, perhaps since her mother had died. As Laura listened to Lawrence's unsteady words on the phone that afternoon, she braced herself for bad news she was sure would be coming. Her great-uncle was past ninety and living alone. Although he probably considered himself fit as a fiddle, she knew it was only a matter of time until his health or his mind would fail. Perhaps this call was to alert her to some condition he had acquired or, worse, to announce his impending death due to a grim diagnosis.

But to her relief, the conversation turned out *not* to be health related. Lawrence had been doing some "cleaning out," as he put it. Would she be able to come help him sort through a few bins and boxes? He added, "Might be things of your mom's still here that you'd like to have."

At the time her mother died, Laura had been pregnant with her first child and had given birth just a few weeks later. That period of time was still a blur in Laura's memory. So it had been left to Lawrence and his lawyer to handle the settling of any of Christina's personal property connected to the farm in New Jersey.

"Really? More papers?" Laura queried. "I thought you took care of all that."

"Well, last month, we had some squirrels nesting in the crawl space under the eaves in the attic," he explained. "The exterminator pulled out a few boxes I had forgotten about. And then the other day, I was puttering around in one of the outbuildings and came on an old trunk I can't remember ever seeing before. Anyway, I just thought if you could break away from your work for a couple of days, it would be a big help to me."

Laura exhaled. She didn't realize she had been holding her breath. How nice that her great-uncle was strong enough to want to entertain company. And she was intrigued by the prospect of discovering some precious belongings that her mother might have left behind. A diary, perhaps, or some jewelry or a native American relic. Laura's heart felt light. Of course she would go! The rest of the conversation was spent working out the details of when Lawrence expected her to arrive and where she would stay.

"The room that was your grandmother's is still the coolest place this time of the summer," commented the old man. "I'll have it all fresh and tidy by the time you arrive." Was Laura imagining it, or did her great-uncle's voice strengthen as they talked? She realized she was smiling as she placed the receiver back in its cradle.

That evening, after her family had finished eating dinner, Laura served their favorite raspberry gelatin dessert with dollops of whipped cream and told her husband, Calvin, about the call. As she shared her tentative plans, Cal could not have been more enthusiastic! The couple was fortunate to have careers with flexible work schedules, making it possible to respond to opportunities like this. Noel had listened to every word of her parents' conversation with great interest and then begged to be allowed to accompany her mother.

"Please. I will be so good, and I can be a helper. Really, I can." Laura looked at Cal for support. He was sensitive to Laura's need for occasional "mommy breaks," and this seemed to qualify as one. Without missing a beat, he suggested that while their mom was in New Jersey, he could take the girls to Pittsburgh. Perhaps they would visit their friends Ben and Nicola Simmons. Nicola had worked with Laura's mother and was also Noel's godmother. That was a special bond between their families. Noel had pouted at first when she heard her dad's suggestion. Then after a moment, her cloudy expression brightened.

"Well, would they take us to the zoo?" There had been innovative renovations to the animal habitats at that facility the previous year, and Cal had mentioned going there as a family the next time they visited Pittsburgh. Little Marial, just three years old, chimed in with a cherubic echo.

"Zoo. Zoo. Zoo," she repeated, rapping the table with her dessert spoon.

"Hmm, maybe a picnic in Highland Park, too," suggested Cal. He would phone Ben that evening to make the arrangements. Laura gave her husband a subtle "thumbs-up" and winked.

"That sounds like a wonderful idea," Laura responded. "I'll enjoy my time working with Uncle Lawrence much more if I know you all are having fun together."

Cal and Laura cleaned up the dishes while Noel took her sister to find their picture books, the ones with wild jungle animals like they might see at the zoo. Eventually Cal put his arm around Laura's waist as she dried her hands on the dishtowel.

Laura leaned against her husband. If her mother had lived, Laura was sure her daughters would have heard many stories about life on the farm in Laurel Hill from her. As it was, they knew nothing of their grandmother Christina's childhood.

The Gardner women were all headstrong and stalwart, and Laura wanted to be able to tell the girls about their ancestors. *If there are some old pictures of my mom or her parents on the farm, I will bring them back to show to the girls.* Uncle Lawrence was Laura's only connection now to the Gardners. She felt a sudden sense of urgency to glean all she could learn about her family. She was worried that she might be running out of time.

Giving his wife a reassuring hug, Cal went off to phone their friends in Pittsburgh. Laura found the girls and helped get them ready for bed. As she kissed each one good night and switched on their night-light, she kept wondering what treasures might be waiting at Uncle Lawrence's place.

CHAPTER 2

One week had passed since the unexpected phone call from her great-uncle, and here was Laura at last, waiting in her car on the Ben Franklin Bridge just outside Philadelphia. "'Welcome to the Garden State.'" Laura read the sign out loud. The clear bright sky precisely matched her mood. Laura was headed to Laurel Hill, the township surrounding the community of Chester Town where her mother grew up.

From the minute she had backed out of her own driveway in the Harrisburg suburbs that morning, Laura had been going over in her mind what she could remember about this family of hers. She was the last child in her line of the Gardner clan, a Quaker family who came from England to the New World in the 1600s to escape religious persecution. She was going to be staying on the farm where the first settlers had lived, and which had belonged to Gardners ever since. She would be sleeping the bedroom of Marial Gardner Martin. Laura's grandmother was known to have had a special way with animals as a little girl. She was hired part-time by old Doc Henderson, the local veterinarian, while she was still in high school. He encouraged her to go on to college, and that was how Marial Martin became one of the first women to receive a doctorate in veterinary medicine. Eventually, she took over his practice and he retired.

Laura's mother, Christina, also flourished growing up in that pastoral setting. She had loved talking about living on the farm. Her stories were so real that as a child Laura always imagined she heard the sounds of chickens clucking in the yard and pigs oinking in their pen. However, Laura knew she was not cut out to be a farm girl. Her drive that day had taken her through the Amish region of Pennsylvania. When the strong smell of freshly applied manure seeped into the car, she was even more positive she would never be comfortable raising a family in the middle of barns and silos.

The Gardners who settled in New Jersey, however, knew nothing else but animal husbandry and farming. They learned quickly to rely on the knowledge of the Lenni-Le-nah-pe, a branch of the Delaware tribe who were already living in the area. Each generation developed stronger bonds with the native people. There was a time when the family needed to lease some of their acreage in order to keep the farm viable. Without a second thought, Laura's grandmother met with the Le-nah-pe elders for advice. A few months later, people from the tribe living in Ohio agreed to move back to Laurel Hill and take over the crop production. *Would any of their descendants still live in the area?* Laura wondered.

Marial lived her entire life on the farm. Her brother Lawrence, Laura's great uncle, was employed by the post office in town. He only moved back to live with his sister at the old homestead after he retired. Christina was in Pittsburgh by that time and returned only occasionally for holiday weekends or summer visits. But she never lost her love of the woodlands, the meadows, the plowed fields, and pine forests. In fact, Laura was named for the plentiful bay laurel shrubs that grew wild in the undergrowth of the pine forests surrounding the farm. It seemed that memories of Laurel Hill were a touchstone for Christina whenever she needed to center herself or regain her peace of mind. But it was never her intention to return there to live.

Laura became aware that as she drove along she was humming a lilting, rhythmic tune. She could not recall the words, but it was a song her mother used to sing to her in the mysterious-sounding Le-nah-pe language. Apparently Christina had picked up chants from the children of the farmworkers. She told Laura that Gardners participated in the seasonal tribal celebrations held near the farmhouse. Laura decided she would ask Lawrence if any of those observances still took place. She realized she should be keeping a list of all the questions she had for her great-uncle.

The closer Laura had come to Philadelphia, the more the traffic volume picked up. She had felt her shoulders stiffening as she drove along the Schuylkill Expressway. In the midst of the stop-and-go travel, she was picturing her mother as a teenager, a time, Christina had admitted, when she chafed at being compared to Marial. She struggled to find an identity of her own in the shadow of her strong, intelligent mother. *I remember having those same feelings about my mother,* Laura mused.

Lawrence had never married, so Christina would have been expected to become the next generation to live on the farm. But as much as she liked gardening, tending chickens, and helping cook meals as a young girl, Christina looked forward to having a career of her own, one that was challenging and enjoyable and preferably away from Laurel Hill. She finished college and obtained a teaching contract that allowed her to escape to western Pennsylvania.

Now here was Laura, returning to the farm her mother had left all those years ago. She maneuvered into the correct lane while in her mind she continued the family narrative. Christina met Jude Andrews, a financial analyst at one of the premier accounting firms in Pittsburgh. The two were married and lived in the South Hills.

As a cloud blew across the path of the August sun, Laura thought about her parents' failed marriage, and her mood grew dark. After a decade of relative contentment in her role as a corporate wife, Christina grew restless. It took a period of brooding before she was able to talk to her husband about the dissatisfaction she felt. Jude was not overly concerned, dismissing it as her midlife crisis. Not long after that he brought home a colorful brochure announcing a four-week career counseling workshop. The sessions were being held nearby, and a member of the company bowling league said his wife was going to go. It really wasn't the response that Christina had been hoping for, but she signed up anyway.

That workshop rendered a surprising outcome: affirmation that indeed there *was* something more for Christina, and it was a call to ordained ministry! She applied to the closest seminary, was accepted, and by her own account felt happier than she had in years. She became one of the earliest women ordained in the region. She and

Jude sold their home and moved into the parsonage of the nearby church where she served as pastor. But over time, all the demands of parish life took their toll. The marriage became contentious. Their relationship grew wearisome. And then, at what seemed the lowest point in their life together, Christina had to tell Jude that she was pregnant.

Traffic slowed again and then came to a stop. A gust of wind jostled the bridge deck ever so slightly. Laura forced herself to focus on the present moment, the muted sunlight, gray puffy clouds, the churning river below her. At this point in remembering the story of her parents' life, her stomach always started to ache. It was a struggle for Laura to keep from blaming herself for what had happened, even though she had not yet been born. She understood the divorce was not about her, but about her parents and their longings or unfulfilled expectations. The end result, however, impacted Laura. Christina had chosen to keep the commitment made to God and to keep the child she was bearing. Jude made a choice as well—to walk away from this complicated, strong-willed Gardner woman. In the process, of course, he abandoned the child he had not anticipated. Laura was destined never to know her father, it seemed.

As traffic started moving again, Laura took a deep breath and then steered her shiny Ford Bronco into the highway lanes marked with the green overhead signs and arrows pointing to the Jersey Shore. The landscape of hazy gray industrial plants, apartment buildings, and shipyards gradually yielded to the lush hues of wooded hills and fenced pastures. Her good mood was slowly being restored by seeing the exuberant patches of wildflowers beyond the guardrails. Shifting her thoughts to her own story, she remembered college, and then graduate school where she met and married an engineering student named Cal Marshall. *And they lived happily ever after.* Laura heard those words in the sing-song voice of her little daughter. Noel was now seven; and baby Marial, named for her great-grandmother, was three.

Just then the sun burst out from behind the clouds, so Laura pulled tinted sunglasses from the tapestry case in her purse. She and Cal had delayed having children, much to her mother's disappointment. *Mom never knew either of her granddaughters.* There it was, another lingering sadness that weighed on Laura's heart. Was that why the phone call from Uncle Lawrence had buoyed her spirit? She was being invited to return to the place her mother loved. If Laura could reconnect with Christina's past, perhaps she would be able to share more fully with her daughters the spirit of the grandmother they never met.

Laura noticed a sign for Plum Hill Township. She was getting close to the Gardner place now. The farm had another name, like Tara in *Gone with the Wind.* What was it they called the old homestead?

Then she remembered. *Bittersweet Acres.*

CHAPTER 3

Laura felt a growing eagerness as she drove on toward Laurel Hill. She wanted to find out more about these stalwart Gardners. But she had to admit it would be satisfying just strolling through the same fields where her mother had played as a little girl, exploring the dark forests or picking fruit from the orchards surrounding the house. Laura recalled the excitement in her mother's eyes whenever the two of them would pack up the car for the long ride across the Pennsylvania Turnpike. A trip to Bittersweet Acres brought comfort and healing, no matter what was happening in their lives at the moment. Christina always said that. Then she'd recite the words to an old Shaker hymn:

'Tis the gift to be simple, 'tis the gift to be free
'Tis the gift to come down where you ought to be
And when we find ourselves in the place just right
'Twill be in the valley of love and delight.

Laura had spent the evening before this trip carefully mapping the route to the "place just right," but she also was confident she would be able to pick out landmarks to guide her. Just at that moment on her journey, a produce stand came into view on the left side of the highway. It had the familiar striped awning, and Laura immediately recognized it as Red Top Market. Her excitement increased. She knew she was close to the farm. Deciding to make a brief stop, Laura pulled into the gravel lot, parking between a table of colorful green watermelons and another mounded high with ears of freshly picked corn. She got out and stretched as she examined the fruits and vegetables for sale. The sun was hot, and she welcomed the shade of the iconic red umbrellas over each stand. Bees buzzed noisily around freestone peaches while flies flitted over quart baskets of ripe tomatoes. Several shoppers were engaged in a discussion with an attractive young woman standing at the cash register and wearing cut-off jeans and a tie-dyed tee shirt. Sitting behind the counter in a corner of the building was an older woman with a leathery face, her thick black hair pulled back and pinned at her neck in a ponytail. She wore a cotton tunic and long skirt, both embroidered with colorful designs. Several necklaces made of shell beads hung around her neck. Laura heard one of the customers speak to her, calling her Granny. The woman smiled widely as the man asked about her family. She stood up and carried an album of photographs over to the counter. Taking a glance over the shoulders of the others, Laura watched as the book was opened to the picture of another beautiful young woman. This one was dressed in some kind of ceremonial garb and holding a baby in one arm. Her other hand was resting on the head of a toddler clinging to her skirt. Behind her, Laura noted, stood a tall man with dark skin wearing in a leather tunic decorated with beads. Granny explained with pride that this was taken at the baptism of her new granddaughter in the Episcopal church in Chester Town.

The conversation ended with waves and goodbyes. Laura stepped forward, presenting her purchases and paying for them. Since Uncle Lawrence probably had plenty of tomatoes and beets in his little garden patch at the house, she had selected some crisp green beans along with a small basket of the sweet "Jersey peaches." She could already anticipate the fruit slices with her morning cereal or surrounding a plate of pancakes and waffles.

"You have a lovely family," Laura commented to the old woman with the photographs.

"So do you," the woman replied.

Laura was taken aback. "I…don't…think we've met…before," she offered hesitantly. Then remembering that in small towns, people tend to know everyone else, she relaxed. "I'm Laura Marshall. My uncle is—"

"Lawrence Gardner of Bittersweet Acres," the woman finished the sentence. Her eyes were sparkling. "We knew you were coming, but we could only hope you would visit us too. Come here. Sit down for a minute."

Laura placed the brown bags with her purchases on the counter and followed the older woman through the doorway to a cool interior room. Signaling Laura to take a seat on the bench beside a wooden table she vanished into another small room which appeared to be a kitchen. Emerging with a pitcher and three glasses full of ice, Granny called to the cashier to join them since no customers were waiting. "This is my niece, Elsa," she said as an introduction. The younger woman took the pitcher from Granny and filled each glass with a dark brown liquid.

"Sassafras tea," Granny explained. "A traditional welcome."

Laura took a sip. It tasted rich and smooth, it's cool sweetness enlivening her taste buds. In the next few minutes, Granny explained that her family had lived for generations on land that they now leased from the Gardners and farmed. They considered every generation of Lawrence's family to be part of their clan and were excited to get to see Laura.

"How long will you be staying?" Granny inquired.

"Just a week, I think, to sort through some of the family documents," Laura replied.

"Well, I am sure our paths will cross again." Laura was not as certain of that, but meeting Granny was a lovely surprise and apparently an answer to her question about a present-day connection between her family and the Le-nah-pe tribe.

"Don't you have children?" Granny inquired.

"Two little girls," Laura responded. She set down the glass long enough to pull her billfold from the shoulder bag on her lap. Spreading out a wallet-size plastic folder on the table in front of the other women, she pointed to pictures of her daughters as babies and then the most current ones. "Noel will be seven in December. Little Marial is already three. And this is me with my husband, Calvin."

As they perused the photos, Laura added, "Marial is named for my grandmother."

Granny looked down again at the little red-haired girl posed on a bench and holding a kitten. "She has Marial's spirit. I can see it plain as day, now that you've said that. The older one looks more like Christina."

Laura could not hold back. "You knew my mother?"

"Of course!" The woman sat back, smiling thoughtfully. "We were in classes together all the way through high school. We also learned the ways of the Le-nah-pe from our mothers and my old aunties." Granny stopped to take a drink of her tea. "In our Pineland Guide troop, your mother and I won prizes with our nature projects and traditional crafts. Your grandmother helped us complete our badge in animal husbandry." Laura was entranced!

Looking out the side window at lengthening shadows, the older woman scowled. "I have kept you too long. Finish your tea and then get on to the farm. Lawrence will be wondering what's keeping you." Laura took one last refreshing sip. Then they all got up and went outside to the market area again. It was much warmer now, even under the awning. Elsa returned to her post at the counter, handing Laura her produce. Laura climbed back in the driver seat, waved goodbye to her new acquaintances, and then ran her fingers through her auburn hair in a futile effort to tame the natural curls. As traffic cleared, she pulled back onto the highway.

Bearing left on Green Tree Road and around the traffic circle, Laura drove past a church with a graveyard, then a sprawling school complex set back from the highway and the old Friends' Meeting House at the next intersection. Laura recognized that building right away. Generations of the Gardner family had been members of this meeting. She and her mother had attended services there during their visits. Laura remembered the hush of the Quaker worship and the mystical anticipation of "a word from the Lord" in the place of a prepared sermon by an elder.

Farther along her route the road names identified some of the local flora: Arbutus Way, Larkspur Lane, Pepper-grass Circle, Spice-bush Drive. Laura was just trying to figure out where Granny and her family might live when she spied something she recognized: a dirt path cut through a field. "There it is!" she cheered aloud. Making a sharp turn, Laura pulled the Bronco into the narrow opening between two weathered fence posts and stopped. There among the tangle of smooth green leaves and shimmering orange-red seeds, she saw a small wooden sign hanging at an odd angle. *Bittersweet Acres* was neatly printed in faded paint. Laura had found the "back road," the one she knew her mother always loved. She drove on, following as it circled around a pond and then meandered between plowed fields, and through clusters of fruit trees, and expansive berry patches. Driving along beside a dense stand of pine trees, Laura glimpsed the undergrowth of mountain laurel, those distinctive glossy leaves gleaming in the shafts of light. Rolling down the windows, Laura felt the warmth of the sun and the afternoon breeze. In her rearview mirror, she saw the dust cloud that rose up behind her even when she went at such a lazy pace. Overhead a bird of prey was gliding in a circle. The insects clicked and whirred as she guided the truck through tall grasses and along the edge of an ancient orchard. The aromas wafting up were sweet and earthy.

This was nothing like Harrisburg with its traffic noise and commercial activity. Industrial parks had sprung up just a mile beyond Laura's cul-de-sac. When she sat on the back deck of her house, watching the girls play on the bright blue metal swing set, she could wave to the neighbors pulling in from the grocery store or listen to television quiz shows blasting from the kitchen of another home. In spite of close-set houses, clogged highways, and the occasional gaudy yard art, Laura enjoyed the conveniences of her suburban existence.

But as she drove through weeds and wildflowers, she found herself becoming acclimated to the serenity. Oddly, she felt as if she were entering a kind of sacred space. The crunch of the tires rolling over dirt clods and bits of gravel, the cheery whistle of an unseen bird, a skittering squirrel chattering in the underbrush: all of it made her smile. *The world is different here*, Laura thought as her shoulders relaxed. She loosened her grip on the steering wheel and allowed the afternoon to wrap itself around her like a familiar shawl.

When Laura's vehicle entered the orchard, the dirt tracks joined up with a well-worn road from the main farm entrance. That was the first time the aged brick house actually came into her view. Laura pulled onto a grassy patch beside the house and turned off the engine. There was not a soul in sight. The stillness added to her delight at having arrived at her destination. For the moment, she remained in the front seat, taking in her surroundings, letting the memories flood over her. "Mom, I miss you," Laura whispered. "Help me to see this place with your eyes, your heart."

Just then the screen door on the side porch swung open, and a tall man emerged, wearing baggy overalls and a well-washed olive green cotton tee shirt. One of his gnarled hands held onto the railing. The other gripped the handle of a handsome wooden cane. Slowly he descended the steps and then turned and faced Laura, his kind smile all the greeting she needed.

"Uncle Lawrence!" she exclaimed as she waved, slid down out of the vehicle, and walked quickly toward him. They embraced and then pushed each other back to arm's length and just stared, grinning.

"My, my, how much you remind me of your mother," he said.

"Aw, thank you. I'm a bit of a mess after that drive."

The two embraced again, Laura noticing this time how thin the old man was. Not frail so much as bony with no padding of flesh. Was he eating well? Eating at all? She would have to do an assessment of him in short order. But now they were chatting and walking toward the house and heading up the steps. "There's someone here I want you to meet," offered Lawrence as they reached the top step, and he pulled open the screen door.

CHAPTER 4

For just a moment, Laura's breath caught. Of course, the man would not be living here by himself! Not at his age. On some level of consciousness, she understood that. But she had not for one minute stopped to consider that someone might be here with him today. Was this a person from an agency that provided support to the elderly? A neighbor or friend from the community who fixed his meals or cleaned the house? A girlfriend? *Oh, dear me!* In that split second, Laura felt another twinge in her stomach as she prepared to discover something about Lawrence's life she had not bothered to anticipate.

As they went inside and turned toward the back of the house, Laura was overwhelmed by her memories. It felt like a summer afternoon when she was ten years old. Her mother should have been waiting for her in the kitchen, bent over the counter and rolling out pie crusts for a fresh apple dessert. The aromas were the same; only today, it wasn't Christina standing in the kitchen. It was a man about Laura's age, she guessed, with tousled blond hair, wearing an apron and sporting a swipe of flour on his damp forehead.

"Laura," said Lawrence slowly, as a way of an introduction, "this is Simon."

"Hel-lo," she replied haltingly. It was the only word she seemed to be able to pronounce at that moment. The young man looked up and grinned at Laura.

"Surprised you, didn't he? He doesn't talk about me much. Wants people to think he is doing fine completely on his own, cooking his own meals, cleaning this place, doing laundry." His smile was utterly disarming. Laura tried to gather her senses. She realized that she had not wanted to believe this relative of hers would need much attention or care. She felt embarrassed that she had never bothered to inquire how he was able to manage living alone.

"I'm sorry," she bumbled. "You're Simon? Hi. I didn't mean to be rude just now. My uncle really is a very private person." Laura narrowed her eyes as she glanced over at Lawrence, who was looking both guilty and somewhat amused as he made his way out of the kitchen. Then turning back to Simon, she continued, "From the looks of that pie you are working on, he is very fortunate to have found you."

Simon held up his fingers, suggesting she wait just a minute while he put the finishing touches on what he was doing. Then he carried the pie to the oven, slid it onto the upper rack, closed the door, and walked to the sink to wash his hands.

"I'm the lucky one," declared Simon, shouting over the rush of water in the sink. He pulled a clean dish towel from a drawer, blotted his hands and arms, and motioned for Laura to pull up a stool at the counter. "I came to Chester Town to teach high school industrial arts. For the first few months, I stayed at the hotel on the main street and then found a nice place to rent in the apartments on Pleasant Valley Avenue." Right away, Laura liked Simon's easy manner and bright facial expression. He seemed willing to chat while the pie was baking, so she asked him all the usual "get acquainted" questions, and he responded freely. Then she asked one more.

"Did you meet Uncle Lawrence in town?" She was not sure how else the two would have met.

"Actually, I overheard some of the other teachers talking about a Mr. Gardner and how his family had lived in the area for generations. I've got some connections in this part of Jersey myself, so I was kind of curious to meet him."

Simon pushed a bowl of freshly picked grapes across the counter to Laura. "We've got an arbor out back there," he explained, pointing to one of the kitchen windows. She selected a bunch and popped one of the sweet fruits in her mouth. Slowly she was adjusting to the idea that there was going to be another person in this space where she had imagined only she and her great-uncle would be. Simon continued, "When I first called to make an appointment to come visit, he said no. Seems his niece had just died unexpectedly." He saw a shadow cross Laura's eyes. "Oh, that would have been your mother." His voice was apologetic.

"It's all right," Laura whispered. After a minute she continued, still in a soft voice. "Mom loved the farm. She grew up here, and Uncle Lawrence had hoped she would come back here to live someday. But I knew she wasn't going to leave Pittsburgh." Laura's voice cracked with emotion, and she lowered her head. "I'd rather not talk about that."

The two sat in silence, caught up in their own memories. Then the kitchen timer signaled that the pie was done baking. Simon slipped on the hot mitts and walked across the kitchen. As he opened the oven door the aroma of rich pastry and warm fruit flooded the room. He went on with his story.

"Lawrence finally called me back one day and invited me to come here to meet with him." Simon placed the pie on a cooling rack. Then he attempted to mimic his employer's tone of voice. "'Don't want a nurse,' he told me. 'Just want to keep Bittersweet Acres going.' Then he walked me all around the place, explaining the various lease agreements he had, showing me what needed to be done to the house and grounds. I fell in love with it all: the scent of pine, the knotty old fruit trees, the quiet meadows, the pond, the house. I felt comfortable that day, with this place and with Lawrence." He stopped talking long enough to brush some egg white over the pie crust and sprinkle sugar crystals on it. "He asked if I'd consider moving out here. I said yes, and at the end of that school year, I gave up my apartment and my teaching job. It's been over five years now that I've been managing things here, including your great-uncle!" He smiled at his little joke, but it wasn't far from the truth. Simon had his own room upstairs and was responsible for the care of the yard and garden. He cooked all the meals, handled the household chores, and dealt with any emergencies that arose. "Like I said, I'm the lucky one."

Laura regretted not having known about her great-uncle's struggles but was pleased that he had found a solution on his own, thanks to friends in the community. She was beginning to accept the reality of "Simon" and felt an immediate fondness for the young man.

As she stood up and turned to leave the kitchen, Simon asked her to wait. He had been fixing a tray with a pitcher of icy lemonade and two glasses while they were talking. "Here. Take this, please. Lawrence will be sitting on the porch now," he informed her. Laura found her way to the front of the house, each step accompanied by the delicate clink of the ice cubes. She pushed open the screen door with her elbow and then stepped out, catching it with her foot to ease it shut again.

The afternoon sun bathed the western side of the house in gold and warmed the weathered cheek of the old man dozing in a wicker rocking chair. Laura's great-uncle wore a contented smile as he slept. It was the same look she'd often seen on her mother's face when she nodded off while working on the Sunday *New York Times* crossword puzzle after church services. Laura placed the drink tray on a small table beside the chaise lounge. She wondered why so many older people who had lived through economic hard times and personal tragedies, reached old age with such serene spirits. Her life, her family, her career were all perfectly fine; and she felt blessed in many ways. But she was never completely able to shake off vague worries about the future. Would her anxious feelings finally disappear at some point? She realized she was staring at Lawrence. His eyelids fluttered, and she feared she had awakened him with her thoughts.

"I wasn't asleep," he admitted.

"Simon fixed us a refresher."

"That's perfect. Would you pour?" She handed him a full glass of tart lemonade. As he took a sip, Lawrence closed his eyes again.

"Laura, sometimes when I sit here in the afternoons, I hear voices," he whispered.

His niece took a long drink. "Really?" she probed cautiously.

"Now don't go and mention it to Simon, because he will have me shipped off to a care home sure as anything." Laura debated if she would change the subject or encourage her porch companion to continue.

"Are they just the neighbors talking, the voices?" That could be a reasonable explanation. She thought of Granny at the fruit stand. She was a neighbor. *Where did her family live?*

"Oh, I never see the people," Lawrence admitted. "I just hear their conversations." He set his drinking glass on the table and rested back in his rocker. "Most times they sound happy. I try to pick out voices I recognize. Sometimes I think it's my sister Marial fussing with your mom about something, or our parents is calling us to dinner. But there are others I've not been able to place."

Laura leaned forward in her seat, holding her glass in both hands, resting it on her knees, and staring into it. She was intrigued and a little unnerved. Was this the real reason he had called her? Was he concerned about his mental stability? She may be in a situation she was not prepared to deal with. After a minute, she looked up and spoke to him.

"Sitting here with you is lovely. I remember loving it here with my mom when I was a little girl and got to play in the woods and the fields. Those days were such a long time ago, it seems." She paused, wanting to open her heart but not sure what words to use. "Uncle Lawrence, I miss my mother, and I want to feel close to her again. Do you think that could happen while I am visiting here with you?"

"I wouldn't be surprised at all, dear." Her great-uncle's eyes looked past her and out into the orchard. "I believe the spirits of those we cherish can be found in places they loved when they were alive. We've got some Le-nah-pe neighbors, you know, and they always talk to their ancestors while they walk through the forest over there." His tanned, bony finger gestured toward the pine trees. "I have been living here for a long time, Laura, and am surrounded by spirits and memories. Every nook and cranny of this house has a special significance for me. The creaky step on the stairs, the door in the pantry that always sticks, these call to mind my parents, my sister, and your mother. I don't want to leave this place or them. Ever." He pulled a rumpled handkerchief from his pocket and wiped his nose. "I have tried to arrange things so I can stay right here to the end of my life." Then Lawrence leaned forward and reached for Laura's hands. "And I want to be sure someone will always be here to take care of this place. That's why I wanted to see you."

Laura felt warm delight at his words, followed quickly by a cold surge of panic. What was he thinking? She had only come for a visit. They agreed she would look at papers, sorting through documents, and deciding what to keep and what to throw away. Her eyes widened and her thoughts became muddled. Was he telling her he wanted her to take responsibility for the farm? When she tried to respond, it came out sounding like mere babble.

"Oh, Uncle Lawrence, Mom always thought of this as her family home. When she would tuck me in each night, her bedtime stories were tales of growing up here with other farm children, and her mom and you. But for me, it's all been just a dream, a wonderful, happy dream."

Laura's mind was racing to grasp what her great-uncle was trying to say. She had a life in another place with Cal and their girls. She had a career and friends and connections. She could not simply give it all up and move here. And certainly not right now. She looked at the old man across from her and saw something in his eyes. Was it hurt? Or fear? What could she say that would be sensitive to his desires and yet noncommittal on her part? "I will always treasure what this place and its history means to our family," she finally offered. "Let's walk the property together while I'm here. Tell me the worries you have in your heart. Then we'll figure out the best way to honor the past and protect the future of Bittersweet Acres." Lawrence released her hands and sat back. Her words seemed to satisfy him.

They both picked up their sweating drink glasses, Laura wrapping hers in a dainty linen napkin. It was embossed with a capital *B* for *Bittersweet* in scrolling red-orange script. A nice touch. In a while, Simon probably would call them to dinner. For now, they would sit quietly, listening to the drone of bees in the wisteria and the chirping crickets hiding in the grass. Laura felt her initial concerns slipping away. She had the skills and knowledge to work out whatever her great-uncle wanted. And perhaps Simon would become her ally in this.

Chapter 5

The sun dipped down behind the cluster of pines, and Laura was coming to realize how life-altering this short visit could become. The surroundings seemed to stir her imagination. Out of the corner of her eye, she thought she saw a figure, an older woman moving gracefully through the orchard in front of the house. She recognized the colorful shawl. Granny, from the fruit market, had worn it. Or perhaps it was the one that belonged to her own mother.

The screen door hinges squeaked, and Laura sat up. Simon had appeared on the porch to retrieve the tray of refreshments, and Laura realized she had been dozing. For how long she wasn't sure, but her throat felt scratchy, and her eyes and cheeks were wet. Had she been crying? It was dusk, and Lawrence was nowhere to be seen. She stood up, dabbing her eyes with the damp napkin clutched in her hand. As she followed Simon into the house and down the wide front hallway, Laura stopping briefly to glance through the door on the left that opened into the spacious dining room. The table had already been set for three, a clue to Laura that Simon was more than just hired help. But what exactly was his role here?

She smiled when she saw two silver candelabra in the center of the wooden drop leaf table. Laura recognized them from the visits when she was a child. On one afternoon in particular, Christina had set out the best china and silver, and she called Laura to help. While Laura was smoothing Wrights' Silver Cream on each spoon, fork, and knife, polishing them to a deep shine, Christina worked on the candlesticks as she explained the tradition attached to them.

They were made by a local silver smith in the 1700s as a wedding gift handed down to a bride in each generation. "They've been in this family as long as I can remember," she had told Laura. "I expect you'll get them one of these days." But when the time came for Laura and Cal to marry, silver was no longer a fashionable gift. So apparently, Christina had kept them wrapped in their special cloth and tucked in a cupboard at the farmhouse. On this first day of Laura's visit, they had been removed from hiding, freshly polished and fitted with pale blue tapers. With white linen place mats, ivy green napkins, and Spode china edged with tiny forget-me-nots, the table was elegant.

Laura's reverie was broken by a series of loud expletives coming from the kitchen. She hurried the rest of the way back the hall and found Simon with his right hand under the faucet, cold water splashing over his reddening fingers and palm.

"I have *got* to get some new pot holders," he muttered, seeming to explain the significant burn. "It's one of those things you don't think about until…well, something like this." Simon pointed to a drawer in the kitchen where he kept a first aid box. Laura pulled out the burn cream. Simon's face showed both a grimace of pain and a look of embarrassment as Laura gently applied the medicine and wrapped the wound lightly in gauze.

"I'm so sorry," they both said at the same time. Then they laughed.

"This is not the impression I wanted to make," Simon admitted. Laura wondered if this man thought that she had come to assess his care of her uncle.

"You don't need to charm me. I'm just going to go through some family papers with Uncle Lawrence, and then I'll be out of your hair." Simon exhaled in a way that indicated relief and something else. They both looked up as they heard footsteps coming down the set of back stairs from the second floor to the kitchen. The gait was distinctive. Simon opened the door, and Lawrence hobbled down the last few steps, his arms laden with a stack of books and papers.

"Don't set them down here while I'm working on dinner," Simon admonished jokingly. Lawrence frowned briefly at Simon and then muttered something under his breath.

"Here, let me help you," offered Laura, carefully lifting a few items off the top of the pile and heading for the parlor. Lawrence padded along behind. Laura stopped and turned.

"Oh, Simon, I forgot. I stopped at the farmers' market on the way in and picked up some things. They're in the brown bag on the front seat of the Bronco."

"Thanks, I'll get them," he hollered after them.

For the next half hour or so Laura and her great-uncle sat side by side on the sofa, sifting through a mountain of memorabilia and chatting quietly. Delicious aromas emanated from the kitchen as Simon continued meal preparations in spite of his recent injury. Soon he came into the parlor and announced that dinner was served. Lawrence straightened the piles of materials and then carefully placed an antique paperweight on each stack. He got to his feet with the aid of his cane and asked if Laura would take his arm as they crossed the hall to the dining room.

In that moment, she pictured the generations of Gardner men and women who had walked arm in arm from the parlor to dinner—the swish of crinolines, wafts of cool air from ladies' decorative fans, quiet voices, knowing whispers. Laura was convinced that the history of this home, this family, waited to be discovered in a dusty box, behind a closed door, at the top of a set of stairs. As the improbable couple made their way to the table, she glanced past her great-uncle and out the front window. The sun was well down, and the lawn was lost in shadow. She saw a momentary glimmer of a light among the trees. *A reflection from the dining room candles*, she thought. Still, the notion that something or someone could be outside the house unnerved her momentarily. Once the three were seated at the table and had observed a solemn, silent pause, which was the Quaker grace before eating, Laura relaxed again.

Simon had outdone himself in preparing supper, especially since using his hand was obviously painful. The fried chicken still sizzled in its delicate breading. The green beans from the farm market had been sautéed lightly and seasoned perfectly. Lawrence was proud of the red beets from his little garden, more tender and sweet than Laura had ever tasted. Thick slices of fresh tomatoes created a riot of color that both nourished the bodies and cheered the souls of the people who this day had begun the transition from strangers to friends. As the apple pie was sliced and served with chunks of cheddar cheese, the conversation shifted from Laura's sharing about her family to Lawrence's orienting her to the house, his daily routine, and plans for their time together.

"I'm an old man," he declared. "I go to bed early and get up early for a walk down the lane. I like to check on the farm, come back, and have my second cup of coffee on the porch while I read my devotions. Then I commence with the chores of the day." Simon chuckled at that and interrupted.

"Lawrence would have you believe he bales hay and milks cows," he offered. "In fact, his 'chores' as he calls them are limited to pulling a few weeds from his well-tended garden patch and going into town for lunch and a haircut."

"Sounds exhausting." Laura laughed. "Not sure I can keep up with you, but I'll try."

Putting down his fork and pushing back his chair, Lawrence indicated that he was finished eating. "Thank you, Simon, for a wonderful dinner. If you'll help me up the steps, I think I will read for a while and then retire for the night. Laura, remember you'll be sleeping in Marial's room. Top of the stairs to the left."

Simon stood up and moved behind Lawrence's chair. He looked over at Laura. "I took the liberty of retrieving your suitcase from the car when I got the beans and peaches. It's in your room waiting for you."

"Oh, thank you." Laura started to gather up plates and silverware and then stopped. She went over to her great-uncle, kissed him on the cheek, and hugged his arm. "Sleep well, Uncle Lawrence. I'll see you for coffee in the morning."

Lawrence smiled, seemingly thankful for her affection, and then headed out of the room, guided by Simon. Laura sat down again and gently smoothed and folded her napkin. She absentmindedly arranged and rearranged the salt and pepper shakers and then snuffed the candles. After just a few hours, she felt quite at home in this place. These two men were welcoming, comfortable to be with and easy to talk to. Her great-uncle was still the pleasant man she had known as a child. She wished she had spent more time with him in his younger days. *Damn, I felt that way when Mom died too. Regrets. I miss Mom so much. Why did I wait so long to come here?*

Laura let out a sigh just as Simon reentered the dining room, breaking into her musings. She stood and helped him clear the table, thanking him again for the meal. Although he protested, she worked with him to get the kitchen cleaned up as well. She was concerned about the burn on his hand. It also was an opportunity for her to make more inquiries about her uncle.

"I am pleased to see that Uncle Lawrence gets around so well."

"He's still mentally sharp," Simon reassured. "I take care of the farm income, but Lawrence keeps his own checkbook."

"When does he see his doctors?" Laura asked, not wanting to pry but eager to assess the level of medical care her great-uncle needed.

"We've got it all here on this calendar." Simon pointed to the wall. There was a picture of the Chester Hardware Store above the page for the month of August. Laura could make out appointments for the dentist, optometrist, podiatrist, and general practitioner. "At first, I was simply dropping him off at the doctor's office, but then he started asking me to go in with him, just to be sure he got all the instructions down. When he was ready to designate someone to make decisions for him, should he become incapacitated, I recommended that he choose a family member. But Christina was gone, and Lawrence did not want to bother you and your family." Simon paused. "If you want to take over now, we can change things."

"Oh no," Laura responded. "I don't want to interfere with what you and Uncle Lawrence have set up. You are here with him day in and day out. So your having his power of attorney makes sense." Then she added, "I am happy to help you in any way I can, though. Perhaps the three of us could visit his lawyer, just to make an introduction."

"Good idea. I'll set it up in the morning."

"Well, I am suddenly quite tired. It has been a long day. A quick call to my family and then I'll be ready to crawl into bed. Mind if I go on upstairs?" asked Laura. She blushed, wondering why she felt the need to ask Simon's permission to leave the room.

"Sure, go on. I want to get a few things ready for the morning, but I'm not a night owl any more, especially since I know Lawrence will be up at the crack of dawn."

"Oh, here, let me take a look at that hand," she remembered. Together, they unwrapped the wound. Simon smoothed on more burn cream, and then Laura gently applied a clean dressing.

"There!" she announced as she gently patted the bandage.

"Thanks. See you tomorrow."

"Okay, then. 'Night." Laura made her way to the front hall, her memories flashing back to being a ten-year-old dashing across the wooden floorboards and up and down that staircase. *I must bring my girls here*, she thought. Placing her hand on the banister, she started to climb the steps and then stopped. Voices. Just whispers but clearly human sounds. Two people talking, one urgent, one calm. Perhaps it was Simon in the kitchen making a phone call. Or could it be Lawrence asleep already. Dreaming perhaps? Then there was silence. She shook her head and continued up the staircase.

The telephone extension sat at one end of a table on the second-floor landing. Several framed photographs were beside it. In the dim hallway lighting, their sepia-toned faces were hidden, but it was clear by the outlines of their bodies that they were all related. Which one was her mother? Making a mental note to examine them more closely in the morning, Laura dialed the number for home. As she waited for her husband to answer, she wished with all her heart that Cal and her daughters could be there with her. She pictured herself tucking their little girls into beds in one of the guest rooms and then sitting on the porch with her husband, enjoying the night sounds and evening breezes.

"Hello, my love!" Cal's voice was cheery.

"Are you all okay?" she asked casually, praying that there had not been a family crisis of any kind. Cal assured her that the girls were doing fine, although they missed her. He had taken them swimming in the afternoon, and the day after tomorrow, they would be going to Pittsburgh to visit their friends. It was all arranged.

"Sounds like fun. Give Nicola and Ben my love when you see them." As the phone call drew to a close, Laura felt as if two worlds were colliding in her mind—her real life in Harrisburg and the one she was experiencing there in Laurel Hill. She realized how easy it would be for her to allow Bittersweet Acres to lure her away from other people and places she loved.

"Oh, Cal, I almost forgot. Uncle Lawrence has a live-in housekeeper."

Laura meant it to sound matter-of-fact, but something in her tone prompted Cal to inquire further. "What's her name?"

"Uh, Simon."

Silence. Then he said, "Should I be jealous?"

Laura smiled. "He *is* a wonderful cook," she teased. "But no."

Then she explained that she was quite tired and asked if he would mind if they talked more another night. He said he understood, told her again that he loved her, and then handed over the receiver to the girls. Laura spoke briefly with each of them, wishing them sweet dreams and repeating their favorite rhyme: *Good night. Sleep tight. Don't let the bedbugs bite!*

Gently replacing the phone in its cradle, Laura sighed and then walked to the door of the room where she would be sleeping. It was partially ajar, revealing plain Shaker-style furnishings. The four-poster bed was made up with a wedding ring quilt she recognized as the needlework of her grandmother. Amazed at how well her memory was serving her, Laura went over to the bed and, without thinking, smoothed a wrinkle from the fabric. It was warm to her touch, as though someone had been seated there, waiting for her, but recently gone! Instinctively, Laura made her way to the window, screened but open to the warm night air. Her eyes adjusted to the dark outside. A light similar to the one she had spied earlier was visible, this time in the cluster of pines along the edge of the side yard. She watched as it moved away, getting smaller and dimmer. Then it was gone.

Turning back toward the room, she noticed her luggage on a small bench next to the bathroom door. She unpacked, placing her things in one of the wardrobes, and then changed into her gown and robe. After washing her face, she brushed her hair and was about to climb into bed when something caught her attention. A small pot of hand cream, identical to one her mother always kept beside her bed, was on the nightstand. The brand was hard to come by these days, so Laura had made do with another kind herself. And she had not packed that one in her cosmetic bag. So where had this come from? Puzzled, she sat on the edge of the bed and opened the jar, lifting a dab of the fragrant balm with her finger and smoothing it on her hands. For a moment, she felt a bit light-headed and then incredibly tired. She crawled under the sheets and was asleep as soon as she laid her head on the pillow.

I hear the faint babble of water. Perhaps it's the stream that runs through the farm property. I picture it splashing over rocks and swirling around tree roots. I follow the sound, making my way to a flat rock outcropping where I find the crayfish and striped bass exploring their underwater world. The air is cool by the creek. I pull a shawl around my shoulders. The colorful wrap gives off the scent of cedar smoke mixed with lavender. It reminds me of my mother. I nuzzle my face in the soft fabric, wondering where my mom could be. Is she lost? I have a funny ache in the pit of my stomach. Looking up, I recall a path, the trail she and I had followed once before. It begins near the stream I am sure and leads into the forest. Just a narrow track made by deer or native people traveling to the next settlement.

I stand up and make my way through the underbrush of ferns and berry bushes. The path is barely discernible. No one has walked here for some time. Brambles scratch and pick at my bare legs, but I keep going, stepping over some fallen tree trunks and rocks that litter the floor of the pine forest. A chipmunk darts across my path and then sits up on a log, staring at me. It is clearly annoyed at my intrusion. Chattering its complaints, it turns and runs off. I follow it with my eyes and then look up.

Behind the laurel shrub branches, I spy an opening in the hillside. The cave! The one I had discovered during the long-ago summers when I came here! I never told a soul about this place. It was my escape from hot days and tedious adult conversations. I would sneak away from the house, pretending someone or something was chasing me, and I had to hide…

I walk through the opening, my eyes adjusting to the dimness. I glimpse charcoal drawings on one of the cave walls. Carefully, I retrace them with my finger. They might have been mistaken for ancient artwork of the Le-nah-pe tribe who once inhabited these woods, but I remember the aroma of the burning wood, the scratching sound of the black end of a burned stick rubbing across stone. I had drawn these figures myself: animals, trees, and birds, adding to the menagerie each time I visited. And now, after all this time, they are still visible.

I sense a presence with me before I see anything. A shadowy figure appears far back in the cave. Squinting in the darkness, I can just make out someone seated on the hard-packed earth floor. Is it a man or woman? I can't tell. As I am watching, a small flame appears in the cupped hands of the figure. No bigger than a votive candle, it gives off an eerie glow. The figure gets up, turns to face the wall, and walks forward. Carrying the small light, it disappears into the rock. I stare for a moment and slowly make my way to where the figure had been sitting. Then I flatten my hand against the place where I had watched the person fade away. The wall is solid.

Mystified, I turn, almost tripping over something on the ground. A small leather pouch, dropped by the figure perhaps, or simply left behind. As I am reaching to pick it up, the wistful sound of a flute begins, enticing me out of the cave. Leaving the item, I make my way into the sunlight. I listen to the melody, thinking I have heard it before, but where? After a time, the flute is quiet. The sun is shining brightly, and I cannot keep my eyes open. The only sound I hear is the repeated call of a chickadee trying to locate its mate.

CHAPTER 6

Laura stirred, waking to find herself in her grandmother's bedroom at Bittersweet Acres and the sun well up in the morning sky. She sat up and threw her legs over the side of the bed. It was so tall that her toes just reached the floor. Her feet found her slippers, and she stood up. Still not completely awake, she walked to the bathroom sink, ran warm water to wash her hands and face, and then combed through her hair to untangle it. "You do look like your mom," she told her reflection in the mirror. As she opened the door from the bedroom, the aroma of fresh-brewed coffee wafted in from the hallway, along with the far away sound of something sizzling in a skillet. Her foot-wear flapped gently on the stairs as she made her way down to the kitchen. When she reached the hall, she heard the sounds of toast popping up and someone scraping a knife across the hot surface of the bread.

"Morning!" Simon's cheery voice and happy eyes greeted her when she arrived in the kitchen. He had already set a place on the small wooden breakfast table: plate, mug, juice glass, utensils, and cloth napkin.

"It smells delicious in here," she replied as she pulled up the chair and sat down.

"Sleep well?" he inquired casually.

"Yes." Then Laura hesitated, recalling pieces of her strange dream. She shook her head as if to clear cobwebs. "I was more tired than I knew."

"I have slept really well almost every night since I moved out here." Simon poured steaming coffee in Laura's mug. "So peaceful and dark. And I love it when the whippoorwills start each evening."

"I remember that!" Laura was surprised that a small detail could conjure up such feelings of joy. "Mom called it her favorite lullaby." Laura picked up the warm mug, hoping not to burn her mouth. There was a hint of cinnamon in the dark liquid, smooth and delicious on her tongue and throat. She set the mug on the table again and reached for the toast. "Where's Uncle Lawrence?" she asked, noting a mug and plate already in the sink.

"Off for his morning constitutional."

Laura used a spoon to smooth apple butter on her bread. She asked Simon about his burn and was pleased to see it didn't seem to be holding him back. She was hungry and watched with interest as he whisked eggs and cream together and then poured them into a hot frying pan for an omelet. He retrieved some crisp bacon that was kept warm in the oven, arranging it and the eggs on a bright orange pottery plate and placing it in front of her.

"Anything else I can get for you?"

"Um, some juice?"

"Oh, sure. Sorry. Orange or tomato?"

"Orange, please."

As he filled her glass, Laura asked, "Did you say your folks were from around here?"

"Sort of. My dad and mom lived all their married life in Philadelphia. That's where I was born. And Dad used to know folks from this area, um, from his work, I think."

"I am guessing he's retired now. What did he do?"

"He got his degree in accounting from a college in upstate New York and then took a job in Western Pennsylvania. When he got an offer from Goldman Sachs in Philadelphia, he moved east and then met and married my mom. They had me the next year."

Laura glanced up at Simon and smiled. He was clearly proud of his parents. He continued speaking as he refilled his coffee mug and leaned against the kitchen counter. "Mom was a secretary in a legal firm but quit when I was born. It was nice, just the three of us, living in the big old house that had belonged to her family."

"Your folks sound like interesting people."

"They really are. Well, were. Mom was beautiful and funny and kind, right up the end." There was a catch in his voice. "She died almost seven years ago now." Simon cleared his throat and took another sip of his coffee.

"I'm so sorry," offered Laura, pausing as if deciding whether she should say more. "That was about the time I lost my mom." She was staring out the kitchen window and feeling the familiar burning sensation behind her eyes. Would her grief ever heal completely?

Simon sat down opposite her, putting the carafe on the braided hot mat he had carried over. "Dad's arthritis is all that has slowed him down. He finally gave up the house and moved into a senior citizen apartment complex on City Line Avenue." Simon took another sip of coffee before continuing. "That was difficult for me when dad sold our home. I had a magical childhood there with them. I still drive by the place when I go to visit him."

Laura was about to ask Simon more when a scuffing sound on the side porch signaled her great-uncle's return from survey-ing the farm. He was cleaning off his boots on the hemp doormat. The screen door creaked open and closed. Lawrence came into the kitchen. When he was in his prime, his presence would have filled the door frame. But now he was thin and slightly stooped, a shadow of the man she knew as a child. Laura got up and went over to give him a hug.

"You smell like all outdoors," she remarked.

"Is that good?" Lawrence responded with a smile.

"You bet it is!" answered Laura.

This was the same "call and response" he and Christina had used whenever they were together. He seemed delighted that her daughter had picked up on that and remembered it now.

Sauntering over to the counter, he laid down his cane and picked up the mug of coffee Simon had poured for him. "It's a fine day out there," he remarked. "You two may have missed the best part of it." He exhaled and then sipped his coffee as he gave a brief report on the state of the farm. "The pond could use some rain. It's getting pretty murky. Those old trees in the front are still putting out a lot of fruit.

Simon, we'll be making our famous apple butter this fall." Then in silence, he devoured the slice of buttery toast Simon handed him.

Laura was torn between wanting to explore the farm and needing to get started examining the documents in the parlor. And she realized her great-uncle's strength was limited. As he headed for the front porch, Laura excused herself to get dressed. Once upstairs, she decided to forgo her usual morning shower, only brushing out her hair and cleaning her teeth before she pulled on jeans and a powder blue tee shirt. When she returned to the kitchen, Lawrence was sitting where she had been, his devotions apparently completed, and Simon was nowhere to be seen.

"Oh, good. You're back." Offering her arm to him, Laura smiled, wondering for a moment if he meant her or her mother. "Shall we ambulate into the other room?" He managed to get to his feet and then leaned heavily on his cane as she led the way into the front room. Laura moved to the windows, pulling open the drapes to let in the late-morning sun.

"When Marial and I were children, Laura, we were never allowed in here. It was kept dark and only opened up when company was coming. But once our parents died and Marial had your mom, all former conventions fell by the wayside." He chuckled at his memories of those times, prompting Laura to picture the brother and sister spoiling Christina. She was about to ask a question, but noticed Lawrence had nodded off in his favorite chair. Her uncle was so full of life she kept forgetting how old he was. After his walk in the fresh air, he would need to rest. Meanwhile, she could set about sorting through some of the items he had placed on the antique oak secretary the evening before. Pulling a legal pad and a pen from one of the desk drawers, she wrote *Questions for Uncle Lawrence* as the title and then set it aside and picked up a leather-bound book that was on top of one stack of papers. It was a family Bible.

"Funny I didn't notice this last night," she commented softly. She carried it with her to the sofa, sat down, and opened the cover. It was quite old, she could tell. She turned the first few delicate pages, smoothing them as she went. It was the version commissioned for the Church of England by King James, completed in 1611. The inscription indicated it was given to Elizabeth Chamberlain, on the occasion of her marriage to Richard Gardner, Wallingford, England, May 8, 1676. The handwriting was exquisite, a contrast to the Scriptures themselves which were quite plain with no decoration or illustration of any kind. The leather cover was crumbling and cracked, and after a few minutes, Laura gently placed it back on the secretary, thinking she might look for some tissue paper later to wrap around it. Perhaps she'd find a small box in which to store it. She jotted a note on the legal pad to ask about Elizabeth and Richard.

Then her glance fell on a cardboard box across the room. It had her mother's name on it in faded ink. She had not seen that last evening either. *How interesting!* Laura thought. She hesitated, curious to see what was inside, yet aware that the collection might stir up emotions for which she was not prepared. After a few moments, she got up anyway, retrieved the container, and then walked back over to the sofa. Sitting down again, Laura slipped off her shoes and pulled her bare feet up under her. She took a deep breath and then let it out slowly as she lifted off the lid of the box. Her eyes widened, and she gasped. There on top of all the other contents was a photograph. Smiling up at her was a young Christina, her hair pulled back in a graceful bun and tucked into a ring of flowers. The lace dress flowed easily from her shoulders. Beside her in the picture was an equally handsome man with light, wavy hair, wearing wire-rimmed glasses that did not hide his laughing eyes. His white suit had been carefully tailored to hug his strong physique.

A wedding portrait! Laura turned it in the light as she tried to identify where it might have been taken. Suddenly, she knew the location. It was right here, out front on the porch. In the background, Laura could just make out an immature version of the immense lilac bush which no doubt still filled the house with its perfume every spring. She turned the picture over. Scrawled across the back she read,

Christina Elizabeth Martin
Jude Michael Andrews
Bittersweet Acres
May 18, 1940

CHAPTER 7

Laura looked away from the photograph of the happy bride and groom and tried to calm her breathing. She could feel a flush of embarrassment rising to her face. This was the only picture of her father she had ever seen! Christina had completely erased him from their lives, and Laura had never pressed her mother for information. She was aware now that she had suppressed any curiosity about him in order to avoid the hurt of being abandoned. She had wanted to prevent upsetting her mother as well. So Laura chose to believe that her father was dead.

In the moment, she fervently wished she had taken more of an interested in her mother's early life. She realized she had always wanted to know more about her father. Could Uncle Lawrence shed any light on who this man had been?

Laura never made the connection between this place and her parents' wedding, and yet it was so obvious. Bittersweet Acres was where her mother had been raised. Of course, she would return here to be married! And when the marriage dissolved, how that sadness must have been felt at the heart of this place too. Turning the picture over to the front again, Laura looked at the faces, one so familiar, the other of a complete stranger. "Did you love my mom?" she asked, and tears crept into her eyes.

"He did," answered a soft, trembling voice. Lawrence had opened his eyes. "I see you found one of your mother's gifts." The old man stretched and yawned and then leaned forward in his chair. "Laura, Christina wanted to protect you from any pain or sadness associated with your father's leaving. But I told her at the time that you deserved to know something about him. So we agreed for me to keep that picture here, just in case you might be interested someday. I thought maybe now you were ready."

Laura put down the picture and the box and went over to her great-uncle. She knelt beside his chair and took his hands in hers. "You'll tell me about him, won't you?" she pleaded. "I do want to know about him now, about them together, about what their life was like, and what went wrong."

Just then Simon appeared at the door of the parlor. "You two interested in some tuna salad and fresh tomatoes?" Laura looked up, her eyes red. "Oh, sorry. I guess my timing is a bit off. It can wait." He turned toward the kitchen.

"No, no. We'll come now," Lawrence called after him. Laura wiped her face on her sleeve, retrieved the picture of her parents from the sofa, and carefully propped it up on the fireplace mantel. Then she handed Lawrence his cane and helped him maneuver his way across the parlor and into the kitchen where Simon had set the table beside the window with two places.

"I have already eaten," he advised, "so take your seats, and I'll bring your plates and drinks and then get out of your way."

Soon great-uncle and niece were sipping their iced tea and savoring lunch. Laura was feeling more composed as she spoke again about her parents. "There was one moment on the day of mom's funeral," she recounted, "when I had this deep longing to know more about my father. It really was the first time I felt any interest in him. But it didn't last. Is that strange?"

"When we lose someone close, Laura, it's natural to want something, someone to cling to. When my dear Marial died, I reached out to your mother to help me deal with it. But she already had you and her church ministry, so after the first few months, I was content with her letters and occasional visits." The old man's voice caught as he felt something, perhaps the ache of past losses. "I never dreamed I would live longer than Christina. That was what I was feeling when I called you, Laura. I wanted to know I still had a family."

Laura was so moved by his words that she set aside questions about Jude Andrews for the time being. Her two little girls and Cal were part of Lawrence's family, and he had never met them. How much life they could bring to this man, this home! The kernel of an idea entered her mind.

"Well, let's freshen our tea and head for the front porch," Laura suggested. Lawrence's mood brightened a bit.

"I can tell you more family history before I doze off again."

Just then Simon came from the garden with a quart of fresh-picked raspberries and three large bell peppers. "Cobbler, fresh lima beans, and zucchini stuffed peppers for dinner," he announced proudly.

"Perfect," responded Laura.

As she and her great-uncle settled themselves on the porch, Laura was surprisingly relaxed. She sipped her drink and rocked gently in the wicker chair. The shock of finding the wedding photo had subsided a bit. Lawrence stretched out on the chaise lounge and seemed eager to launch into a genealogical monologue.

"Bittersweet Acres has been in our family for so many generations that folks around here just refer to this as the Gardner place."

Laura leaned forward. "I found an old Bible that belonged to Elizabeth and Richard Gardner!"

"Yes, given to them on their wedding day, as I recall. They brought it with them all the way from England. We can trace a family tree starting with them and adding all the children, husbands, and wives. I've got most of the birth and death dates somewhere. But let me just share the short version with you now." The old man's voice went hoarse, so he took a long sip of his watery tea.

"My dad's name was Lawrence, which makes things confusing from the get-go." He chuckled. "That Lawrence married a teenager named Sarah Budd. It was standard practice back then, so don't be too shocked. They had two stillborn babies, Isaiah and Samuel, and were about to give up on having a family when along came my sister Marial and then me five years later."

Laura was aware of the high rate of infant mortality in years past, but it still touched her heart.

"Marial ended up married to Josiah Martin, another local Quaker, and the two of them lived here on the farm with our parents. They sent me off to business school, so I got my degree and found a job managing the Chester Town Post Office. I could have lived here with them, but instead I bought a little house on the western end of Kings Highway, closer to where I worked. Are you still with me?" Lawrence smiled.

"I think so," Laura encouraged. "I'd love to visit Chester Town while I'm here."

"We can do that. Simon and I will have to run errands at some point. You can drop us off and venture a bit on your own, or we can drive you around."

"I heard my name." Simon appeared in the doorway with a fresh pitcher of fruity iced tea.

"Uncle Lawrence has just agreed to take me on a tour of the town," Laura announced.

"Well, okay, but it's going to storm later," replied Simon. "So not this afternoon. When we do go, we can make that stop to meet with our lawyer." As Simon refilled their glasses and then turned to go inside, Laura explained to her great-uncle that she wanted to introduce herself to his solicitor, if that was all right with him.

"Oh, good," he replied. "You can see how we have things set up." Then he called after Simon. "Come sit with us for a bit. I'm just getting to the good part of my family history."

"I really should…"

"Hogwash!" Lawrence surprised both younger people with his comment. "You work too hard, Simon, and spend entirely too much time by yourself. Just keep us company. I'll get sleepy soon, and Laura will want someone to entertain her."

They all gave a relaxed laugh and settled back, Laura in her rocker, Lawrence on the chaise lounge, and Simon in the porch swing. The katydids were humming loudly. The weather would be changing.

Laura was not sure how much Simon knew already about his employer's life. "We were just at the point where you, Uncle Lawrence, were settled in town and my grandmother and grandfather lived here with their parents."

"Marial had her veterinary practice and Josiah farmed. Your mother came along in 1911. Little Christina stayed close to her mother. She learned how to recognize the rhythms of the farm. 'For everything there is a season,' as they say."

Laura knew the reference and allowed the ancient wisdom of Ecclesiastes to surface in her mind:

> *a time to plant and a time to reap*
> *a time to break down and a time to build up*
> *a time to weep and a time to laugh*
> *a time to mourn and a time to dance*
> *a time to seek and a time to lose*
> *a time to keep silence and a time to speak*
> *a time to love and a time to hate*
> *a time to be born and a time to die.*

"So what happened after Josiah died?" Laura asked. A shadow of sadness formed on Lawrence's face. Simon was puzzled. The old man took out his handkerchief to wipe his nose, and then he told the story Laura had heard countless times from her mother.

"It was the year after I finished school, Simon. A summer thunderstorm set one of the neighbor's barns on fire. Josiah directed them to take water from our pond. All the men around here ran to help fight the blaze." He stopped. After all this time, the memory of the event was still difficult for Lawrence to bear. "At some point, the fire caused the walls to collapse. One of the beams fell right on top of Josiah and killed him instantly."

"Oh, how awful!" Simon's response was genuine.

Laura had been raised without a father, but she knew it must have been much more difficult on the farm in those days.

"I can't imagine Marial caring for your elderly parents, keeping up her practice, and raising a child on her own."

Lawrence spoke quietly. His energy seemed to be fading.

"I tried to be of some help myself when I could get off work. Then after our parents were gone, Marial and Christina stayed right here all by themselves. Even though it was unheard of at the time, it worked out fine. Those two were kindred spirits, sensitive to nature, aware of the delicate balance between health and sickness, nurture and carelessness, stewardship and waste." Lawrence paused, lost in his thoughts or perhaps simply tired. Laura could not decide which. After a minute, he continued. "They both had so much patience! That was what it took to care for the garden, the chickens, and occasionally piglets or lambs. It wasn't easy, but they were truly happy to be together. I, on the other hand, was not that adept with farmwork, and Marial kept encouraging me to continue my business career. There were plenty of neighbors and friends who remembered Josiah and were always ready to help out."

"Speaking of neighbors," Laura interjected, "Mom told me about a family of Le-nah-pe who lived near here. She said she used to play with their children, who were about her age." She turned to tell Simon the story of Christina's playmates, and a few minutes later, when they stopped talking and looked back at Lawrence, he had drifted off to sleep. Smiling, Simon nodded to Laura, and the two slipped quietly down the porch steps together. The breeze had picked up a bit, and it seemed a perfect time for a walk, so the two headed off in the direction of the pond.

It was still hot, but the scent from the pine woods was delightful. The two meandered silently down the narrow trail of stones and earth. They reached the wooden bridge over the stream at the upper end of the pond, and Simon stopped on one side to stare into the tea-colored water. Laura leaned over the opposite rail, gazing into the creek as it trickled gently along. "Have you ever wondered what it was like here? You know, when the first Gardners arrived?" she mused. "They faced so many unknowns in this country. How were they going to make a living here on this land? It couldn't have been easy."

"I had those same questions when I first came to stay with Lawrence. All this part of New Jersey was inhabited by the Lenni-Le-nah-pe tribe. The first settlers were probably wary of the people with dark skin and mysterious customs who were living here. I knew nothing about them, so Lawrence encouraged me to begin reading anything I could find."

"What did you learn about the Le-nah-pe?"

"Well, the native people were nomadic, roaming these forests, fields, and seashores, sustained by the wise use of the gifts of the Creator. The way I understand it, the Le-nah-pe camped by the ocean in the summers, catching and eating all kinds of sea food, preserving the fish, and gathering shells which they made into beads for trading. Then when the weather turned cool, they moved inland, making their home in the forests where they hunted game and gathered berries and nuts and spent the winters."

"But wait. Didn't they farm too?"

"That was later. Some clans decided to settle in one area and build more permanent shelters. They cleared small patches of the land, planting corn, squash, and beans. Other families continued making seasonal migrations to the sea shore and back. But they all came together in the fall each year for their thanksgiving feast and traditional ceremonies. Lawrence has a couple of informative books on Le-nah-pe culture at the house. I'll help you locate them."

Laura turned and was about to thank him but instead tapped his shoulder. He came and stood beside her as she pointed to a mossy log wedged against the bank of the stream.

"Look!" she whispered. All the time they had been talking, she was staring, unseeing, at a dark mound on the log. Just then to her surprise a green-and-yellow-striped head poked out from it. Two stout front legs with bright-orange markings emerged next from within the sturdy shell.

"*Chrysemys picta*," he stated proudly. "It's one of the few scientific names I can remember and pronounce." Laura noticed he blushed just a bit. "The Eastern Painted is the most colorful turtle living here in the Pine Barrens. It's the one I picture when I read the Le-nah-pe creation stories." Laura looked puzzled, so Simon proceeded to speak, using the soft lyric voice of a native storyteller to relay the legend. "The Great Spirit created the world when a large tortoise raised its back out of the water and it became land. A tree sprouted on the land, and from its roots, a sprout produced the first man. Then another sprout appeared and produced the first woman."

Laura laughed with appreciation for his attempt at drama. "A man of knowledge and talent," she chortled.

"Thanks. Yeah, I like these Eastern Painted guys. They hang out around the lakes and ponds and marshes, looking for things to eat, like worms or snails." The two humans stood side by side, watching as the turtle stood on up on all fours and then moved slowly down the log, eventually sliding silently into the stream.

"Must be time for his dinner," Laura offered.

Simon glanced at his watch. "Speaking of which, I need to head back to the house and get to work on *our* supper." Laura silently gave thanks that it wasn't going to be snails!

"And I have more notes to make on my mother's childhood." Laura was sure Lawrence would have awakened by now. She and Simon walked a bit more quickly back the path, paying no attention to the butterflies hovering on field flowers and birds calling greetings across the meadow. They found the old man right where they had left him on the porch, but he was awake, sipping from his glass and fanning himself with the evening paper.

When he saw them, he smiled. "I wondered where you two had gotten to."

Simon climbed the steps to the side porch and disappeared into the kitchen. Laura joined her great-uncle again out front.

"Sit down, child," Lawrence invited. "Now where did I leave off in the story?"

He must have read my mind, thought Laura. As he talked, she realized she was actually beginning to piece together the Gardner ancestry. Lawrence informed her that somewhere in one of the boxes was a framed document, a copy of the actual land grant from the British Crown to the acting governor of West Jersey, as the region was named. The date on it was 1683, he thought.

"There is another interesting paper I want us to find and keep. It's a copy of the ship's manifest for *The Shield*, one of several passenger ships carrying people from England to the colonies in the seventeenth century. It lists Richard Gardner, along with Elizabeth and two sons.

"That trip must have been terrifying for the adults, let alone the two small children," Laura put in. She continued to be amazed at the strong hearts and wills of her family.

"They had to make a choice: leave England or be imprisoned for their faith," reminded Lawrence. "It was a risky journey, that's for sure. And in spite of terrible conditions on board, Richard did his best to protect the little family, praying for safety from danger and disease while they huddled in the dank hold. After many weeks at sea, ships like *The Shield* and *The Kent* anchored near the mouth of Ancocas Creek to let the passengers disembark. All that the Gardners had with them were a few coins, one knapsack, and the belongings they could fit in a wooden sea chest. That was it. When they finally stepped off their ship, they knelt right there beside the dock and offered prayers of thanksgiving for their safe passage."

"That's a great story, Uncle Lawrence." Laura would enjoy telling that one to Noel and little Marial. "Now remind me how they found *this* place," she asked, gesturing to indicate the grounds around the house. Laura was not sure how far the farm was from where they had come ashore.

"Ah, that was a blessing of being part of the Quaker community," Lawrence explained slowly and deliberately. "All the English Quakers who settled along the Delaware made their home together in the wilderness. The first to arrive tried to clear the land so they could have farms, like they did in England. But the forests were thick with trees and shrubs, and they didn't have proper axes. It was really rough going." The old man winced and rubbed his shoulder, as if he felt in his bones the suffering of his ancestors. "Other folks arrived later with carpentry skills and better tools. There were plenty of scrub pines, red cedars, and black oak trees. So they began to build rough log cabins clustered in small settlements. When the Gardners landed, Elizabeth reportedly took the money she had been given by their English benefactor and used it to rent a small lean-to on the edge of the village of Chester, and that's where the four of them lived. At least in the beginning."

A bright flash of lightning, followed by loud rumbling thunder marked the arrival of a summer storm. The rain began, a gentle shower at first and then a deluge pounding heavily on the metal roof. Laura could hear Simon, tending to the open windows. The two stood up and made their way inside.

"Am I getting you lost in the details, Laura dear? I don't want to bore you with ancient history."

"Not at all!" she responded. "I admit it is a lot to take in, but I enjoy trying to imagine how life was for folks back then."

"Well, you can find some old sketches and pictures of the early settlements in some of the books here in the parlor. There are also good references in the library at the old Meeting House." Lawrence sat down heavily in his favorite chair while Laura perused the shelves of books along the wall near the fireplace.

Lawrence seemed relieved to be getting to the end of this part of the story. "It was old Billy Penn who gave out land grants to Quaker settlers, and Richard Gardner got this place: one hundred acres of hills, forest, and meadow lands with a stream meandering through it. The native people referred to this area as Laurel Hill. The forests are lovely in the springtime."

The lightning became more frequent, the thunder sharp and close. Laura pulled out an old atlas and sat down close to Lawrence. His voice sounded tired, but there was one more important fact he was determined to share.

"Elizabeth was the one who chose the name for this place." The rain blew noisily against the windows. *Bittersweet Acres*. Laura remembered seeing the plant by that name growing wild at the entrance to the farm. She had noticed more on her walk that afternoon. The vines draped themselves over fence posts and wrapped their branches around tree trunks. At this time of year, the leaves were a deep green, pointed and glossy, and the clusters of yellow and orange berries hung heavily on the tips of the smooth stems. She imagined that the colorful fruit lasted throughout much of the winter to feed birds and other wildlife.

Laura had also seen a list of Elizabeth Gardner's children. She tried to remember who they were. Two boys made the journey from England, and then came a baby girl named Elizabeth, who was still-born. William was next but lived less than three years. A daughter Sarah died before her first birthday, and a son Joseph also died as an infant. Then finally, a boy, Jonah, was born. So much hope and yet all that sorrow.

"No wonder she chose *Bittersweet* as the name for her home," Laura mused aloud.

Simon's voice broke through her reverie.

"The Latin for bittersweet is *Celastrus scandens*," he shouted from the doorway and over the din of the storm. "Native people chewed the bark of that plant for medicinal purposes, especially female problems. They say the taste is bitter at first and then turns sickeningly sweet. Oh, and dinner is served."

CHAPTER 8

Eventually, the rain abated, and the storm moved off. Laura felt a cool breeze blow across her as they sat at the dining room table. Simon was serving dessert—the fresh berry cobbler—and offered to tell Laura some of the history of the farmhouse itself. She took a fork full of sweet fruit and tender crust, noting to herself that Simon enjoyed every opportunity to share some of his historical knowledge. It seemed to Laura that he had become part of the Gardner clan by virtue of his employment.

"When the family settled here," Simon recounted, "Elizabeth befriended the Le-nah-pe, allowing them to continue to hunt and fish on the property as they always had. It was the Quaker way to interact with those already here and learn from them how best to use the land they had been given." Simon stopped to scoop a spoonful of berries from his plate and eat them. "Richard and the other men in the area built the first structure on this property. It was the modest log cabin we use now for a garden shed." Laura pictured the family of four living in such a tiny space. "Later, the Gardner men learned the new trade of brick-making that had sprung up near Chester Town. One of them designed this house and decided to build it here next to the orchard."

"Laid most of the brick himself," Lawrence put in.

"It was the first of its kind, and because it was well constructed and understated, it became the model for many other Quaker buildings."

"So there are more houses like this one?"

"Sure. I'll point them out to you when we take a drive," Simon continued. "By the turn of the century, the children began to move away. Finally, only one son, Thomas was still living here. He married Ann Percy, the daughter of one of the families in their Quaker meeting. They had five children—all of whom lived, by the way—and raised them here in this house. Help me here, Lawrence. Thomas's oldest boy was Jacob, right?" Lawrence nodded as he picked up the story from there.

"Yes, it was Jacob who inherited the property. Then his youngest son Aaron loved the place so much he was chosen as the one to inherit the farm. That's when Jacob built the addition on the house. For Aaron and his family."

Seeing Laura's puzzled look Simon told her that the other part of the house was almost hidden from view now behind lilac bushes. "But when you walk around back, you'll notice a slight difference in the color of the bricks," he added. He went on to explain that Aaron eventually had opened up a doorway between the two parts of the house.

"Laura, once your mother was grown and had moved away," Lawrence added, "Marial and I closed off the other side again and she lived over here."

"By the way," Lawrence shifted the subject of the conversation slightly, "you might enjoy finding out more about Aaron. He kept a journal of his plans to increase crop production, maintain hunting grounds, and guard the water supply. It's here in the house somewhere." He noticed Laura's eyes brighten. "I believe Aaron also kept written records of the meetings he held with local farmers and members of the Le-nah-pe tribe. He invited them all to gather here from time to time to talk about the environment, you know, native plants and animals, soil, climate, seasonal pests and the like. He was concerned about the impact of over hunting certain species, like beaver, for example."

Lawrence became pensive as he pushed his dessert plate to the center of the table and leaned back in his chair. "People in each generation of our family have been like Aaron, caring for the land. Marial was the one of us who loved this place from the start. It has taken me a bit longer to appreciate the precious gift we have been given."

Simon indicated that there were some herbs and other plants in the garden that may have been growing there since Aaron planted them. "I did the research to figure out which were for cooking and which had medicinal properties." He got up and disappeared into the parlor. He returned in a few minutes and handed a book entitled *Historic Gardens of Chester Town* to Laura. "You might enjoy reading about some of the homes I'll be pointing out on our drive through town." Laura opened to the table of contents, but as she was browsing through the pictures and diagrams, she realized she was getting drowsy. Simon's meals had a way of creating in her a sense of contentment and satisfaction. Laying the book on the table, she yawned and stretched, which proved a welcome signal to Lawrence, who then announced his own weariness. It had been a long day.

While Simon helped her great-uncle up the stairs, Laura excused herself to make a call to her family. This time, she decided to use the telephone extension in the kitchen in order not to disturb Lawrence's bedtime routine. She dialed the number, longing to hear her husband's voice and those of her children. Noel would share the full account of their day, and the giggles from little Marial would soothe her soul. And there was that eagerness within Laura's heart to share the seed of an idea planted in her mind that morning.

"Cal, there is something about this place that is, well, enchanting. Does that sound strange?"

"No, dear. Not in the least. Lots of mysteries exist in those piney woods." Laura knew he was referring to the legend of the Jersey Devil, shared with him years ago by Christina. Local folklore said a woman known as Mother Leeds had twelve children and, when she found herself pregnant once again, cursed the thirteenth child. It was born with hoofs and wings and flew off into the pine trees where it still lives, terrorizing local populations when the moon is bright and the air is still.

"Well, as a matter of fact, I did see lights in among the trees last evening, and it feels a bit odd being in this historic house. But..." She paused before continuing. "Remember the night after mom's funeral when we stayed in her parsonage?"

Cal nodded and then realized he had to speak. "Yes. You were quite pregnant and distressed, and I tucked you into bed in her guest room."

"And you rubbed hand cream on my fingers to soothe me to sleep."

"That's right!" He pictured himself holding the little white jar.

"Well, there's a small pot of mom's hand cream here. It was on the nightstand when I arrived. It's as if she's telling me *she's* here." There was silence on the other end of the phone. Then a gentle cough.

"Laura, you may be imagining things."

"Oh, maybe, Cal. But I felt like I was supposed to come here for some reason. And then dear Uncle Lawrence started talking about how wonderful it will be for me to take over this farm when he dies or maybe sooner!" She took a breath. "Cal, I feel like I am facing some kind of life-changing decision." Laura hesitated. She was being shown a future that she did not seek, and perhaps did not even desire. She wanted her husband's help to process what was going on. "It's a little frightening to think about. Not just his dying but my having so much responsibility for the legacy of my family. How can I choose living here when it might mean leaving you?" Her words sounded irrational, and in speaking them, she finally understood why she was so anxious. Cal, who was not used to hearing this level of panic from his usually levelheaded wife, managed to keep calm.

"Aren't you overreacting just a bit?"

"Oh, I am sure it would never come to that, so, yes, I guess I do sound a little crazy." At that point, she laughed, and her demeanor became brighter. "I've been thinking a lot about my mom, of course. Oh, and guess what?" Her voice revealed her excitement. "I found her wedding photograph. It was taken right here at the farm."

Cal could sense that Laura was dealing with a lot of emotions, so he remained quiet and listened as she continued to talk about her family: the first Gardners and the old Bible, their friendships with the Le-nah-pe tribe, the building of the farmhouse, the death of her grandfather, even seeing the turtle on the log. Her next words were telling.

"I am happy here, Cal, in a way I haven't been since Mom died. And I wish you and the girls were here with me." Then she told him her idea. "Do you think we could come back together? A long weekend this fall or maybe over the Thanksgiving holidays? I'm pretty sure Uncle Lawrence will enjoy the company." When Cal did not respond right away, she continued. "Just us spending time here. It's important."

There was something new, an intensity in Laura's voice that her husband had not heard before. This was more than an offhand request, he was sure.

"It sounds like a nice idea. I am sure the girls would have fun. Let me see what I can arrange." Laura heard a hesitancy in his words. But they were both tired, and at this point, all she wanted him to do was consider it. Cal then reminded her that he and the girls were heading to Pittsburgh in the morning.

"Well, we won't talk for a few days, then. So think about it, please. You have the number here if you need me for anything."

"We'll be just fine," Cal reassured her. "And, Laura, you will be too. I love you."

"Love you too. 'Night."

Laura hung up the phone, surprised at the sense of relief she felt just sharing her idea with Cal. Her Harrisburg family would be enjoying time with friends for a few days, and she was free to focus on her other family—the Gardners. She planned to take full advantage of the promising opportunity.

The house was quiet as she made her way through the downstairs hall. Laura revisited the parlor to retrieve the garden guide and then remembered the wedding photo on the mantelpiece. She picked it up and slipped it in between the pages of the book. Turning off the lights, she experienced what she had felt the evening before: a strangely powerful wish to bring Cal and the girls to the farm.

As Laura started up the stairs, the voices began again. Whispers but a bit louder. This time, she could tell they were women. Standing still, Laura strained to hear something, anything that was being said. The words flowed together, over top of each other, swirling like the water in the stream. She could pick out three distinct strains this time. *It's like listening to one of Bach's inventions*, she thought, remembering her childhood piano lessons. Her teacher always said, "Find the theme, and follow it through the entire piece, no matter where it appears." There was one sound, not quite a word, that Laura picked out again and again. Then the conversation faded away. Laura continued up the stairs, went into her bedroom, and quietly closed the door behind her. *If this place were haunted, I think I would feel fright*, Laura observed. *But I am sensing curiosity, as if spirits are coaxing me find something…or someone.* She made her way to her bathroom, turned on the light, and then prepared for bed by showering, brushing her teeth, and combing out her hair. She slipped on her nightgown and without much thought sat down in the rocker. Pulling the photograph of her parents from the book, she touched her mother's image gently and then rested the picture against the mirror on the dressing table. Opening the book Simon had handed her, immediately she became engrossed in stories of early Chester Town.

"It began with a sycamore tree," the narrative reported. "Settlers disembarking from *The Shield* headed to this place and reached it after days of slogging through swamps full of holly and climbing across hills beautified by lush blooms of laurel." Apparently, upon their arrival, the first Quakers planted a tree which was alive when this book had been printed. She hoped it was still there.

Skipping forward a few pages, Laura read an account of a tavern established before the Revolutionary War, which was a stagecoach stop on the Kings Highway to Philadelphia. In the next chapter, she read that the boundaries for local family farms were often described by trees and plants. "Samuel Burr's orchard runs from the corner of Chester Pike to a stake fifty paces from the white oak tree." Laura wondered if Bittersweet Acres had been surveyed in such a manner. She came to another passage describing "two houses built in a garden nine hundred feet back from Springhouse Road. There is a quaint stone well at the center, a rose arbor lovingly tended by the residents, a charming children's playhouse, and a walled terrace with apple trees." A footnote indicated that the owner was apt to serve tea to passersby in the gazebo!

Laura looked forward with new interest to her pending excursion into town.

But as her eyelids grew heavy, she put down the book and turned out the bedroom lamp. The moon's light shone through her open window, flowing across the wide plank floorboards and up onto the bed covers. On the nightstand, the pot of cream was glowing as if iridescent. Laura went over and picked it up, opening the lid, breathing in the fragrance, and dipping her fingertips into the cool contents. Smoothing the balm on each hand, she was overwhelmed by the aroma of spices and the sense of a loving presence quite near her.

"Momma, I know your spirit is here," she whispered.

A whip-poor-will was just ending its lullaby as Laura snuggled beneath the soft sheet and drifted to sleep in the moonlight.

The sound of a horse whinnying! I run to the fence, holding several small apples I've picked from the orchard. I remember to flatten out my hand as I reach toward the massive beast, allowing him to nibble the fruit without catching my fingers in his teeth. As he is finishing the last bite, a shadow falls across me from behind. I turn to see a tall, brown-skinned woman standing behind me. This figure has a cape made of a thousand turkey feathers draped across her shoulders, and for a moment, I think she might actually be a bird.

"You left something behind. You must return and get it." The voice is stern but more anxious than angry.

Is this the figure I had seen before, bent over the light in the cave? No, this person is flesh and blood. She is reaching out to me. I climb down from the fence and then hesitantly take the woman's strong calloused hand. Together, we walk to the stile and climb over the fence and into the meadow. As we come to a stream, I notice a brightly colored turtle make his way out of the water and onto the bank to sun itself. The woman speaks softly to the turtle, almost like a prayer. Then she speaks to me.

"The Great Spirit created the world. All the earth was covered with water. Then a large tortoise raised its back out of the waters, and it became the land which we now occupy." I listen intently to the mellow tones of the creation story and hear something of the timbre of my own

mother's voice speaking. The faces are different, but the voices are the same—the dark woman's and my mother's.

The story ends and the woman motions for me to follow her into the forest. We walk single file, following the narrow deer track where teaberry plants and blueberry bushes are plentiful. The chipmunk is standing guard again. This time, it sounds as if his chattering is repeating "bittersweet." My guide points to the cave where I like to play. The aroma of warm pine surrounds me as I make my way up the small bank. I turn back a moment later, but the dark woman is nowhere to be seen.

I enter the dim space, and the cool air envelopes me. Waiting for my eyes to adjust, I remember the other visit, the shadow figure, a small flame revealing my charcoal drawings, a fading presence. A disembodied voice echoes in my mind. "You left something behind. You must return and get it."

On the floor of the cave is the leather pouch. I recall having stumbled over it before. I squat down to look at it more closely. Opening a flap of material, I see it contains a wooden doll, hand carved from a single piece of wood. It is dressed like a Le-nah-pe woman in a tunic of soft tan doeskin. Around its neck are strings of tiny shell beads.

Picking up the bundle with care, I stand up and walk toward the entrance to the cave. I hear a drum beating, muffled and distant, but with a distinct rhythm. Then the sound of the flute begins. A signal? A summons? Unsure what to do, I tuck the leather package under my arm and make my way out into the sunlight. The music seems to come from the direction of the setting sun, but the trail leads only in the opposite direction. I hesitate for a moment and then turn and follow the path back to the stream.

CHAPTER 9

Laura was jarred awake by a sudden loud crash and clatter beneath her window. The sun was already up, and for a moment, she did not know where she was. The drums and flute song from her dream faded as shouts and muffled expletives rose on the breeze from the backyard. She threw back the coverlet and dashed across the room to see what was happening. There in the grass sat an old man, holding his ankle and grimacing. His overalls had blotches of red on one side and down the legs. Simon stood over him, his face showing both concern and annoyance. Beside them on the ground was the rickety wooden ladder that Laura remembered seeing up against the house. Now it had several rungs broken, and shreds of denim fabric were caught in one side rail.

"Oh, Uncle Lawrence!" shouted Laura. "Are you all right?"

Without waiting for an answer, she pulled on her robe, wrapping it around her as she dashed down the stairs and out of the house. By the time she reached the scene of the accident, Lawrence was lying back quietly, and Simon was checking him over.

"A nasty scrape and a badly twisted ankle," the younger man announced.

Laura grabbed a pillow from the chair on the back porch, placing it carefully under her great-uncle's head. She looked up at Simon for some clue as to the seriousness of the injuries and was slightly reassured by his calm demeanor.

"I'll get the first aid kit and clean up your wounds. Then we'll call the doctor and have him look at the rest of you." Simon was clearly a take-charge person. "Laura, will you sit here with him for a minute?"

"Sure."

Simon disappeared into the house, and Laura turned to Lawrence.

"I'm fine," her uncle muttered, clearly uncomfortable and unhappy to be stretched out on the grass in front of Laura. "When I was out for my walk this morning, I noticed that darn spot Simon missed when he repainted the shutters last month. So I got the can of red paint and thought I could just...ouch!" He grabbed his side.

"Lie still," Laura ordered gently. "When I woke up, I heard shouts and then saw you from my bedroom window. I was so frightened. From up there, I couldn't see that all this red on you was just paint!"

Simon was back with the medical supplies. Laura reached for them. "Here, Simon. Let me do that while you get in touch with doctor." Simon tried to protest and then relented. Laura was silently reprimanding herself for her overreaction, and yet any injury at Lawrence's age could be serious. Once she had cleaned and bandaged the cuts and scrapes on his leg, she checked the swelling in his ankle and knew they should ice it right away. He'd need an X-ray, no doubt.

Simon returned to the yard carrying ice cubes wrapped in a tea towel. With Laura's help, he was able to maneuver Lawrence to a sitting position. Then they got him standing up on his uninjured leg. Simon steadied the seemingly weightless frame while Laura dragged the chair from the porch, placing the cushion back on the seat. Then she supported her uncle as he sat down again, quite gingerly. An apple crate from under the porch became an ottoman of sorts, elevating the injured ankle of the older man. Tenderly, she applied the ice pack. Laura was becoming apprehensive about how the rest of this day would unfold.

"I'll get dressed as quickly as I can." She hurried into the house and up the stairs. Pulling her hair back in a headband, she grabbed her jeans from the wardrobe, smoothed a few wrinkles from a plaid cotton shirt as she slipped it over her head, fastened on her sandals, and took a quick glance in the mirror. Earrings! No time. Grabbing her purse, she scrambled down the stairs and outside.

The two men were talking quietly and looked up approvingly as she approached.

"Nice," offered Simon. Laura reddened slightly, pleased that she could pull herself together so quickly. "Let's get him to the car," he added. Lawrence looked directly at Simon and grimaced. Was he angry or worried? Laura was not sure.

They both helped settle the older man in the backseat, his leg propped up and the ice pack on his ankle. Laura climbed into the front seat as Simon started the engine of the boxy silver Volvo.

"It's a turbo," warned Simon.

"So let's get a move on," urged Lawrence impatiently from his position in the backseat. He winced in pain. As they pulled out of the yard and onto the dirt road, Simon explained to Laura that they had found this car at the local used-auto dealer's place several years ago, in great condition, with low mileage and lots of pep. The reliability of this model was legend. The truth was that both men had fallen in love with the car.

"Lawrence likes the roominess and these large windows," Simon pointed out. "The sweet engine was my bonus." They turned onto the highway and picked up speed. Lawrence spoke again.

"We thought it would do fine for the short trips into town or Simon's excursions into Philly. And I enjoy our occasional drives on back roads through the Pines to the shore on the weekends." Laura glanced up at the mirror on her visor. Her uncle's face was pale under the weathered tan. Simon accelerated just a bit and followed the flow to traffic around one of the jug handle intersections for which New Jersey is famous.

"We're meeting your doctor at the county hospital, Lawrence." The driver's voice was firm but gentle, signaling that there were to be no arguments about it. The entrances to the medical facility were well marked. Simon pulled in at the emergency department and turned off the engine. He and Laura got out, and while Simon went for a wheelchair, Laura opened the back door of the car and assisted Lawrence in sliding across the seat. She looked up as the two people accompanying Simon announced that the hospital staff would take over. Stepping back, Simon and Laura watched as the man and woman in medical attire deftly maneuvered Lawrence into a wheel-chair and then through the doors. Laura followed them while Simon moved the car.

After the initial triage interview, Laura and her great-uncle were taken into an examining room. Simon arrived just as a middle-aged man with wire-rimmed glasses joined them. He introduced himself to Laura as Dr. Serene. *What a lovely name for a health care professional!* she noted. Directing his words to Lawrence, the doctor continued.

"I wanted to see you in here because of your age." The older man winced again, pained by the comment as much as his injuries. Dr. Serene did not seem to notice. "Let's have a look-see."

He asked Laura and Simon to step out into the hallway and then closed the door.

"Are you okay?" Laura asked Simon, noting his edginess.

"Yeah, just feeling like I've let Lawrence down. He knows better than to get up on that broken ladder. But I should have been more careful." He scuffed his shoe on the floor like an embarrassed little boy. "It's tough. He has a mind of his own, and I don't want to take away all of his independence."

Laura listened as Simon gave a measured account of the difficulties of being a full-time caregiver for her great-uncle. Until that moment, Laura had not given much thought to the burden he had assumed with his job. She admired him all the more.

"Oh, Simon. It's not your fault. If anything, I have been a distraction to you both."

Just then the door opened, and the doctor invited the two back into the room.

"We've cleaned up the leg wounds and put a little stitch in the large one... The ankle has a serious Grade 3 sprain, which means torn ligaments. An ice pack will bring the swelling down. Then we'll get him in a splint. It's going to stay pretty painful for a while. I've also ordered an X-ray to check for cracked ribs." Then he turned to the patient. "I'm admitting you, Lawrence, just until we get all the tests done and we are sure no other bumps or bruises are going to appear."

Simon tried to reassure the old man. "Good idea, don't you think? I'm not sure I can get you up the steps at home anyway right now."

"Oh, I guess you can keep me here, Doc, if you really think it's necessary," responded Lawrence dejectedly. "Just for a day, though. I have company to entertain." That was Laura's cue.

"Well, Simon was going to show me around town and take me to meet your solicitor. We can keep the garden weeded and watered for a couple of days, if necessary." She paused. "And I promise to stay close to Simon until you get home again." As soon as she uttered those words, she blushed. It sounded more intimate than she intended, and she hoped Simon did not read anything into her comments.

A nurse arrived, pulled up the sides of the gurney, and then guided Lawrence's bed into the hall and over to the elevator. Simon went along, turning back and indicating for Laura to wait for him in the lobby. The doctor came and stood beside her.

"He's one tough guy, and I am pretty sure there won't be any problems. But because of his age, we have to be cautious."

"Thanks," Laura managed. She was dazed by the entire experience and unsure of her role in what was happening.

"I'll have orders written up for you before we send him home. For the ankle, it's rest, ice, compression, and elevation, along with a pain reliever. Once the splint comes off, we'll show you exercises for him to do." Laura started to explain that she wouldn't be in town that long but let it go, listening instead to what the doctor was telling her about her uncle's condition. "This is one of those ankle injuries that can put even young folks out of action for months, and it's also likely to be reinjured somewhere down the line if he doesn't take precautions. Try to keep him immobilized as long as you can." Laura noted a sly twinkle in Dr. Serene's eyes. Apparently, he knew Lawrence all too well.

His tone changed slightly, showing more worry. "Laura, I'm concerned about the ribs. If we find they are fractured, he could develop breathing issues pretty quickly. But we'll know more about that tomorrow." Then he reached over and took Laura's hand. "I am so happy to meet you. Lawrence has been fretting about what will happen to the farm once he's gone. But now you are here, and that means a lot to him, I'm sure."

Laura was about to emphasize that she was just visiting, but she was too weary to continue the conversation. Dr. Serene disappeared behind a door labeled Staff Only. She walked to the drinking fountain, swallowed some water, and then found a chair in the lobby. As she wrestled with what the doctor had said, the elevator doors opened, and Simon stepped out. His stride revealed the same exhaustion she was experiencing, now that the adrenaline rush has ebbed. She stood up and met him at the hospital entrance. They walked in silence to the Volvo.

"Let's get some lunch," Simon said glumly as he unlock the car door.

CHAPTER 10

The Cuckoo Clock was the popular German restaurant in Chester Town. Simon was silent as he pulled into their gravel parking lot. Laura was also too tired to speak. The couple exited the car and found the front door. Inside, Laura immediately understood the significance of the name of this place. A riotous cacophony of ticking came from over thirty quaint, hand-carved wooden timepieces from Bavaria hanging on the wall behind the bar. The larger ones resembled chalets adorned with tiny dancing figures in dirndls and lederhosen. Others displayed idyllic scenes from farm life with chickens, cows, or sheep. Smaller clocks had the familiar shape of a little birdhouse with a small hinged door in the center.

Laura slowed to admire one miniature timepiece with two delicately carved wooden birds in flight. She was sure all of them would produce the iconic "cuckoo" call on the hour and was relieved when Simon chose a table for them on the shady outdoor patio, which overlooked a stream. It would be quieter there.

The waiter provided iced water almost immediately, followed in a timely manner by their entrées. Laura had selected a salad called Castle Neuschwanstein: broiled salmon on assorted greens with radishes, caramelized almonds, and balsamic vinaigrette dressing. The bratwurst on potato roll was Simon's favorite, he told her. It was smothered in onions and peppers and served with a large helping of warm German potato salad.

As they ate, Laura read aloud to Simon from the colorful brochure at the table. "The common cuckoo, native to Europe, had long served as a natural marker of time, a welcome harbinger of spring. Its familiar calls denoted the coming of the new season and warmer weather." Skipping down a bit, she found a lovely quote from a British naturalist. "There are few who do not feel a thrill of pleasure when the first cuckoo is heard in a lovely spring morning. Mellowed by distance, borne softly from some thick tree whose tender and yellow-green leaves are but half-opened, it seems to assure us that, indeed, winter is past."

Simon indicated that the owner's family came from a village in the Black Forest. "He's got clocks from each of the most famous German clockmakers: Hermle, Hans, Rombach und Haas, Anton Schneider," Simon informed her. "A couple were carved by his relatives who worked in the factories. It's quite a collection." Apparently, the owner also had a sense of humor because each clock was set just a second or two off from the others. At one o'clock, Laura and Simon were treated to a full minute of chimes and cuckoo calls and clock doors clicking open and shut. Laura giggled as she imagined spending New Year's Eve in the place.

Simon looked at her and smiled back. For a moment, his concern for Lawrence disappeared, and he focused on the woman sitting across the table from him. "Let's not to go back to the farm just yet," he suggested. "Shall we take that grand tour of Chester Town I promised you?" Laura was feeling refreshed after the meal and her glass of chilled Riesling.

"I'd love that, if you are up to it. Just let me visit the rest room first." She walked across the patio and into the bar, admiring the clocks again. The quiet of the ladies' room with its aroma of delicate lavender potpourri soothed her spirit. She finished up with a thorough hand wash and a splash of cool water on her face. Looking in the mirror as she blotted her cheeks dry, she realized that, in spite of no time for makeup that morning, her skin looked amazingly clear and smooth. She searched in her purse, found and applied a bronze lipstick, and then put a dab on each cheek and blended it in. *That's better*, she observed. She turned and headed back to the patio. Simon stood, having paid the tab in her absence, and escorted her to the entrance and out to the car. Both seemed to have renewed energy since eating lunch.

"First stop, the lawyer's office."

Laura's stomach lurched. She had hoped for more notice. Given the events of the morning and her attire of shirt and jeans, she was hardly dressed to impress. For a split second, she wondered if Simon had planned to make this meeting awkward for her. But the man already was pulling in and parking in front of a yellow brick office building with the brass nameplate on the door: *Kevin L. Perkins Esq.* She flipped down the car visor and quickly checked her hair while Simon sat there grinning.

"What?" Her tone expressed her irritation.

"Oh, nothing. Kev will love you."

Laura got out, gathering her thoughts as Simon meandered to the parking meter and deposited two quarters. Then they walked together into the building.

The foyer was dim and cool. A large wood desk marked *Reception* was unattended.

"Perhaps he's not in," suggested Laura. "We can come back another…"

"Kev! We're here!" shouted Simon. Laura winced and frowned.

A door to their left flew open. A balding, pudgy man clad in neatly pressed khaki slacks and a bright-green Chester Links golf shirt strode quickly toward them.

"Simon, you are early, as usual."

The lawyer shook Simon's hand while turning toward Laura. "Lawrence's niece, I presume. Hello."

"Great niece," she corrected and immediately wished she had not said it.

"Of course. Yes. Well, come in. Come in."

Kevin ushered them into his well-appointed office, pouring iced water in crystal glasses and indicating they should sit on the leather sofa beside the window. Laura took a deep breath and tried to calm her nerves. After all, she, too, had her *juris doctor* degree and a successful law practice. Then Laura remembered something her mother said about going into awkward situations.

"You can't cry when you are drinking water," Christina had admonished, "so be sure to have some handy when you're nervous." With a grateful heart, Laura took the glass Kevin handed her. Simon

73

indicated that they had just come from the hospital. He shared the story of Lawrence's fall. The lawyer expressed concern at the news and immediately turned to Laura.

"Then it's good you are here to discuss your great-uncle's legal affairs. You do know that I was the one who handled things when your mother died. My condolences, by the way. Then Simon brought Lawrence in about a year ago to make a few changes." Laura was feeling at ease discussing legal matters and was eager to know what those "changes" might have been. She ran through her standard list of inquiries, and Kevin was ready to respond to each one. Yes, he had a list of Lawrence's bank accounts, investments, insurance policies, etc. His office had a copy of the will, and the original was kept in a safety deposit box at Chester Town Banking and Trust. Kevin then picked up the Gardner file from his desk and sat down opposite Laura, handing her each document in turn.

"Here's the durable power of attorney." Lawrence had designated Simon as the person to act on his behalf, Laura read. Should Lawrence become incapacitated, Simon will have the authority to take care of everything for him: buy or sell real estate, manage investments, operate the farm, handle taxes, represent him in lawsuits, and apply for benefits. "You know the drill. If we want to change that person, Lawrence just has to let me know. But I wouldn't wait too long if that's what he has planned." That sounded ominous at first, but Laura knew Kevin was referring to the need for the person to be physically and mentally competent in order to revoke a POA. At this point, she was comfortable with these arrangements as they stood.

"Next," the attorney continued, "we have a health care POA. Again, you see Simon is the one to make any and all health care decisions for your great-uncle if he is not able to make them himself." Laura scanned the document. She did not know if Simon and Lawrence had discussed potential health issues. Had they agreed on a course of action that would be taken in case of a crisis? She would talk to both of them about that later.

"This is fine for now," Laura said, placing the papers on the table. Then it occurred to her that it was possible Simon might quit working at the farm at some point or move away. She did not want anything left to chance or to the whim of an uncaring court official. So she looked up. "Kevin, I think I'd like to be identified as the backup agent for both of these, just in case Simon is, well, not available. Does that make sense?"

"As the relative, sure," the lawyer answered and then looked at Simon, who nodded approval. "I'll draw it up that way and bring it by for Lawrence to sign next week. And I just noticed a typo, Simon. My secretary misspelled your last name in both of these. I'll have her change that right away." He scribbled some notes on a sheet of paper and clipped it to the documents. "Now we have this letter of intent which was written some time ago, before your mother's death, and isn't a legal document as such, but Lawrence wanted it in the file as his personal directive." He handed it to Laura. She noted it was still addressed to Christina as executor and beneficiary. Kevin continued, "Lawrence is worth quite a lot. We should probably get clarification about which of you he wants to handle the distribution of his assets. When he gets home from the hospital, give me a call. I'll come by to go over this and make the necessary changes."

Laura pondered the necessity to put a monetary value on history and memories and relationships. Suddenly, tears began to well up as a wave of grief washed over her. She did not want to continue this discussion with Kevin. She was developing an affection for her great-uncle and the farm. This was not the time for her to consider his death and all that it would entail. She found a tissue in her purse and blotted her eyes.

"Kevin, I appreciate so much your taking care of all this. I had always assumed my mother would be having this conversation with you."

"Well, you need to give credit to Simon for encouraging your uncle to get things cared for." Laura did not correct him this time.

"Oh yes, I do," Laura affirmed. "He's here on the scene. I am not, at least not yet." *Where did those words come from?* Somewhere in Laura's mind was a suggestion that all that might change!

"I'm glad to hear you say that," Kevin replied brightly, "since at this point you are the beneficiary to the entire Gardner estate." Laura let those words sink in for a minute. Christina was the only member of the generation after Marial and Lawrence, so she would have inherited the farm. But now that she was gone, it would be given over to Laura! No wonder Uncle Lawrence had been pressing her yesterday to tell him she would look after things. Again, she was embarrassed by her lack of awareness of how much her visit meant to him.

Setting aside those thoughts for the moment, Laura opened her purse again and pulled out the leather case holding business cards. She scrawled her home telephone number on the back of one and handed it to the lawyer. "Once I'm back home, please don't hesitate to contact me. I'm sorry it took so long for us to meet." She took another pleasant sip of the cool water while silently admiring the elegant glassware.

Kevin clipped her card to the files, put them back on his desk, and picked up his card to give to Laura. "I don't suppose you golf," he stated with a tinge of disappointment.

"No, but my husband, Cal, likes *to think* he does."

"Well, when he is back here with you, have him give me a ring."

Simon sensed the meeting was over and stood to move toward the door. A few more words of farewell and then he and Laura returned to the sidewalk outside the law office.

"That went well." Simon seemed content that something had been crossed off his to-do list. Laura wanted to make a comment but decided instead to ask him about their plans for the rest of the day.

"Do you still want to show me around town now?"

"Sure. Since we have time on the meter, we can walk a bit, if you feel like it."

"Great. My muscles need a good stretch."

They walked to the corner and turned west. The shady sidewalk was cooling off as the sun lowered in the sky, and they stopped to read the bronze plaque beside an old sycamore tree. It was the one planted by the first Quakers that Laura had hoped to see! Simon slowed again as the two reached an old building with a decorative wooden sign: *Cox's Tavern.*

"This was the old stagecoach stop," he informed Laura. She remembered reading about it in the garden book. "There were hitching posts across the front, and the porch was a favorite gathering place for townsfolk." He directed her attention around to the side of the two-story wooden structure. "That porch was the entrance to the original bar room in the back. No women allowed." Laura stepped back to get a better look at the entire structure. She tried imagining a carriage ride from Philadelphia to Chester Town and an overnight in this quaint hotel over a noisy saloon.

"Who lives here now?" she asked.

"The McCoy family bought it around 1900. Over time they have added indoor plumbing, upgraded the kitchen, and made it their family home. It has been well cared through the years, but I am afraid when the last son, Clarence, dies, it will be torn down and replaced by a modern office building." There was a hint of sorrow in his voice.

"Does Uncle Lawrence have any photographs of how 'old' Chester Town looked?"

Simon thought for a minute. "He may, and I am sure the historical society has a collection as well."

"Ooh, I'd enjoy spending some time there."

As they continued their stroll, Simon pointed out a number of attractive old homes with narrow alleyways between them. Standing at the certain angle, Laura could glimpse the backyards, some with grape arbors, others with aged wooden barns or outbuildings, and most overflowing with flowers. This town was heaven for gardeners. *And Gardners*, thought Laura.

Simon looked at his watch. "Let's head back to the car before we get a parking ticket. Then I can drive you around town a bit." He paused and added, almost apologetically, "Laura, I really want to check on Lawrence before we head back to the farm."

She heard the concern in his voice. "Well, why don't you just leave me here and you go visit him?" she suggested. "I can walk around a bit more, browse in some of the shops, and soak up the ambiance of the town. Pick me up in, say, two hours?"

"Do you mind?" Simon was almost euphoric. "I know you want to see him too."

"Yes, I do. But I also don't want to overwhelm him right now. Give him my love, and tell him I will come by in the morning. I think he'll understand."

"Okay. Thanks. I'll meet you at the other end of the street under the town clock."

"I can find that." Laura smiled as she watched Simon turn, stride away, and disappear around the corner. Her affection for the man surprised her. Then she glanced again at the old tavern before moving on. *So much history on the verge of disappearing forever*, she mused. Would she be able to keep that from happening to Bittersweet Acres?

Most of the shops on both sides of the main thoroughfare were in fact old homes that had been restored or renovated. Many had impressive landscaping and historic registry signs. With their inviting front stoops, leaded casement windows, and decorative stained glass transoms, it was obvious that the look of the street had changed very little over time. Vintage clothing items were displayed in one window, toys and games in the next, then the drugstore with cards and gifts, a shoe store, and one displaying copious artists' supplies. There was even an original one-room log cabin with candlelights in each window. *Piney Woods Soap and Candles*, said the sign. Laura wanted to explore each one, but instead stopped in the pharmacy to purchase a few picture post cards of the town, and took mental notes of the shops she would visit on her next trip.

Strolling past a hair salon and a quaint used bookstore Laura came to a church building with intricate stone work and a tall steeple with a carillon. *This must be the church in Granny's family photographs*, she remembered. She gently pushed on the wrought iron gate leading to the entrance garden, and was pleased to find it opened easily. She felt as if she had been transported into an old English vicarage. A boxwood hedge lined the flagstone walk and a well-tended rose garden was laid out next to the building. When she reached the front door of the church and pulled on the handle, it also yielded to her touch. Her breath caught as she entered the cool darkness of the sanctuary with familiar aromas of beeswax candles and furniture polish. The door closed quietly behind her, and she walked down the center aisle. Late afternoon sunbeams penetrated stained glass windows, casting pale light across the pews. Laura recognized scenes from the life of Jesus in some windows while others depicted what she thought might be famous figures from Anglican church history.

Slipping into one of the rows, she let herself become lost in the pleasure of the moment. She thought of her mother, the first woman minister Laura ever knew. Laura always considered the church building as home, filled with love and beauty and mystery. On this afternoon, she was feeling nostalgic knowing that this town was where Christina grew up. Laura was coming to understand better why her mother never lost her love of the family farm and why she chose that country cemetery outside Pittsburgh as her final resting place.

Her thoughts drifted into a prayer. "God, I sense your spirit here in this sanctuary and in this community. Is this where you want *me* to be?" Her reverie was interrupted by a door opening and closing and then footsteps coming up the aisle toward her. A shadow in priestly garb swished past and climbed the steps leading to the lectern. She could not make out the figure's face clearly, but she was sure it was a man. He opened the large Bible, ran his finger down the page, and then began to read.

> *Jesus said, "You know the commandments: 'You shall not murder; You shall not commit adultery; You shall not steal; You shall not bear false witness; You shall not defraud; Honor your father and mother.'" The woman said to him, "Teacher, I have kept all these since my youth." Jesus, looking at her, loved her and said, "My dear, you still lack one thing; go, sell what you own, let go of your money, and you will find a heavenly treasure. Come, follow me."*

That was not the way Laura remembered that passage from the Gospels. She knew the person Jesus addressed was a lawyer, but it would not have been a woman. Laura was puzzled. Was the message for her? Was she the one lacking one thing? The priestly shadow raised his head and spoke directly to Laura.

"Honor your mother. Honor your father." Then he closed the book and disappeared through a door in the chancel area. *Why did this man speak to me that way?* Just then, there was a humming and a buzz followed by the notes of a scale being played on a pipe organ. Her thoughts were muddled. Had she been dozing? Laura checked the time. It had been almost two hours since Simon had left her. She stood and quietly slipped out a side door so as not to disturb the musician's practice. That exit opened on a brick path through the garden. It circled around the side of the building, went through an arched cloister, and led into the parish graveyard.

As Laura walked among the tombstones, the memories of her mother were strong. What was happening to her? Being in the sanctuary seemed to amplify a spiritual connection to this town and to her family. She felt a tiny bubble rising inside her. Contentment, perhaps? As she let herself out through the wrought iron gate, she could still hear the organ playing. It was an old Shaker hymn she recognized, her mother's favorite—"Simple Gifts."

CHAPTER 11

Back in front of the church, Laura was greeted by a whiff of freshly baked bread emanating from the German Bakery, a shop just a bit farther down the block. *Perhaps Simon would enjoy a break from being her pastry chef.* She found the door and went inside, accompanied by the tinkle of a tiny bell. A jolly old gentleman with rosy cheeks and white whiskers appeared behind the glass cases. He smiled broadly and invited her over to sample the fresh batch of warm cookies he held on a tray. She thanked him as she selected one and took a bite. Then licking the gooey chocolate from her fingers, Laura introduced herself. When she commented that she had eaten a marvelous lunch at the Cuckoo Clock, the baker's grin widened.

"That's my cousin's place," he replied with a thick German accent. "He's Albert Bruchhausan, and I'm Johnny. We've been friends with the Gardners ever since our family moved here from Camden." When she told him of Lawrence's accident, he was visibly worried. She had to reassure him that the hospital stay was cautionary.

"Simon is with him now, and I've been on a walking tour of Chester Town." She asked Johnny if there was anything he made that her great-uncle especially liked. The baker nodded and pulled out a sheet of thin white cardboard from under the counter. He adeptly folded it into a box, locked the sides into place, and then proceeded to fill it with rolls and assorted sweets. Laura watched as he layered a small fruit pie, some strudel, crumb buns, and cookies between sheets of wax paper. Then he closed the lid and wrapped the box with string which he snapped off and tied in a secure bow. "How much is all this?" she inquired.

"No charge!"

PENELOPE GLADWELL

"Please…"

"This is all good medicine for your sweet uncle. And for you and Simon too. Take good care of my old friend, and let me know how he is doing."

"Simon will be in touch, I am sure. Thank you so much. This is most kind."

"You'd best be on your way, Liebling. There is an impatient fellow waiting for you across the street." Laura looked out through the storefront window. Sure enough, Simon had parked the car, gotten out, and was leaning casually against the passenger side of the vehicle. Her heart jumped, which surprised her. She was genuinely happy to see him. Leaving the bakery, she waved to Simon, stood at the curb until the traffic was cleared, and then carried the bakery box to the car.

Simon shook his head in feigned anguish. "I should have warned you about Johnny," he teased as he opened the car door for Laura. "He loves pretty faces, and his baked goods are to die for." Blushing slightly and carefully placing the box on the floor, Laura inquired about her uncle.

"Resting comfortably," Simon replied as he walked to the other side of the car. "The doctor found hairline cracks in two ribs which he wants to watch. They'll do more tests tomorrow. So that gives us time to arrange things at the farm."

Laura wanted to ask him what he meant by "arrange things," but Simon was already getting in the driver's seat, so she climbed in her side. The interior of the Volvo had quickly filled with the aroma of sweet rolls and bread.

"Let me show you a few of the old brick houses I mentioned before."

They pulled away from the curb and made a right turn at the intersection. The next street on the right took them into a charming tree-lined neighborhood. Simon assumed the role of tour guide, explaining how, as the abundance of wood in the cedar swamps ran out, later settlers turned to other building materials. "This county became well-known in the mid-1700s for its artisan bricklayers." He slowed the car, pointing out unique architectural features on some of the homes. One had a Flemish checker-board pattern, another a zigzag border, and then another with a diamond design. Laura noted that one house even had dates and initials worked into the brick on the gabled end.

Like the Bittersweet farmhouse, these were all large square buildings with smaller structures attached. Simon was correct; the trained eye could distinguish which parts had been built first by examining the color of the brick. It looked to Laura like the original floor plan had become standard: the first floor had a center hall with rooms on each side and a staircase to the second floor. The number of bedrooms could vary from three to four. A shed on the back probably held the original kitchen. It was only the addition of porches or gables that gave the row of houses any individuality.

Simon turned several more corners and then pulled over to the curb. "Here's the place Lawrence bought when he came back from college." It seemed to be a two story version of the farmhouse! Laura rolled down the window, as if to breathe in the history of the place. Set back from the street, it had a flagstone walk up to the front. This porch was small, yet it still seemed welcoming. The front yard was more garden than lawn, with yarrow, coneflowers, and other perennials smartly positioned among ground covers and annual blooms. A picture flashed into Laura's head: the flagstone patio beside her mother's parsonage in Pittsburgh! Christina had recreated this very space for herself in a city far from the people and places where she was raised. *Oh, Momma, were you homesick?* Laura wondered.

"The folks who bought this place from him are members of the meeting and have honored Lawrence by keeping up the flower garden. He asks me to drive him by here once in a while so he can admire it." Simon turned the car around in the driveway and traveled west for several miles. On her right, Laura noted the entrance of what had once been a gated community. Stone pillars had supported a decorative grillwork of wrought iron that had rusted through. Only a weathered verdigris plaque was visible. *Mount Vernon Farms.* Laura gasped.

"What's wrong?" Simon was alarmed and slowed the car as he reached over and took Laura's hand.

"No, no. It's all right." Catching her breath, she explained, "I just had a momentary flashback. Mom is buried in a place called Mount Vernon Cemetery. It has stone pillars just like those." After another minute, she swallowed and said, "I was not expecting that." Simon had pulled to the curb and stopped. He turned to face Laura.

"Grieving is a strange process, isn't it?" Simon offered. "The smallest thing can trigger a wave of emotion and at the oddest times."

Laura recalled how she felt in the lawyer's office and realized Simon had noticed it too. She appreciated his sensitivity. She must ask him to share more about *his* mom sometime. She released his hand and they continued driving through town.

By the time Simon pulled into the farm lane and parked the car beside the house, it was dusk. Laura gathered up her purse and the box of bakery items, got out of the car, and made her way into the dark kitchen. The place felt empty without Lawrence. She set everything down on the counter and went up to her room. She wanted to freshen up a bit before eating any dinner. It had been a long time since she awakened that morning to the cries of her injured great-uncle.

Meanwhile, Simon carried in an armload of groceries, letting the screen door slam behind him. He had stopped at the supermarket for the usual staples and a few special items the nurse had suggested having on hand for Lawrence's recovery: chicken soup, Jell-O, and whole milk. Once it was all put away, he grabbed a pad and pencil and sat alone at the counter, jotting down the things he needed to accomplish in the next several days.

Laura was upstairs stretched out across the big bed in her grandmother's room, trying to imagine growing up on the farm, raising a daughter alone in this house. A gentle tap on her door disturbed her thoughts. She sat up. "Who is it?" she asked, though she realized at once that it must be Simon.

Through the closed door, he told her he had heated up some home made vegetable soup and asked if she wanted to eat. "I've tossed together a bit of salad too."

"Oh, thanks," she replied. "Come on in. I must have dozed off." Simon pushed open the door and stood leaning against the jamb.

Her stomach gave a twinge. "I really am hungry, and that soup smells delicious."

Laura looked at Simon's face. She could tell he had been crying. "What is it?" She was alarmed. Sliding off the bed, she went to him, reached for his hand, and then guided him to the ladder-back rocker near the window. He collapsed in it, and Laura took a seat on the dressing table bench beside him.

Regaining his composure slightly, he started to apologize, but she signaled *no need*.

"I was chopping up a green pepper from the garden," he began, "when it occurred to me that at some point Lawrence would leave..." His voice trailed off.

Sitting in silence, Laura saw the vulnerability of this man, so strong and capable yet filled with deep caring for her great-uncle. In many ways, he was closer to Lawrence than she was, and today had to have been difficult for him.

"Laura, we assume people will be around forever, don't we?"

She knew all too well the truth of his words. After her mother died, she had regretted not spending more time with her, not being involved in her life. A blessing for Laura had come these past few years in getting to know her mother's friends.

"Today was one big wake-up call for me," he continued. "For the first time I realized just how fragile Lawrence is. I've been forced to think about what my life would be like without him." His eyes filled with tears again.

"Oh, Simon. I had no idea what you were feeling today. It was thoughtless of me to demand..."

Now he waved off *her* apology. "Actually, you were the perfect distraction." He looked up at her and for a moment his disarming smile returned, then faded. "But once we came back here, the house seemed lifeless, and I felt unsettled. Puttering around in the kitchen usually comforts me, but tonight nothing I did would relieve my sense of dread."

In another moment, he seemed to gather himself. Standing up, he suggested they go eat the soup. Laura agreed. He motioned for her to go first, but as she drew beside him, she put her arm around him and gathered him close to her. He relaxed, sobbing lightly, resting his head on her shoulder. Laura gently rubbed his back and whispered, "We'll get through this. Really, we will." The whip-poor-will's song floated in through the open window, seeming to echo her promise.

CHAPTER 12

Sitting side by side at the kitchen counter, Laura and Simon were moody as they each consumed large bowls of beef broth laden with a variety of summer garden vegetables. They made quick work of homemade rolls from Johnny's bakery and the salad of mixed greens. Laura shared how overwhelmed she felt dealing with inheritance issues at the lawyer's office.

"I understood today how much responsibility I have to the Gardner family. What will I do with a farm? With all the possessions that are going to be left here when Lawrence..."

After a long silence, Laura realized they both might be better off focusing on the immediate concerns.

"What have you written on this tablet?" asked Laura, pulling the yellow legal pad over to her place.

"My to-do list for the morning," Simon explained. "I've asked a couple of folks to come help us."

"Ah, the *arrangements* you mentioned this afternoon."

"As soon as Doc Serene saw the extent of Lawrence's injuries, he told me he'd not be able to get upstairs for quite a while. I was thinking *maybe never*. So we're going to open up the addition tomorrow and fix a place for him to stay on the ground floor over there."

Laura could hardly contain her eagerness to focus again on the Gardner family history. She wanted to explore the rest of the old farmhouse, maybe visit rooms and cubbyholes where her mother played as a child. Her energy for the task seemed to cheer Simon as well.

"We'll start early," he warned. "The Peters from next door are coming. Did you know them? And the Coxes. They'll be arriving here by six thirty to start airing out the place. We want to make a good start before the day gets too hot. And then you and I can run into town and check on Lawrence at lunchtime."

"Okay." She felt her spirits reviving. "I'll set my alarm clock. Coffee and strudel at dawn."

"Laura," Simon's voice became tender. "I am so grateful for you right now. This business with Lawrence was not something I saw coming. I'm afraid it caught me off guard." He reached over and put his hand on hers as he had in the car. "Thank you."

After a moment, Simon withdrew his hand, gathered up the dishes, and cleaned up their meal while Laura watched. All the clatter and splashing in the kitchen became background noise as Laura dealt with the emotions she was feeling. First there was Uncle Lawrence. Plenty of elderly people had a fall and never quite recovered. She, like Simon, was confronted with the possibility that this was the beginning of a steep decline of her great-uncle's health. She wanted more time with him before his...she stopped short, not able to bring herself to think *death*.

And then there was Simon, so easy to be with, pleasant, and caring. She felt as if she had known him all her life. In the midst of the chaos of today, her feelings for him had become pleasantly ambivalent. She was happy to be with him and yet sensed how dangerously close she was to hoping their friendship could become something more. It was all so confusing. She missed her family and wanted to talk to Cal about the accident, her feelings, everything. But he was in Pittsburgh with the girls, so she wouldn't contact them.

The telephone on the wall rang out, jarring Laura and bringing her thoughts back to concern for her great-uncle. Simon answered, "Hello?" His voice was anxious. Then he relaxed and handed it to her. "Your husband," he mouthed silently.

"Cal? Oh, I am so glad you called!" Laura turned to stare out the kitchen window into the dark. After quickly ascertaining that her family was still in Pittsburgh and that they all were healthy and having a good time, she began to share the events of her day, starting with Lawrence's accident. Simon wiped the last drips of water off the countertop and then quietly exited the room using the back stairs to the second floor.

"I just don't know how this is going to end for him," she finally added. "We'll find out more tomorrow."

Cal had listened, knowing that his wife was a strong woman, like her mother. Still he wished he were there to support her. "Take whatever time you need, my love," he said. "The girls and I are going to head home in the afternoon. I'll call you once they get settled in bed tomorrow night. By then you'll have more information and time to think about what you need to do."

Always calm and sensible, Cal knew just what Laura needed to hear. She hung up with a sense of reassurance that she would not have to face whatever happened alone. As she remembered Simon's confession earlier, she was keenly aware that, without Lawrence, he *would* be adrift. The farm would belong to Laura. Where did Simon fit into that future scenario? A tender ache returned to her heart. Looking around the kitchen, she realized how graciously he had honored her privacy by leaving the room. *One of the good guys*, she thought warmly. *We'll figure something out together.* Turning off the lights as she went, Laura made her way through the hall, into the foyer, and up the front staircase. The moonlight shone through the transom over the front door, lighting the pathway up to the second floor. Weariness overcame her, slowing her ascent. The three ghostly women's voices were speaking again. As she reached the top step, she leaned against the banister, listening intently to the lilt of what seemed to be a pleasant conversation. Tonight she was able to understand one or two sounds, a word that each woman spoke in turn and which seemed to excite them.

Laura also detected anticipation in the tone that evening, as if the word spoken was the name of something or someone holy. She said it in her mind, determined not to let the strange word slip away. As the conversation around her faded, she hurried into her room, found some paper on the dressing table near the lamp, and printed how it sounded to her: *g a h m u i n.* Tomorrow, she must mention it to Simon.

Her long-overdue hot shower was soothing. She ran the soap over her tired arms and legs, shampooed her hair, and then rinsed by letting the water pour down over her head, calming her entire body. *Honor your father and your mother.* The ancient words recited by the priestly figure that afternoon flowed through her thoughts again as she stepped out of the steamy bath and wrapped herself in a clean, fluffy towel. Laura believed that this visit to Bittersweet Acres would be a way to honor her memories of Christina, but since she had known nothing of her father, she was at a loss to understand how she could fulfill that part of what seemed to be a directive. Slipping a nightgown over her head, she went to the dressing table, picked up the wedding photo, and looked again at the man in the picture. She felt no animosity toward him, nothing at all, really. She put the photo back and walked over to the bed. The nightstand held a copy of the New Testament, along with the little pot of hand cream. Laura thumbed through the Gospels, looking for the reading she thought she had heard in the church that afternoon, but it escaped her search. Instead, a piece of parchment fluttered to the floor, and she bent down to pick it up. It was some sort of blessing.

> May the stars carry your sadness away,
> May the flowers fill your heart with beauty,
> May hope forever wipe away your tears,
> And, above all, may the silence make you strong.

She read it again and then slipped the page back in the Bible, wondering if the source of this quotation was Quaker or Le-nah-pe. As she smoothed fragrant lotion on her hands, a breeze made the leaves of the tree outside her window rustle softly. For a moment, Laura thought she could hear her mother's gentle voice humming. More wishful thinking. She lay down on her side and pulled the covers up over her shoulders. Moments later she was fast asleep.

I am lying on a rug in the corner of a large room; and an older woman with a sour face is rushing around looking behind pots and bowls, turning up woven mats. She is dressed in a leather skirt and leggings edged with colorful threads and beads. Her moccasins are also dec-

orated with vibrant embroidery. Clearly, she has misplaced something precious, and it distresses her.

"Where is my ow-tas?" Her cries of anguish fill my ears. Sitting up, I try to remember what I am doing in this place. The woman whirls around and points a dark, gnarly finger in my direction. "You have done this!" she screeches. "You, Bead-Child, where have you hidden my ow-tas?"

I had been told to clean up the house for a festival. I spent the day sorting through possessions, determining to whom each item belonged, and putting everything in its proper place. I do not know what an ow-tas is, and therefore, am not able to answer the accusations of the woman.

"What does it look like?" I ask.

"Like my grandmother, of course," replies the woman sharply. The name of this crone is Roaring Waters. Somehow I know that, and she is clearly unhappy having to explain that ow-tas is a medicine doll. "I must have her with me, or we will all become sick."

Oh, the doll! I know exactly where it is. I had found it wrapped in doe skin on the floor, tripped over it, in fact; and when I saw the sweet face and the lovely outfit it was wearing, I decided to keep it. I put it in the basket I had just finished weaving the day before and tied it up in one of the rafters.

I point up. "There, in my basket," I say.

Roaring Waters sighs with relief and then climbs up on one of the beds to cut down the doll. Her mood softens as she cradles basket and all in her arms for several minutes and sings quietly to the little wooden figure. Then without speaking to me, she leaves the house.

It is impossible to go back to sleep after that. I hear the drums out in the forest begin their beating. Then a flute joins in. There is the shuffle of feet, barely audible on the carpet of pine needles outside the door. A parade, perhaps, or a dance. I get up, pushing aside the drape covering the doorway and peering out through the opening. The clearing where the house stands is filling up with people. Most are strangers to me, with bronze skin and black hair. All the people are gathering around Roaring Waters, standing close or seated at her feet. When the music stops, several women take the doll from its basket. They remove the old clothes and dress the doll in a beautiful new outfit with leather leggings and skirt, a robe of rabbit fur, and a beaded clasp holding her hair in place. At this point, the entire community begins to sing. Some young men have rattles made of turtle shells, and they shake them in time with the song. Roaring Waters wraps a cord around the medicine doll's waist and ties her to a long pole.

I watch as women form a line, dancing along behind Roaring Waters and the dangling medicine doll. The parade circles the area, pausing before the door of each home. Someone repeats the words of an ancient prayer for the well-being of the family living there. When all the dwellings have been blessed, the dancers return to their seats. Then taking loose the ties from around the doll, the older women puts it in the basket and hands it back to me. "Keep her with you always." She smiles, and for a moment, her face is the face of my mother! I thank her and walk back to the house, holding the doll like it was a real child. I crawl onto my rug, place the woven cradle beside me, and hum a lullaby to the doll as I fall asleep.

CHAPTER 13

When Laura's alarm began to buzz, it was just daybreak. She awoke remarkably refreshed for having such a strange and vivid dream. Images of a festival drifted through her thoughts as she pulled on khaki shorts, her favorite peach tee shirt, and a matching headband to hold back unruly wisps of hair. Sitting in the rocking chair to put on socks and tennis shoes, Laura went back over again the events of the day before: the uncle's fall, the hospital visit, lunch with Simon, and the happenings on her walk through Chester Town. She pictured Simon sitting beside her yesterday, admitting how much he loved his life here with Lawrence. Her heartbeat quickened briefly. She sat back against the chair and sighed. This visit was not turning out the way she had it planned at all! A few quiet days looking through documents, sorting out memorabilia, then home; that was all she had expected. Suddenly everything was complicated, and her thoughts were a jumble.

Well, perhaps some physical activity would clear her head. Today was all about preparing the farmhouse for her great-uncle to return home. But it might also be a good time for her to talk to Simon. She determined to watch for the right moment to have an honest discussion with him about the future.

By the time Laura went down to get her coffee and pastry, two strangers were already standing in the dimly lit kitchen. They greeted her guardedly, as if they were not quite sure who she was. Wayne Peters and his wife, Julia, owned the farm next door. Their family had lived there almost as long as the Gardners had been at Bittersweet Acres.

Through the screen door, Laura could see Simon standing on the side porch beside a tall sandy-haired man in a tee shirt and jeans. Facing the two men was a woman with a sturdy build, skin of bronze, and long black hair tied up in the back. She had a colorful woolen shawl around her shoulders. The woman from the fruit stand!

As Laura filled her coffee mug, the Peters couple expressed their concern over Lawrence's accident.

"I've warned the two of them that they needed more help, but they won't listen," declared Wayne. "We'll have to get this place cleaned up and safe before we leave today." Julia was only a bit less judgmental.

"We still remember back when Marial and her daughter lived here. It wasn't easy for them, but the place was in good order. Two men, well, I don't need to say more, do I?"

Laura took a sip of coffee, set her mug down, and held out her hand. "I'm Laura, Christina's daughter."

Julia reached for Laura's hands and held them between both of hers. "Oh, of course you are! It's probably been years since we last saw each other. You've aged beautifully." After a pause, she continued with a little more warmth in her voice. "Your mother was such a special person. In spite of her country upbringing, she made it in the big city. I am truly sorry she is no longer with us."

Were these two people always so annoying? Laura could not tell whether they were sincerely concerned about Lawrence or just worried about what might happen to the land once he died.

"Julia, we sound like a couple of Jersey farm hicks." Wayne laughed. "Laura, what we are trying to say is that we are sorry that Lawrence got old and needs help. We are also sorry they won't let us do more to assist him. Simon is quite good with him and has done his best at keeping up the grounds but—"

"The thing is we all were so looking forward to having Christina come back here one day to take over the place." Julia did not seem the least bit aware that she was interrupting her husband. "Once she died, everything turned out to be, well, different."

Indeed, it has turned out differently, thought Laura with a brief trace of bitterness, *for so many people.*

"Laura, do come visit us before you leave. We'd love to show you around our place and talk about your mom if you want to."

"That's very kind," she responded. "Let's see where we are at the end of today. I really want us to get Lawrence home as soon as we can." They nodded their understanding.

Laura picked up her coffee and walked quickly out onto the porch. Simon greeted her with his usual smile. "Oh, good. You're awake. And you've talked to the Peters. Laura, these are two more good friends from the meeting—Elizabeth and Randy Cox. This is Laura, Lawrence's great-niece."

Shaking hands, Elizabeth gazed directly into Laura's eyes. "Hello, again!"

"Granny, um, Elizabeth, hello."

The woman's gaze remained steady as her smile widened. "Please, call me Liz. It's short for Elizabeth. And coincidentally, the lizard is my spirit guide."

"We had tea together at the market the other afternoon!" Laura explained to Simon. Then she addressed Liz. "I am so glad to see you again." She sensed that this woman held the key to some secret in her mother's life. Laura wondered if the dreams she had been having were connected to her somehow. Simon managed to break her train of thought, something he seemed to do routinely.

"Are we ready to get started?"

Wayne and Julia joined the group on the side steps of the main house.

"We've got all the windows wide open over there," announced Julia. "It's not as musty as I thought for having been shut up so long." Laura caught Liz and Julia exchanging a knowing glance. There were boxes of cleaning supplies on the picnic table in the side yard. Simon rattled off the list of contents and asked if there was anything else they thought they might need. Since there were no additional suggestions, each one picked up a carton and marched in single file around to the opposite side of the house. As they paraded past the broken ladder, Wayne nodded to indicate he would move it. Simon mouthed, "Thank you," and walked on.

The rosy glow of the rising sun was filtering through the pine trees when Laura first stepped into the section of the old farmhouse referred to as "the addition." It had been built in the mid-1800s, and Laura recalled that its first occupants were Aaron Gardner, his wife Rebecca, and their children. Once more, she sensed how close this family had always been. Standing there in the great room, she found herself wondering what her own life might have been like if her mom had decided to move back to the farm at some point. Perhaps Christina would still be alive, living in the original building, and she and Cal and the girls would be right here, right next door. *Bittersweet. That is how all this feels right now*, Laura realized, and she forced her attention back to the present.

The main floor was surprisingly tidy, Laura observed, but it would need a good dusting and vacuuming if Lawrence were going to live there for a time. As Julia pulled the cushions off the sofa and chairs, the men carried them out onto the porch, where she took up the task of hitting them rhythmically with a sturdy wire rug beater.

"Where shall *we* start, Liz?" asked Laura.

"Let's see what's in here," responded the Cox woman. She headed for the kitchen and proceeded to pull items from the cupboards, as she prepared to wipe out the cabinets and wash up the plates and glasses. Laura followed her and began emptying the drawers, all of which contained crumbs and droppings from the frequent visits of field mice. She filled the sink with hot soapy water and dropped cutlery and other utensils in it to soak.

"I doubt that Lawrence will do any cooking here, but I can't stand a dirty kitchen," Liz explained. "Maybe Simon will want to fix some of their meals over here until things get sorted out." Laura could picture the two men actually moving into the addition one day, perhaps even renting out the larger part of the house. Then her thoughts went to a more grim possibility: that Lawrence would not live much longer, Simon would leave, and she would have to put the property up for sale. She shook her head, hoping to clear such ideas from her mind.

As the two women busied themselves, Laura decided it might be a good time to learn more about Le-nah-pe traditions and the strange words she thought she kept hearing. Gathering up her courage, she addressed Liz. "What do you believe about dreams?"

Liz stopped what she was doing, turned, and stared at Laura. "You've been sleeping in Marial's room, haven't you?" Then she resumed her work as she spoke. "Laura, my people believe that dreams are our own prayers blended with another reality, the spirit realm. We must pay close attention to the messages they bring."

"Well, I have had dreams and visions off and on since I was a little girl," Laura confessed. "Mom and I used to talk about them. And I have had one every night since I've been here. They are, well, intense. I'm not sure if I should be excited or alarmed."

"You spent time here as a child, so you probably encountered our spirit world for the first time when your heart was tender and receptive. Now that you have returned, a familiar channel is opening up in you again."

Laura was silent. She was not sure how much to share with her companion. But Liz coaxed her to continue. "Can you tell me what's been happening to you?"

"Well, first, there are the voices on the stairs. Women talking," Laura began. "I can't quite understand them. But last night, I did pick up one word from their conversation: something like"—she pulled the paper from her pocket—"*gahmuin*."

Liz finished wiping the counter. She turned around and walked over to where Laura was standing. Pulling up kitchen stools, she motioned for the two of them to sit down.

"*Ga-mwing*, perhaps?" The old woman pronounced it slowly and clearly.

"Yes, that's it. What does it mean?"

"That is the name of the Le-nah-pe fall harvest festival. It used to be held each November at the full moon. It was when my people would say *wa-ni-shi*, thank you, to our Creator."

"Oh, like Thanksgiving."

"Well, not exactly." Laura noticed that as Liz spoke, her eyes sparkled, just like the eyes of the women who danced around the medicine doll in her dream. "People who belonged to our tribe traveled long distances to be here for ga-mwing," Liz commented. "They built shelters near the Big House, where the chief or *sa-chem* and his family lived during the festival. Then for twelve nights, there would be ceremonies with songs and dances. The meal was important, of course, but there were days of celebration filled with prayers and singing and dancing. And there was the big deer hunt, when they sent out men to kill game for the winter." Liz grew silent as childhood memories flooded back to her. "My parents told me they always looked forward to the evenings when those who had been given visions sang them to the community."

"Sang?" Laura wondered if the chants she heard her mother sing had been part of someone's vision song.

"A special rattle made from a turtle shell was passed around the room. If someone had been given a vision during the past year, they would not pass it on but would shake it. The drummer played while the person told their vision with music. When they were finished, they sat down and handed the rattle to the next person."

"That would take a long time," Laura guessed.

"Yes, sometimes the ceremony continued until dawn the next day!"

"You said there was a Big House here?"

"Yes, over in the clearing in the pine forest. The site was rebuilt every year, starting in late summer, so that it would be ready when the sa-chem arrived at the beginning of November." Liz got up and returned to her cleaning as she described other traditional ga-mwing ceremonies. Laura took it all in, intrigued. A bright ray of sunlight burst through the kitchen window, and Liz turned to face Laura once again. "After Marial's husband died, she knew she needed help to keep the farm going, so the next fall, she consulted the sa-chem. After prayers and conversations, he contacted our family. We had been living out near the Pennsylvania and Ohio border at the time, but my father agreed to come back here to work the land. It was Marial who insisted that we live in this part of the house."

"So that's how my mom grew up with Le-nah-pe children for playmates!" New appreciation for her mother was growing in Laura's heart.

"Not everyone around here thought that was a good idea," cautioned Liz. "But Marial was determined to share this place with those who originally lived on the land and who knew and respected it. Your mother grew up learning the ways of the Le-nah-pe. She became quite adept at using herbs for cooking as well as medicine. Christina was particularly fond of sweet grass and yarrow. She put them in everything!" The expression on Liz's face indicated her delight with each memory she was sharing. "I can see your mother standing right here in a shaft of morning sun with her favorite wooden bowl and muller. She spent hours grinding seeds to a fine powder. Did she ever teach you the ditty she made up?" Liz did her best to sing it for Laura.

Lotion and potion, elixir and balm,
breathe deeply the magic, breathe in and be calm.

Laura thought of the little pot of cream in her room. That bedtime routine was something Christina had invented for herself as a child! The contents of the jar here at Bittersweet Acres gave Laura the pleasant feeling of being in a meadow in the fall, of being with her mother. Unlike the commercial product, this one had a scent that was, well, hypnotic, inviting calmness. Perhaps that was what was encouraging her dreams.

A loud thump and shouts from upstairs cut off the women's conversation. Rushing from the kitchen, they joined Julia, who had been fussing over the placement of sofa cushions but was now standing at the foot of the stairway.

"We're okay," came a voice from the second floor. "Just dropped part of the bed we were dismantling." Then Wayne and Simon appeared, maneuvering a solid wooden headboard into position before starting down the stairs. The women stepped aside as the men descended and then watched as they leaned the heavy piece gently against one wall.

"Need some help up here!" Randy called down.

"Just catching our breath," responded Wayne. Turning to Julia, he added, "We are getting too old for this." The men disappeared up the steps again. And Liz returned to the kitchen. Meanwhile, Laura approached the cedar headboard. As she ran her fingertips across the smooth surface, dim memories from her childhood rushed to surface. She recognized the warm orange hue and the creamy streaks in the grain. As a little girl, she had slept in this very bed! Was it in a guest room? The attic? She could not quite picture where she had been. But she remembered the aroma of the cedar permeating the mattress, the pillows, the quilts as she napped. The act of recall made her dizzy. She found a seat in one of the chairs Julia had just finished reassembling, trying to regain her equilibrium.

Eventually, all the parts of the bed had been carried down, bolted back together, and positioned in one corner of the great room. Simon insisted that its occupant must have a full view of the old orchard and the farm road through the front windows. Liz finished up her kitchen tasks while Julia swept and straightened the rest of the living space. Laura cleaned and freshened both the bathroom upstairs and the powder room on the first floor. It was just a few minutes past eleven when the six of them gathered outside on the shady porch steps.

"Thanks, everyone," said Simon. "The place looks great." He pulled the piece of yellow lined paper from his shirt pocket, unfolded it, and glanced at the list he had made earlier. "Yep, I think we have the place ready for Lawrence's return."

If he is able to return, Laura thought sadly.

Wayne and Julia said goodbyes and headed home, walking through the meadow and disappearing into the pine trees. Liz said she would lock up, so the others walked out into the yard. Laura noted that the broken ladder had been moved and was partially hidden under the grape arbor. It was close to lunchtime by then and Simon had chicken salad, fresh tomatoes, and soft rolls waiting for the four of them. They all filled plates and carried them to the picnic table. Simon ate quickly and then excused himself to go wash and dress for the trip to town. Laura could tell he was eager to get to the hospital.

"I'm sure the nurses would call if there was any problem with Uncle Lawrence," she had offered reassuringly.

"I know, but we've got the box of sweets from the bakery." His voice trailed off as he headed inside. Turning to the Coxes, Laura encouraged them to have second helpings, and they did. After they cleared the table, the three of them moved to the front porch, where there was a delightful breeze. Settling back in the wicker chairs on the porch, they exchanged comments about finding even ordinary chores so tiring. After a while, Randy indicated he would be taking a nap when they got home. Laura noticed Liz frowning. There were household duties waiting for him there, she guessed.

"Will you be coming to worship in the morning?" the woman inquired of Laura. "I'm sure the folks will want to meet you and to hear the latest news about Lawrence."

"I think so. I'd like to visit the Meeting House again. Does Simon attend?" Randy nodded.

"Lawrence has made him a 'regular,' so I expect he'll be willing to escort you too."

"Well, I will mention it to him."

"Come on with me now, Randy." Liz was standing with her hands on her hips. "I need to get a few minutes of work out of you before you collapse."

"Yes, dear." Randy smiled as he stood, and Laura joined them as they walked down the gravel driveway to their vehicle. After a round of genuine hugs, the couple pulled away in their pickup truck, leaving a gentle cloud of dust to settle on the wildflowers beside the road. Laura returned to the kitchen. She was running the water to rinse off the glasses and utensils and did not hear Simon enter the room. He touched her shoulder. Laura jumped.

"Oh, Simon! You startled me!"

"So sorry. I just wanted to let you know I'm ready to leave now. Don't you want to come with me?" Laura explained that she would have to shower and change clothes and Simon could be there and back before she was ready.

"Besides," she hesitated, "I really need to make some headway on that stack of memorabilia in the parlor. That's the reason I'm here, after all. Tell Uncle Lawrence I'll be in to see him tomorrow. Maybe we can bring him home together."

"Will you be all right here on your own?"

Laura wondered why he thought she would *not* be okay but let it drop.

"You go ahead. Stay with Lawrence as long as you wish," she replied. "There are plenty of leftovers in the fridge here if I get hungry."

"Okay then. Here's the county hospital phone number if you need to reach me." He put a slip of paper on the counter. Laura watched as he went out of the kitchen. When she heard the *click* of the screen door as it latched behind him, she turned and finished cleaning up from lunch.

CHAPTER 14

Wiping her hands on the dishtowel, it occurred to Laura that being alone in the house offered a unique opportunity. Her desire to explore more of the farmhouse had been piqued that morning as she had worked with everyone over in the addition. The aroma of cedar still lingered in her imagination. Where did she nap in that bed? Her memories of the house were those of her childhood. What would she discover now, as an adult, in closets and behind closed doors?

As she walked past the parlor and approached the staircase, her heart began to race. She felt as though a force too strong to resist was luring her upstairs. What else might be here in this house that would help her better understand her mother, her great-uncle, her family? Ever since she had arrived, she sensed that this building held answers to her many questions. Would it give up some of its secrets this afternoon?

There were no voices today. It was as if the spirits gave silent permission for her to pursue her quest for discovery. At the top of the stairs, she paused beside the table in the hall. Picking up one of the photographs resting there, she held it toward the window so that she could make out the faces. This was another wedding portrait, one taken of a couple standing in the parlor near the fireplace. The bride bore a striking resemblance to her mother. "Marial and Josiah," she whispered aloud. She replaced it on the table and held up the next. Three figures stood together, a man in work clothes, another in a business suit, and a woman holding a baby. Laura smiled slightly, touching each one and naming them: Josiah, Lawrence, and Marial. The baby was Christina. Even then, there was a hint of a glow radiating from the child. Or was that a trick of the camera? Laura returned the photo to its place and then bent down to get a good look at the third picture. It must be her great-grandparents standing in front of a horse-drawn carriage. They were on their way to worship, she guessed. *My family*, Laura thought, and a longing filled her heart. She wanted to put photographs of Cal with her and Noel and little Marial here, right beside their forebears. *When I come back for a visit, I'll bring them*, she decided.

The second floor of the original farmhouse had three bedrooms. Marial's room, the one where Laura was staying, was the largest one. It contained two large wardrobes, a chest of drawers, the dressing table with a bench, and the rocking chair. But the four-poster bed dominated the room. The two windows in front overlooked the porch roof and the orchard. The back windows provided a view of the meadows and the pine forest. A portion of the room had been walled off years later to create a spacious bathroom.

Across the hallway were the two other rooms. Laura took for granted this was where Lawrence and Simon slept, but the doors were kept closed. From the landing there was a dark hallway which she discovered took her to a set of narrow curved stairs. This back part of the house was built on when an indoor kitchen replaced the old outdoor cook house. These were the steps Lawrence had taken a few nights ago. What else was back here? Behind one door, Laura found the linen closet. Another revealed a well-appointed bathroom, probably shared by the two men. There was a third door, one with a distinctive clear glass doorknob. Seeing it immediately jogged her memory. As she turned it, she knew exactly what was behind this door: the steps to the attic! Pulling it open, Laura slowly climbed the familiar stairs. At the top, she paused and looked around. The large area had once been both a comfortable guest room and play space for children. Now it was stuffy and quite warm. One section was a jumble of odd pieces of furniture, paintings with gilded frames, and fringed lampshades. The other area appeared to have been put in some sort of order recently but was nonetheless crowded. Laura slipped between boxes to reach a wicker baby buggy pushed up against one wall. It held an assortment of homemade rag dolls and cloth animals, along with wooden blocks, a bag full of marbles, and cars from a toy train. She remembered there being a doll house up here, right beside a big bed with a fluffy down comforter. This was where she had slept as a little girl!

Laura had already started back down the attic stairway again when she heard the telephone ringing. She scurried the rest of the way down and back to the second-floor landing to answer it. It was Simon.

"I'm just now getting to see Lawrence. He has been having breathing therapy and some adjustments to his ankle splint. But he looks pretty well."

"I am so happy to hear that," Laura responded, her voice tight and breathy. "Did you tell him about his new bedroom?"

"Not yet. We'll cross that bridge in a little bit. Laura, will you look for Lawrence's reading glasses. He thinks he left them on the table by his bed and is annoyed that he didn't bring them with him. Oh, there's Dr. Serene. Got to go."

Before she could say anything else, the phone went dead. She hung up the receiver and walked across the hall to her great-uncle's bedroom. Turning the white porcelain knob, she gave the door a gentle push. The curtains were open to the afternoon sun which streamed across the braided rug. It was made long ago by one of the Gardner women, no doubt, and the once-bright colors were now faded with age. The furnishings throughout the room were plain but not uncomfortable in appearance: a simple Shaker-style bed and matching dresser made of dark cherrywood; a ladder-back rocker, twin to the one in Marial's room; and a clothes tree where two sets of overalls were hanging. She walked over and sat down in the rocker. On a small table, Laura glimpsed several books about lakes and streams in New Jersey and the pair of wire-rimmed spectacles she'd seen Lawrence wearing. Laura took another unhurried look around. *Uncle Lawrence's space*, she observed. It fit his needs perfectly. This was where he wanted to be, at the end, here with his belongings and his memories, in the place where he still listened for the voices of his parents, his sister, and his niece Christina.

Carefully picking up his glasses, Laura went out into the hall and quietly closed the door. She didn't know what she had expected to find in Lawrence's bedroom, but she felt satisfied that nothing about her great-uncle was a mystery. He was the simple Quaker man he appeared to be.

She stopped in front of the other door. Simon's room, she thought. A tiny flicker of apprehension entered her mind. That man, she realized, was still a bit of an enigma to her. Her feelings for him were confused at this point. She liked being with him. They seemed to have a lot in common. And yet there was a subtle edge to the relationship, something Laura could not pin down. It was as if sometimes the two of them were competing for Lawrence's attention and approval. Yet they cooperated when the occasion required it. She genuinely liked Simon and admired his kindness and his care for her uncle, but Laura had a gnawing feeling that there could be some ulterior motive behind his presence on the farm.

With that thought, she stared at the door to the second room. This was her chance to look behind the curtain, so to speak, and get a better idea of who this man truly was. Putting her hand on the cold doorknob, she turned it and pushed, but the door did not budge. Locked. *Damn.* In an instant, Laura's mind invented a series of nefarious explanations for his presence at the farm and the locked door: a con artist preying on the old man, perhaps, or an ax murderer looking for an opportunity to wipe out her family. Each of the schemes she imagined became utterly ridiculous the moment she considered it. Cal would tell her she was overreacting.

"Laura," she told herself, "how many days have you been here? You and Simon have eaten together, taken walks, visited town, worked with neighbors. People trust Simon, and so should you. There is no real reason to doubt who he is. This is a remote farmhouse. He might want to lock his door here just because of the location." Laura stared at the knob and muttered aloud, "I just want to know more about you. Just to be sure. Just to protect my uncle." *And myself,* she added silently.

She remembered noticing a metal ring of keys in one of the drawers of the parlor desk. Perhaps one of them fit the lock on this room. As she went downstairs, the voices were whispering again. Were they trying to encourage her? She reached the parlor and carefully set her great-uncle's glasses on the mantelpiece. Taking a deep breath and hurriedly opening and closing each drawer she found what she was looking for. Grasping the heavy key ring, Laura rushed out into the hall and up the staircase again.

Na-che-si-mus? she heard as she passed through the voices.

Na-che-si-mus! Laura stopped to listen and then repeated it several times in order to remember what they were saying. *Na-che-si-mus!* She could ask Liz what the word meant tomorrow when she saw her after worship. Reaching the top of the stairs, Laura stopped and stood in front of the locked door. Her hands were shaking. She had to find out about Simon right now. His phone call suggested that he would be away for perhaps another hour. Holding the ring out in front of her, she fingered through the keys, searching for one most likely to fit. There were several that looked as if they had been forged generations ago. Selecting one, she placed it in the opening and tried to turn it. Nothing happened. Another. No. She sensed a slight panic rising in her and fumbled and dropped the entire bundle onto the wooden floor with a loud clank. Stooping over, she picked them up, muttering, "*Find the key. Find the key!*" She stood up again, forcing her shoulders back. Laura was determined to gain entry to this room. At last, she chose one that caused the lock to yield with a quiet click, and the door eased open.

CHAPTER 15

When Simon finally drove up the lane and pulled onto the gravel to park the car, Laura had been sitting in the parlor for about twenty minutes, ostensibly looking at documents. In truth, she had been listening impatiently for the sound of the man's return. He tromped up the porch steps and came in, heading straight for the kitchen. Laura heard him whistling softly through his teeth as he set down several grocery bags and put away their contents.

"Laura?"

"In here, in the parlor," she responded.

"Wine?"

"Yes, please. There's some white chilling in the refrigerator."

"Perfect. Just a sec."

Laura stared at the door, wanting to see what Simon's face revealed when he entered the room. His smile was disarming as always, just turning up the edges of his mouth; and his eyes, though tired, were happy. He walked over to the coffee table and set down the wine bottle and two glasses. Then he took a seat in the chair across from Laura.

"How's Uncle Lawrence. Is he better?" she asked a little too casually.

"Yes. We can pick him up tomorrow afternoon." There was relief and a lightness in Simon's voice as he filled their glasses with the pale gold Riesling. "So what did you do all alone in this old farmhouse for hours?" Laura could tell his spirits had been buoyed by the visit to the hospital, and she did not want to ruin his mood. What had she done that afternoon? Her answer to his question might not be something he would hear as good news. She struggled to control her emotions. Like an excited little girl with a big secret, she scooted to the edge of her seat, planted her feet firmly on the floor, and then took a deep breath.

When she did not respond right away, Simon grew curious. He leaned forward a bit and looked at her with concern. "Well, I hope you weren't sitting in this gloomy room missing me the entire time!"

Taking another breath and exhaling slowly, Laura shook her head. "I'll tell you in a minute. But first there is something I want to *show* you." Laura's look became troubled. She picked up the garden book Simon had given her and opened it to the place where she had slipped in the wedding picture of Christina Martin and Jude Andrews. She handed it to Simon. Slowly, deliberately she inquired, "Have you ever seen this picture before?"

Simon reached over and took the photograph. She watched his reaction. He smiled as one does when first looking at someone else's vacation pictures. "Is this your mother?" he asked with hesitation.

"Yes, that is my mother, Christina, on her wedding day. The picture was taken right out there on the front porch." Laura paused. "And that's my dad."

Simon smiled. "Nice couple."

Laura peered at him over the top of her wine glass, watching his face intently as she sipped the sweet cold beverage. Then she set her glass back on the table. Suddenly her words burst out, an unrestrained confession. "Simon, this afternoon, I decided to explore the house on my own. But one of the rooms upstairs was locked, and I remembered the set of keys I had seen here in the desk. So I retrieved them, unlocked the door, and went into the room, which I discovered was yours." She dropped her head and took in a breath.

Her words seemed to hang in the air for a moment. When she spoke again, her voice was filled with apology.

"I know it was wrong. I should have waited for you to come home." There was an odd silence in the room. The face across from hers was difficult to read. Simon seemed to be trying to remember what was locked in his private space that Laura might have found interesting. He finally spoke.

"Well? What did you find," he offered, "besides rumpled bed-sheets and my dirty socks?"

Taking another deep breath, Laura reached under a stack of papers, withdrew something, and thrust it toward him. "This. This is what I found."

It was a framed snapshot of a middle-aged couple sitting on the front porch of Bittersweet Acres. The woman was dressed in a peach linen outfit, which set off her wavy blonde hair. The man was in a summer suit, his tie off and shirt collar open.

Simon sighed. "That's it?" He seemed genuinely puzzled by her outbursts. "It's just a picture of Mom and Dad. I keep it on my dresser." He glanced at it again and then set it on the table.

Laura sat up straight and narrowed her eyes as she looked directly at Simon. Her words were more calm and measured. She could see he had no idea what she was talking about.

"I have spent the last half hour trying to make sense of this," Laura began. "Your mother and father were here, on this farm. They knew Lawrence."

"Sure, yeah. A vacation, I think. When I finished school and found a teaching position here, Dad gave me this picture of them and encouraged me to visit Bittersweet Acres if I ever got the opportunity. Then I heard Lawrence was in need of help, so I jumped at the chance."

"Your dad relocated to Philadelphia in 1952 and married your mom. You were born a year or so later, right?"

Simon nodded. "Uh-huh. I told you that. What is this all about?" Simon still could not figure out what Laura was trying to say. He picked up the picture of his parents again. "I keep this photograph of my folks," he explained in a wistful voice, "to remind me of the time when they both were happy and healthy. I like to think of them together, before Mom's illness took so much out of her and out of Dad too." His eyes grew wet. Laura waited for several minutes and then spoke.

"My mom and dad divorced in 1952, when she was already pregnant with me."

Laura's story, the one she had believed about her mother, her family, her entire life, had been rewritten that afternoon. And so had Simon's, but he had no idea.

She felt dizzy. Was it the wine, or just the effect of her mind struggling to sort out what she had come to realize? When Simon put down his own picture and picked up the wedding photograph of Laura's parents, she tried again.

"Simon, I had never seen any pictures of my dad until Uncle Lawrence gave me that one the other day. I recognized my mother and the front porch of this house. But the person with her is someone I have never known, the man she divorced before I was born. That's my dad."

Her companion nodded okay but showed no glimmer of recognition.

"Go ahead. Turn that picture over," Laura urged.

Simon followed her instructions, read the inscription, and then blinked twice. He slumped back in his chair.

"What are you saying?" His voice was soft, almost childlike.

Now she spoke in a deliberate, slow pace. "Simon, I thought your last name was Anders. That's what the attorney meant when he referred to the typo he has to fix. Your last name is Andrews, isn't it?" She paused. "The man in that picture, Jude Andrews, is your father, isn't he?" It was when Laura had compared the two photographs that she had realized the truth. "My mother was married to *your* father. That's what I discovered this afternoon while I was alone in this old farmhouse."

The air in the room was thick with unspoken thoughts and feelings. When Simon remained silent, Laura leaned forward a bit and added, almost tenderly, "Simon, I am your half sister."

After a minute, Simon stood up and walked over to the front window. In his mind, he was trying to absorb all the facts he had just learned. His father had been married to Christina. He and Laura were siblings. He was part of this family. He did belong here. It was as if the final piece of a jigsaw puzzle, the one that makes the picture clear, had finally been located, hidden in the corner of the box. By Laura's putting it in place, the image had emerged. Turning to face

Laura, he could not decide whether to laugh or cry. Laura jumped up and walked over to him.

"Simon, I am struggling to take all this in, too, but I really think this is incredibly good news. Don't you? Until today I did not expect to ever know anything about my father. Now I find out he is alive and you will be able to introduce me to the man who has been a ghost for all these years…if you want to."

"This is unbelievable!" Simon verbalized quietly. Still puzzled he continued. "Lawrence told me about your mom, and her living in Pittsburgh, but I never once made a connection to my father. If I had known…"

"What's unbelievable is that no one said anything to us, even hinted about our parents."

The two stood there, staring at each other, their minds whirling as they tried to take in what this meant for them. Finally, Laura spoke.

"The only people alive now who could have known all this are your dad, um, *our* dad, and…"

They both spoke his name at the same time. "Lawrence!"

Laura added, "I wonder *when* Uncle Lawrence put it all together."

Simon's brain was racing now. "Was it his plan all along? Having me living here? Then inviting you to come visit? What was he trying to do?" Laura walked over to the fireplace.

"I think," Laura was figuring it out as she was speaking, "that he wants to tie up all the loose ends in this family before he becomes too old or too ill to make it happen."

Picking up their wine glasses the two went into the kitchen, lost in their thoughts as they prepared and ate a light meal of salad and artisan bread. Suddenly tired, Laura suggested they straighten up the kitchen in the morning. Side by side the two climbed the stairs and then parted with a brief hug. Laura waited until Simon went into his room and then she entered her bedroom and closed the door. She wondered what dreams might come to her this evening.

I feel waves of emotion surging in and around me. I am standing on a rope bridge across a deep mountain pass. Holding on to steady myself, the rough hemp scrapes and tugs at my palms. I take a step forward and the planks beneath my feet start to sway. It is frightening, and I feel helpless to do anything. Forward or backward, my steps only create more nauseating movement. If I stay in place much longer, however, I will rub my hands raw.

"Don't look down," I tell myself and immediately my gaze drops to my feet. The depth of the gorge becomes visible through the slats in the bridge. Swooning a bit, I regain my equilibrium and force myself to look up and turn to face what is ahead.

Standing at the far side of the chasm is the figure of an old man emerging from the shadows. I am trying to focus, to identify him when a sharp whistle pierces the air. Then it quickly transitions to a familiar lilting melody played on a flute. I see sparks of light glimmering around the distant form, fireflies dancing in time to the music. I take a step forward, drawn toward the vision, and immediately set the bridge swinging again. Fear overwhelms me as I brace myself and grab a tighter hold on the rope.

Just then, the music fades, and I feel a different sensation: rhythmic footfalls shaking the planks. Someone is approaching, coming toward me from behind! I try to see, but the ropes twist wildly. I fall down to my knees. Blood oozes from my wounded hands as I struggle to right myself, but I fail to pull up to a stand. I am sure I will be killed by my assailant or tumble off the bridge to my death. I scream one word, "Na-che-si-mus!"

"I am here," responds a calm voice I recognize. "I am here. You are safe now, and we are together." Strong arms pick me up, and a young man steadies me against his body. He reaches around and touches each of my palms, which seems to ease the pain. Then he slowly, tenderly turns me to face him, and says, "It's all a dance, really. Just a dance. But once you begin, you have to keep going."

I am unsure what he means.

"Look into my eyes and follow my lead."

Then the flute begins again, this time along with a steady drumbeat I have heard before. With uncanny grace, we move together in time to the music and in harmony with the swaying of the bridge. We make our way to the far end of it and are standing again on solid earth.

I collapse into the arms of my rescuer.

"How did you find me?"

"You called me. Na-che-si-mus. Little brother. I am your brother, and I will always be here for you now." He takes a blanket and wraps it gently around my shoulders. I am still shivering from the trauma of being stranded over the precipice. This blanket is soft and smells of spices and lavender. We find a thick bed of leaves under a nearby tree and sit down side by side. I rest against my brother and listen intently as he tells me stories about his father…my father. The moon is full and bright. The only sounds are his soft voice and a whisper of tree branches in the gentle night wind.

CHAPTER 16

Laura lay still, listening to rustling leaves as they became the familiar sizzle of bacon in a frying pan. The aroma of brewing coffee filled the air around her. She stretched and rolled over, noting that the smooth comforter was awry and her pillow was on the floor. The memory from her dream faded only slightly as she made her way to the bathroom. Today was Sunday. Sabbath. Today she would worship at the Quaker meeting and then go with Simon to pick up Uncle Lawrence from the hospital.

Simon.

Lawrence.

Laura was unsure of the message of her dream, and even more preoccupied by what the revelations of yesterday meant for her. A brother. A chance to meet her father. More than all the books and historical documents stacked in the parlor, it seemed that her own story was what she was sorting through on this visit to Bittersweet Acres.

What might be her great-uncle's explanation for his part in all this? Why had he not mentioned who Simon was? To either of them? He had to have known about their relationship for some time. What did he think their response would be? Before this visit, he probably didn't know Laura well enough to be able to predict her reaction. And once he fell off the ladder, there wasn't a good time to bring it up.

Stop, Laura told herself. *You can deal with all this later, after worship, once Lawrence comes home.*

She patted dry her freshly washed face and stared in the mirror. Her mother's image stared back at her as she mouthed the words of her long-ago dream. *You will find your father someday, and he will be proud of you.* Laura spoke out loud. "Oh, Momma. I hope so."

Down in the kitchen Simon was whistling a tune as he set the table for their breakfast. As Laura came in, he stopped. "No, keep going," she encouraged. "I love that tune, although I can't remember where I've heard it before."

"It's something I learned from Liz's niece, Elsa. She says they used to sing it at one of the Le-nah-pe festivals. We can ask her if you want to know the name."

"Are there other native folks who attend the meeting besides the Cox family?" Laura was curious.

"Yes, at least a dozen, maybe more. Many Quaker families today have some connection to the tribe by marriage or work or shared land rights."

As she enjoyed eating the fruit compote and cheese and bacon quiche Simon had prepared, Laura kept reminding herself that this was her brother. He was a sweet guy, funny at times, self-assured most of the time. She had to admit that she had liked him from the start and had been comfortable being with him. But she had never had a sibling. This was going to take some time to get used to.

As Simon refreshed their coffee, she found herself trying to recall all her interactions with this man over the past several days. Would she have behaved differently if she had known he was her brother? Her thoughts were swirling again as she stirred the cream into her mug.

"I am doing the same thing," Simon broke in, seeming to read her thoughts. "Do you want to talk this out some more instead of going to worship?"

"Oh, that would not help just yet. The service will give me time to think. And we'll not find many answers until we get Uncle Lawrence home. He has a lot of explaining to do." Laura tried to sound stern, but it came out in a way that made them both laugh. She was picturing them questioning the old man as if he were a naughty child.

"Okay, well, I'll tidy up here while you finish dressing. We'll leave around quarter to ten."

Laura gave Simon a gentle hug and peck on the cheek. Then she picked up the morning newspaper from the counter and went up to her room.

She put on her yellow flowered sundress, sat at the dressing table, and examined the riot of cosmetics spread across the top. Moisturizer, foundation, cheek and eye colors, concealer, mascara—all a part of her daily routine at home. But today they seemed unnecessary. She could apply a dash of blush, swipe a pale lipstick across her lips, fluff her hair, and she was ready. *Tis a gift to be simple*, she mused.

As Laura bent over to tie on her sandals, her eyes scanned the Sunday newspaper headlines and stopped short when she read: "EPA Renames New Jersey 'Toxic Waste State.'" The article highlighted ongoing deliberations between the US Environmental Protection Agency and state authorities concerning the funding to clean up the contaminated properties and waterways. New Jersey had received more Superfund money than any other state in the nation. Laura took the paper with her over to the rocking chair and sat down. She became heartsick as she read of the pollution from coal tar waste. Leaking chemical drums had been illegally stored or dumped, contaminating ground water. As many as fourteen thousand properties were cited. Federal government monies would never pay to mitigate all the offenses.

She was starting to read a related editorial highlighting the increasing numbers of childhood cancers in the state when she heard the distinctive toot of the horn on the Volvo. Setting the paper aside, she grabbed her purse and went downstairs.

As Simon guided the Volvo down the farm road, Laura tried to shift her focus from the headlines to holiness by recalling the instructions for a Quaker meeting her mother had once given her.

"Worship begins, dear, when the first person enters the room, so try to be quiet and unobtrusive when we go in. It is okay to smile at someone. But do not speak aloud if you can help it. We will sit in silence and clear our minds. That's called 'expectant waiting.'"

Become still, inside as well as outside? Open your heart to Holy Spirit? Find your personal deep stillness? Between all the r lations of yesterday, the strange dreams she was having, and the

ronmental horror she had just read about, Laura was not sure she would be able to clear her mind this morning.

Simon pulled in beside the historic sandstone Meeting House on Laurel Hill Road and parked right next to Randy's pickup. Laura was eager to see the couple again and to discuss her dreams with Liz. She found them already seated inside the meeting room, so she and Simon slipped in that row and sat on the wooden bench beside them. Liz reached over, took Laura's hand, and gave it a warm, loving squeeze. Did the woman know what was in Laura's heart on this Sabbath day?

Looking around, Laura noted that they were seated in the section originally built in 1760. The pews, wide wainscoting, gallery, and wooden columns also dated from the eighteenth century by the looks of their unadorned construction. Light streamed in through the clear window panes, which Laura noticed were uneven from the "running" of the glass over time. This room was just as she had remembered it, probably just the way it was when her mother came as a little girl with Marial and Josiah and Lawrence. Sitting quietly as other worshipers entered and took seats, Laura could picture the Gardner family, generations of them, arriving each week in hopes of finding spiritual help for their daily lives. *That's what I want today,* she prayed.

At some point, Julia and Wayne came in and sat in front of Simon, but they turned only slightly to acknowledge the friends seated behind them. Laura clasped her hands together in her lap, straightened her posture, and looked around the room. Who were all these people? How long had they been coming to this place to wait quietly for God? She noticed that some had warm bronze faces and straight black hair, like Liz. Others might have had English or Scottish heritage, their cheeks a healthy pink. Farmers, business people, families with children sharing silence, listening to the silence.

After about fifteen minutes, a man and woman stood up together and escorted the children into another part of the building for Sabbath school classes. Laura thought of her daughters and all the things she loved about them. Then she found herself thinking about what they were like on the inside. She had never really taken the time

to consider their dreams, ambitions, or gifts. But on this morning, she wanted to do just that.

She looked at her hands and noticed she had unclasped them. They lay open, receptive and inviting on her lap. She pictured people floating, one by one, into her palms, forming a circle, dancing together. Her daughters, Cal, Christina, Lawrence, Simon, Jude, she welcomed them all and somehow felt she was also part of their dance. It was a beautiful image. She watched until it slowly faded away.

Then Laura thought of the newspaper article again. In order to clear her mind, she envisioned the words floating up off the page and into the air. She listened again to the silence. All remained quiet until one of the members stood in place and began to read a passage from the Psalms. Laura had noticed Bibles on the benches but had not been led to pick one up. She listened to the words of this ancient hymn.

> The earth is the Lord's, and the fullness thereof
> The world, and they that dwell therein.
> For He hath founded it upon the seas, and estab-
> lished it upon the floods.
> Who shall ascend into the hill of the Lord?
> Or who shall stand in His holy place?
> He that hath clean hands, and a pure heart;
> who hath not lifted up his soul unto vanity, nor
> sworn deceitfully.
> He shall receive the blessing from the Lord,
> and righteousness from the God of his salvation.

As she listened, Laura found she was able to set aside her usual objections to King James English and male references to God. She heard the old words in a new way, a message about the stewardship of the earth. The world belonged to the Creator, and humans were placed here to care for it. Those who were charged with protecting the land and the air and life on the planet must remain clean and pure of heart. Self-interest, greed, and carelessness would take a toll on all the people. Gradually the silence returned inside her.

After a time, someone began to sing quietly. At first, it was difficult to hear. Then the single voice was joined by another. The words were a language Laura had heard only in her dreams, but the melody was one she now associated with Bittersweet Acres. Assuming it was a Le-nah-pe chant, Laura let the music flow over and around her as other people joined the song and the sounds repeated. *Like a three-part invention*, she mused. Her mind wandered to the voices she had heard on the farmhouse staircase. She slowly came back to the present as one by one the singers dropped out until finally only one voice remained. Then it, too, ceased, and the room was filled with only the sunshine and the silence.

How long they all sat in quiet waiting Laura could not be sure. It was as though time had stopped for her. She imagined the first people planting crops, fishing, hunting. She remembered her dreams of the medicine doll, the dancing and prayers to Mother Earth. The experience was pleasant and beautiful, like the afternoon when she stood with Simon watching the turtle on the log. Eventually, she knew she would stir; but for the moment, all she felt was contentment and joy.

One of the elders stood and Wayne turned to shake hands with Simon. The others in the meeting took their cue that worship had ended. Everyone stood then, greeting those around them with handshakes or hugs and then walked with them out the doors and onto the porch. Several clusters of neighbors formed, sharing the news of the week or inviting each other to join them for a meal later in the day. Simon drew a small crowd, as people inquired about Lawrence's health, and he took the opportunity to introduce Laura as Christina's daughter. He and Laura had agreed not to mention their newly discovered relationship until they had a chance to talk with Lawrence.

As they walked to the car, Liz caught up with them. "Laura, did you have a message during worship this morning? What is troubling you?" Clearly, the woman had a gift of insight.

"I'm afraid I was a bit distracted, even though I tried to stay centered," Laura confessed.

Turning to Simon, she asked, "Can I have a minute to talk to Liz?" He nodded yes, and the two women walked together and found a seat on one of the benches at the end of the Meeting House porch. "Liz, I read the article in the paper this morning about the hundreds of court cases related to pollution of the state's drinking water. I had no idea."

"The Le-nah-pe have been aware of it for many years, even before the first reports of sicknesses in the children. It took a long time for officials finally to begin to pay attention to what we all were saying. By then fish were dying and the land was already being destroyed." A sadness filled the old woman's eyes.

"Are the farms around here safe?" Laura thought of the garden markets along the highway, a livelihood for many families. She worried about Bittersweet's soil, the farmer leasing the land, even Lawrence's tomatoes and beets.

"It's only a matter of time. But up to now, the major pollution had been limited to counties over along the coast. The soil there is dead, and money alone will not bring it life again." Liz looked directly at Laura. "That is why this year we plan to hold a fall ceremony as our ancestors did. We will pray to the Creator to show us how to heal the soil and the water and restore Mother Earth's bounty. Those who participate in the ga-mwing will share their dreams and visions with us at the festival. We will speak together of what we need to do. We will also dance with the medicine dolls to keep our own families healthy. Perhaps you will be there?"

Laura had so much to ponder, as well as the thoughts stirred up in the time of worship. Liz seemed to understand and stood up to leave without waiting for an answer. "We will talk more another day. You need to deal with Lawrence today." Laura wondered for a moment what she knew about the family circumstances. Was she referring to getting the uncle back home from the hospital? Or something else?

"Liz." Laura touched her friend's arm and whispered, "I have learned another Le-nah-pe word. Na-che-si-mus!" The old woman's eyes brightened. She grinned and squeezed Laura's hand as they walked in silence to the parking area. Randy helped his wife into the truck. Simon opened the door for Laura. The two couples waved to each other and drove off in opposite directions.

CHAPTER 17

Simon suggested to Laura that they stop for lunch on their way to pick up Lawrence. They turned off the highway, following a narrow blacktop road overshadowed by tall pines. Eventually they came to a cluster of buildings, shops, and businesses hidden among the trees. The sand and gravel of the parking area crunched gently under the tires of the car as Simon turned in and followed the signs directing them to the restaurant: Pirate's Cove. He found a place to pull in and stop, but it was some distance from the front door. Laura observed the nautical décor, including a gang plank walkway with piers and ropes for handrails. The dream! Laura felt a twinge in the palms of her hands, but when she looked down at them, the feeling disappeared.

Simon had called ahead for reservations, probably while she was getting dressed that morning, and they were escorted to a table beside the large window which overlooked the water.

"That's the Ancocas," Simon announced, pointing to the tea-colored creek flowing gently below them.

"The one where the settlers first landed!" Laura remembered excitedly.

"It's the most prominent waterway in the county. For generations, people have traveled it for both commerce and recreation. Here." Simon pointed to the map on the back of their menus showing its headwaters in the pitch pine land of Ocean County. "The north branch meanders for about thirty miles through a forest of mostly maple, hickory, and oak. Finally, the main stem widens and flows out to the Delaware River."

"Is the water in all the creeks in South Jersey that color?"

"No, not really. In the Pinelands, the water picks up its distinctive color. There are tannic acids in much of the plant life, in particular the Atlantic white cedar tree. Also the riverbeds have naturally occurring iron in them. Not too far downstream from here, it will turn more blue-green."

Laura studied the map and then looked at the pictures of wildlife surrounding it: Painted and box turtles sunning themselves on fallen logs; herons and kingfishers standing in river coves; white-tailed deer; beavers; wood ducks; mallards; and Canada geese.

"Such interesting natural resources. I had no idea!" she marveled.

"The variety of trees and animals is amazing," Simon added. "Do you like to hike? There are miles of creek-side trails. And if you have a canoe, the water is pretty serene."

Laura liked being here with Simon and longed to explore this place and learn more about its history and its resources. As she gazed into the creek a plastic jug bobbed its way along the bank before getting hung up on a low-hanging tree branch. That brought her thoughts back to the newspaper headline.

"Simon, how long have people allowed the region to remain polluted?"

As they ate the lightly broiled seafood they had chosen for lunch, Simon shared some of the history of the state's environmental issues. He added that he was part of an action committee formed by the Le-nah-pe and other concerned citizens.

"Lawrence has been involved almost from the start. Those casual drives through the pine barrens I told you about were never just a pleasant outing." Simon went on to elaborate. "A small settlement in Ocean County had three beautiful cedar lakes and clusters of vacation homes. The Gardners had close friends who lived there. It was an ideal escape from the hectic city life for people from Camden and Philadelphia. Families could rent cabins in the summer and spend time swimming, fishing, riding bikes, and playing in any of the little parks. It was also an easy drive over the causeway to Long Beach Island and the ocean."

He stopped talking long enough to take a bite of his fresh flounder and then picked up the story. "Chemical companies in North

Jersey offered good money to land owners in the Pines who would let them store industrial waste on their property. No one thought about the possibility of coal tar sludge and other by-products seeping into the ground."

The waiter brought the check, and Laura took another drink of iced water. She was sullen by the time he reached the end of this story. "You know the results," Simon continued, "There were fish kills in the streams. Bacteria in the lakes made them unsafe for swimming. When you put industrial waste in sandy soil, it isn't long before you are smelling or tasting it."

Simon glanced at his watch. "We've got to go now to pick up Lawrence. He'll be cross with us if we don't get there soon." Laura nodded in agreement, and they got up to leave the restaurant.

"So tell me the truth," she demanded as she noted the memorabilia on the walls and in a glass showcase by the front door. "Were there actually pirates in these parts?" She sounded skeptical.

"Oh yes!" Simon shot back with a grin. "That part of the story is on an insert to the dinner menu here. Pirates freely roamed the streets of Philadelphia in the 1600s. In fact, every town along the Delaware has a tale of buried treasure in their history."

At that point, he broke into his best imitation of Long John Silver. "Avast ye! Merchant ships a-plenty sailed out to the West Indies from 'ere. Buccaneers would be hidin' in coves like this, a-waiting to intercept vessels and steal their booty to resell. Then they'd bring all hands and make their way into the city, hangin' out in taverns 'til they'd be three sheets to the wind. Aye, they'd hide their treasure anywheres they could, even under floor boards of churches. Sea dogs like Capt'n Kidd and Blackbeard were all familiar to folks back then." As he opened the car door, he uttered a gruff. "Arrgh, me lass! Heave ho!" Laura was still laughing as she buckled her seat belt, and Simon backed the Volvo out of the parking space.

CHAPTER 18

Lawrence was patiently waiting in his room for release from the hospital. He was seated in a chair beside the bed, clothed in his usual overalls and a comfortable tee shirt, this one a rusty orange. His hair was combed neatly to the side, and someone had taken the time to give him a shave.

"We took the scenic route," Simon apologized from the doorway.

"Am I glad to see you!" An easy smile appeared on the old man's face, and he reached out toward Laura as she walked over to him. "Help me up, and let's get going."

"Uncle Lawrence, I am glad you are well enough to come home. It's been, well, interesting at the farm without you." From his expression, she knew that he could tell something was up.

"Uh oh," he remarked. "You two have been conspiring against me, haven't you?"

Simon stepped closer and in his most conciliatory voice explained that Dr. Serene had given strict instructions for Lawrence to avoid stairs. Period. "I know, it sounded extreme to me too, but I think you are what they call a "fall risk" right now. Once you are out of the splint for a while, we'll talk about getting you back in your own bedroom."

"So I'm sleeping on the sofa. A fine kettle of fish." Lawrence clearly was annoyed.

"Oh, no, Uncle Lawrence," Laura explained gently. "We've fixed up the great room in the addition for you. The cedar bed's been brought downstairs, and the whole place is clean as a whistle." There was such joy in Laura's voice that it managed to squelch any complaint he might have tried to make.

A nurse arrived with the paperwork for discharge. After reviewing with Simon the things to do and not do, the list of prescriptions and dosages, and the date for a follow-up appointments at Dr. Serene's office, she called for an orderly with a wheelchair. "Hospital requirements, I suppose," muttered Lawrence in feigned displeasure. In truth he knew he was not strong enough to walk to the front door, even with a crutch or his cane. Simon helped him get settled in the chair and then left to get the car. The orderly wheeled Lawrence to the elevator, followed by Laura, who carried the small tote bag with his personal items and home care instruction papers. They arrived at the entrance just as the Volvo pulled up. Lawrence thanked the hospital staffer and asked him to convey his gratitude to the others who cared for him. Once he was comfortably in the front seat, Laura climbed in back, and Simon started the car.

"Straight home, right?" he asked.

"Please," Lawrence responded. "I am eager to see what you two have done to our place." Laura noted his use of the inclusive pronoun. *Our place.* Yes, Lawrence had been waiting for this day. He had created the legacy he so sorely wanted.

As the three rode through town, Lawrence pointed out a landmark or two, for Laura's benefit. Just as they made the turn onto Laurel Hill Road, he instructed Simon to pull off to the side.

"See that large black walnut tree?" He gestured ahead about a hundred feet, on the left-hand side of the road. "It's known as the Pirate Tree."

Simon turned to Laura. "We were just talking about pirates after lunch, weren't we?" His smile was genuine. Laura waited for the story that she was sure Lawrence was about to tell.

"It was Blackbeard himself and his crew that buried silver and gold right there, on a dark, stormy night. In order to guard the treasure, the old pirate required the services of an outlaw, whom he summarily shot to death with a magic bullet. The pellet left no wound, they say, and he was buried close by in a standing position, ready to fight any who dared to dig up the treasure. And it's all still there, they say, every doubloon of it, to this very day."

Lawrence tried to look serious, but Laura and Simon were already chuckling as she commented about how much of New Jersey history and legend she had yet to discover. Simon put the car in gear, and Lawrence dozed off as they made the short trip back to the farm.

The great room in the farmhouse addition turned out to be a perfect spot for recuperating, and Uncle Lawrence settled in without a fuss. Simon had unlatched the connecting door to the main house, propping it open with a cast iron doorstop in the shape of a sheep. The opening was plenty wide for a wheelchair to scoot through. So on his first evening back home, Lawrence ate in the formal dining room. Dinner consisted of his favorite chicken pot pie with a tossed salad. The crust was flaky, the gravy smooth and rich with the pleasant aromas of rosemary and just enough thyme. Carefully chopped carrots, potatoes, and peas were tender and colorful on the plates. The pitcher of iced tea got passed around as they ate, and Lawrence regaled the young folks with details of his brief hospital stay, more than perhaps they really wanted to hear. But it was all in good fun.

When the peach cobbler was served, the old man took one bite and then laid down his spoon. "Okay, let's talk about what's really on your minds."

Simon and Laura exchanged glances, each hoping the other would begin the conversation. Laura took the lead.

"Uncle Lawrence, exactly *when* did you realize that Simon's dad was my dad too?"

The old man leaned back in his chair, took a deep breath, and let it out slowly. He was searching for a good place to begin his all-important tale.

"So you found me out, did you? Well, it's like I told you. I moved back here to be with Marial sometime after Christina was married. Eventually we updated the addition to the house and took to renting it out to folks for vacations. Made us a little bit of extra money, you know. At one point, a group of business men from Philadelphia stopped in. They'd been calling on some new customers here in Chester Town and were kind of interested in Quaker history. They wanted to visit our place since it's an authentic old building on an original land grant." After a taking another long breath, he continued.

"Well, there was this fellow in the group that Marial and I recognized right away, but he didn't seem to know who we were. It was Jude Andrews. He'd filled out some, with a little silver in his hair, but his eyes were as bright as ever. Anyway, we were on the front porch talking. Jude was looking around, and all of a sudden, I could see that it was coming back to him. He was standing right where he and Christina had been married! We didn't say anything, and I sure didn't want to embarrass him in front of the others.

"The next day, he came back, alone this time. We had a good talk, and he explained to us as best he could what had happened between him and Christina. He told us about his new wife and their son. I wanted to tell him about you, Laura, but Marial said no. You both have to understand that Jude and Christina had made an agreement when they divorced. They would live their own lives and not maintain contact with each other. The baby, that's you, Laura, would not be Jude's responsibility. He was free to follow his heart and his dreams. Your mother sent him away with her blessing and kept you for herself as *her* blessing." Laura could feel tears welling up. She reached for her glass of tea. Lawrence spoke again.

"In the end, we invited Jude to come back any time and to bring his wife if they ever wanted to get away from the city for a while. Jude did call a few months later, and he and his wife spent a long weekend over there." He motioned toward the addition. Lawrence paused, took a bite of dessert, and a sip of the hot coffee Simon had poured from the carafe on the table.

"Simon, I can't tell you how happy I was when you came by one afternoon to talk about working here. I could see the family resemblance to your parents right away, and you have many of your father's mannerisms. But I didn't hire you just because I knew your dad. I wanted you to learn to love this place and perhaps one day become someone who would help take care of this land. Marial was gone at that point, of course. With Christina's untimely death...I was afraid of losing everything." Lawrence's demeanor became distraught and he turned to Simon. "Laura had her career and her family. I didn't know if she had any interest in dealing with Bittersweet Acres, but I needed to find out. I had to give her a chance to meet her dad if she wanted to. And I thought the two of you should get to know each other. I did a lot of soul searching on my morning walks, and one day, it occurred to me that maybe together the three of us could come up with good solution to my concerns. The phone call to you, Laura, was to be my attempt to tie up the loose ends in this family. If you had not wanted to come, then that would be my sign to let it all drop."

Laura wiped her eyes and reached for her great-uncle's hand. "I am so glad you tried," she said. "Since Mom died, I have wished a hundred times that I had some tangible way to stay connected to her. I have fallen in love with this farm, and you have given me the chance to meet a brother I never knew existed." She paused, happy to see peace returning to her great-uncle's face. "Perhaps I'll even get the opportunity to meet my father."

For the last few years, Laura had wondered about the man who abandoned her and her mother. Now she knew that not only had he found love with another woman and continued to be successful in business but also happily fathered another child, a son. Building a relationship with Jude Andrews at this point might be too painful for either of them. But Uncle Lawrence seemed to think it was worth taking a chance.

Then it was Simon's turn. He got up and moved his chair over beside Lawrence's wheelchair and then sat down. "You were very courageous to try to resolve all this. I wish you had told me a sooner, but I suppose Christina's spirit has been orchestrating this whole thing. You know, during your conversations with her out on the porch?" He looked knowingly at Lawrence. "I understand now why you and I have become such good companions, Lawrence. And then meeting Laura this week is just …well, whipped cream on a delicious cobbler!"

Lawrence indicated he was ready to retire to his room about then. Simon wheeled him through the hall doors to the great room and helped him get into ready for bed while Laura cleared the table. A few minutes later, Simon called to her. She let the pan she was scrubbing sink back into the soapy water and dried her hands. It was good to have her great-uncle back home, and she was delighted to be able to tell him good night in person. Simon had turned on a small lamp on the bedside table, and Laura thought the room looked cozy. Lawrence was propped up on several pillows with his glasses up on his forehead. Apparently, he intended to catch up on some reading before going to sleep. He laid his book across his stomach and reached for both Simon and Laura.

"Please don't be upset with me."

"We understand, Uncle Lawrence. Really we do," Laura replied, and Simon nodded. "You did things the way you thought best."

Simon looked at the old gentleman he had come to love. "I still have to work through my thoughts and feelings, but in time it all will be well. Now get a good night's sleep. We are both close by if you need us before morning."

Simon squeezed his hand and left the room. Laura kissed her great-uncle's cheek. "Shall I close the curtains on the windows?" she asked.

"Just those over there," he answered, pointing to the ones that face the pine woods. As Laura pulled the drapes together, she saw once again the single light, wandering among the apple trees and then disappearing. *I must ask Liz about that*, she thought. Turning back to the dimly lit room, she watched Lawrence calmly turn the page of his book as she padded softly through the doorway.

The rest of the house was dark except for the one lamp on the table at the top of the stairs. Simon had gone up to bed, she assumed. Laura checked the front door to be sure it was secure and then started up the staircase herself. There were no voices this evening, just a quiet rustle, like someone settling down to sleep under quilts and coverlets. Laura smiled with recognition. Uncle Lawrence! She realized that any sounds made in the room next door could be heard from a certain location on the steps! Someone in that part of the house, meeting and talking, would have created the muffled conversations that had so unnerved her. Another mystery was coming clear. She was almost giddy with all the revelations of today. But she was also dead tired.

As much as she wanted to share all this with her husband, she walked past the telephone without stopping and went into her bedroom.

What other mysterious occurrences had simple explanations? After taking a warm shower which she found remarkably soothing, Laura donned a cotton sleep shirt, her last bit of clean nightwear, and made a mental note to do some laundry in the morning. As she sat at the dressing table and ran a brush slowly through her hair, she stared into the mirror, looking for any resemblance she might bear to her father and to Simon. What about her children? Did the girls carry traces of their grandfather that she had never recognized? She had uncovered an entire gene pool to be explored.

Picking up the pot of hand cream, Laura dreamily made her way across the room to the big four-poster bed. The quilt was smooth, unrumpled by any secret visitor. She scooted up on the mattress, plumped the pillows gently, and then slipped her feet under the cool sheets. Opening the jar, she took a deep draft of the now familiar aroma, lavender and spices. The image emerged from yesterday, young Christina grinding herbs with native women and singing,

> *Lotion and potion, elixir and balm,*
> *breathe deeply the magic, breathe in and be calm.*

The contents in this little pot were always the same: cool, smooth, creamy white. Yet its effect seemed to change depending on the mood of the one applying it. The night she arrived, Laura had been too excited to sleep, and yet when she applied the lotion, she immediately dozed off. The following day, she had been deluged with her family history. She came to bed needing to sort out all the threads of the Gardner tapestry. And in the process of the nighttime ritual, her mind cleared and any lingering doubts about coming to this place vanished. On Friday, she had the strange encounter in town with the priestly man. When she came home, she heard more clearly the voices on the staircase speaking Le-nah-pe. Like her mother, she was learning to reconcile traditional faith with other more mystical belief systems. As she sat in her room that evening, massaging her hands, all the strains flowed together into one message. She realized spirituality was not separate from life but the very heartbeat of existence.

Tonight as she closed the lid on the little pot of hand cream and set it on the nightstand, Laura experienced the sensation of being surrounded on all sides by loving beings offering silent reassurance that she was unique and cherished and blessed. It was a feeling she had not known before, and as she closed her eyes she prayed that it would never leave her.

I hear footsteps coming. Then ugh! I am drenched in cold water from a pail! Who did that? Wiping my face on my sleeve, I see the room I am in is bathed in light from the fireplace. A harsh voice is hollering at me. "Get up, Bead-Child. You are a miserable brat. I don't want to see you here." I am barely awake and shocked and confused but manage to stagger to my feet. I still cannot see the face of the person speaking, but the message is clear. "You must leave this place and take your flea-bitten possessions with you." I scurry about, gathering up my blanket, a pair of moccasins and the basket containing my medicine doll.

Then the figure comes toward me. The hands hold out a cup of water and a slab of meat. "Before you leave, you must eat what I offer you." I turn and run out of the house in anger and fear. I am not wanted here. I will run away. But how can I live in the pine forest on my own? I stand in the clearing, not sure what to do or where to go.

Then another figure comes out of the woods. "You must go back," I hear. It is the voice of a young girl. I recognize Elsa, the girl from the fruit market. "Don't you know," she remarks, "that you must eat and drink before you cover yourself with ashes?"

I think she is another tormenting spirit at first. Then I realize this is some kind of ceremony, and she is here to help me. Together we go back inside the house. I take the meat and drink from the dark one who is still standing in the same place. When I finish eating, Elsa gathers soot and charcoal from around the fire and tenderly smears them across my face and down each arm. Then she leads me out of the house again.

"You don't know what to do. I can see that. So listen and I will tell you." Her voice is gentle but serious. "Follow Turtle Creek through the gardens until you come to the mound of stones. Look for the place where

overhanging rocks form a shelter. That is the best place to fast and receive power. That is where you may find your blessing."

I understand her now. Today I start my quest for a vision. How silly of me to have forgotten! Elsa cautions me not to eat or drink anything else during the day. "And be sure to remember all strange things and what you see or what you dream."

In the next moment, I am on the path through the garden. I keep walking until I reach the creek. In time, I come to a great mound of rocks. There in the shelter of the overhang, I make a nest of dry leaves and grass and spread my blanket over it. For some time, I sit there cross-legged in the cool darkness, waiting for another helper of the Le-nah-pe Creator to come to visit me. Eventually, I slump down and pull the cover over me to ward off the damp. I fall into a troubled sleep.

When I wake again, the sun is bright, and I am thirsty. I hear a sound overhead, the whooshing of wings and then a rustling of feathers. I sit up and see a large bird with a dark head, gray-blue back, wings long as its tail, and brownish-white bars beneath. It has landed directly in front of me. It has a hooked beak edged in gold. It is a falcon.

With a few strutting steps, it comes toward me. Without speaking it tells me to be vigilant, that positive changes are coming to my life. It asks me to trust that I have all the tools and knowledge to fulfill my mission. It warns that I must not hold back but act quickly. Then it flutters back into the open and flies off, soaring and circling above me as I stand up. The voice in my heart whispers, "Soar high. See your world with greater vision."

Chapter 19

In the distance, Laura heard someone quietly calling her name. "Laura, Laura dear, are you awake?" She rolled over on her side, expecting to feel the rough blanket and hear leaves crunch beneath her shifting weight. But the cover was smooth and her bed quiet. Without lifting her head, she opened her eyes and scanned her surroundings. The bedroom door was open. Her clothing was in a pile by the bathroom where she dropped it all the night before. When her gaze reached the rocking chair, she knew whose voice she had heard.

"Liz," she muttered sleepily and then sighed deeply, sat up, and stretched. "What are you doing here?" Her brain was in that place between sleep and waking where nothing makes any sense. The old woman got up and came over, sitting on the edge of the bed and taking both of Laura's hands in hers.

"Good morning." She smiled. "You were so restless we could hear you downstairs. Lawrence suggested I check in on you." Liz reached around behind Laura, arranging the pillows as a backrest and then lowered her gently against them. "How are you feeling?"

"Oh, I had the most interesting dream," Laura began, leaning back and allowing her eyelids to droop to a close. Then a moment later she sat bolt upright. "Liz, what does it mean when a falcon appears?" Her words were intense.

Liz was again holding her hands. She slipped them together and gave them a reassuring pat. "Sit back, and I will answer all your questions." Laura did as she was told, and the other woman slid off the bed, walked across the room, and then carefully moved the rocking chair over closer to Laura. "I hope you are not frightened."

Curiosity, not fear, was what Laura felt. She kept thinking of how much she identified right then with the story of *Alice in Wonderland*. Things were not as they seemed. Would they ever return to normal?

"I feel fine," she answered. "I just need someone to explain what is happening to me. Please."

"Then let's start with the falcon," Liz suggested. "If that is your spirit guide, it is an indication that you are independent, an agile thinker with a sharp mind. You know how to work out problems and are three steps ahead of everyone else." Laura listened intently and then responded.

"This visit has become quite disconcerting for me. When I arrived, I was confident I could help Uncle Lawrence with whatever he needed and then return home to my family. But all the voices and dreams here have made me wonder if I will ever go home. What is real, and what is an overactive imagination? I feel so powerless to make sense of it all."

"When falcons hunt, they are fearless," Liz continued. "They soar overhead looking for quarry. When they see what they want, they flatten their wings against their bodies and plummet down in a free fall." That image resonated perfectly with what Laura was feeling. "At just the right moment, they open their wings again, slowing their speed, then pull their feet up in front of them and grab the chosen prey." Liz leaned over, tenderly tucked Laura's hair behind her ears, and then took her face in both hands. "People with a falcon totem have impeccable timing and know just when to strike." Laura thought that was probably what made her a good lawyer. "Conquering challenges, taking charge, mastering whatever comes into your path: these are all attributes you have already. Perhaps the falcon wants you to be more selective in what you seek or be more discerning of what is important to you."

Laura closed her eyes again, pondering the words of her wise friend and sorting through the event of the past days for connections. What was important? That was not something she had stopped to ask herself for a long time. Her life in Harrisburg, the law practice, Cal, and the girls—those things had been her life's purpose. Then last week, she added helping Uncle Lawrence and finding her roots here in New Jersey. Now it included meeting her father and growing her relationship with her half brother, Simon. And there was the issue of land and water contamination that she had just learned about from reading the newspaper. She felt overwhelmed.

Liz sat back down in the chair and patiently rocked, humming the same tune Simon had been whistling the other day. Its familiar melody was soothing to Laura's troubled soul. She asked herself again, *What is important?*

"Can you tell me about other dreams you've been having?" Liz sensed that the telling of them would help Laura gain clarity.

"Well"—Laura was searching for a way to summarize what she remembered—"in the first dream, I went into a cave somewhere here on the farm, and I saw a shadow figure walk through the wall. Then the next night, a woman guide appeared and took me back to get the medicine doll that was left for me in the cave. In the following dream, I was part of a festival where everyone danced with the medicine doll. The night after I discovered that Simon and I are related, I dreamed of a deep mountain pass and the frightening bridge I had to cross in order to reach my father. Then last night, I was fasting alone, and the falcon appeared to tell me that important change is coming." She stopped there to think if she had left anything out. "And then there are the voices on the staircase, talking in Le-nah-pe."

Liz stopped rocking. A look of amusement came to her face. "That last part is simple," she offered. "I told you we started planning for the ga-mwing already. Those of us who live nearby have been meeting regularly, and Lawrence lets us use the other side of this house for our gatherings. So I have a key. Elsa and Julia and I have been discussing the festival preparations almost every evening, and you have heard our chatter through the walls!" Her laugh was soft. "Did you see mysterious lights in the forest too?"

Laura nodded, a little embarrassed when she sensed there was a logical explanation about to be revealed. "We are repairing the great house for the sa-chem. Folks gather the tree branches, grasses, and bark each day after work and carry them to the site of the building. Sometimes they get delayed. When they have to work after dusk, one of us must carry a lantern to show the way. Usually it is me since I am too old to do much else." Again, Liz chuckled gently. Then she grew serious.

"Laura, I can help you discover the stories behind the symbols and signs in your dreams because they are from our Le-nah-pe tradition. But you alone can decide what they mean for your life."

"Why are all my dreams here images from your culture?" Laura asked.

"That is my doing," Liz confessed. "Remember the sassafras tea I served you at my market stand? It contained herbs that are said to open channels in people's hearts to native ways. Then Elsa brought the pot of cream to the house and put it in your bedroom. It holds a special potion, made from a recipe your mother created all those years ago. It helped Christina find her way through difficult days and eventually to discover her life purpose."

"I never saw Elsa here!" remarked Laura.

"She often does housework for Lawrence and knows this place well. The other night, she came into this room through a secret passage just as you were finished talking on the phone by the stairs. When you hung up, she had no time to escape. So she put down the lotion where you found it and hid herself in one of the wardrobe closets. Once you were asleep, she came out, and since it was dark, she lit a candle she had in her pocket. Then she left the way she came in. Here. I'll show you."

Liz struggled to a stand and then helped Laura out of bed and into her robe and slippers. Together they walked to one of the bedroom walls. Liz instructed Laura to place her hand flat on a wooden panel over what appeared to be a knothole and give a gentle push. As she did so, there was a quiet click, revealing the latch to a pocket door. Liz slid the door open, and stepped into the hall above the great room in the addition. Laura looked down to see her great-uncle sitting in a chair and eating his breakfast!

"Good morning!" he called up to the two women in a cheery voice. "Coffee's getting cold."

Laura turned to Liz, who seemed to be enjoying her role as the one who revealed all that was mysterious. The older woman nudged her. "Go on downstairs," she urged. "I'll be down in a minute."

Bewildered, Laura stepped across the threshold, went down the steps, and joined Lawrence below in the great room. Behind her, she heard the faint scrape of the once-secret door gliding shut.

"You're looking well today, Uncle Lawrence," Laura remarked as she sat down in the chair beside her great-uncle. "How does your ankle feel?"

The old man nodded. "Fine."

"I did not realize the house was joined on the upper floor as well."

"Marial's idea. It was Elizabeth's family that came here to live once Josiah was gone. Liz's mom, White Wolf, and Marial became good friends. Their children were like one happy family, sharing meals together, spending evenings by the fire here in the great room or playing up in the attic on rainy days. It was just easier to have another door between the two homes, so I helped some fellows put it in." Lawrence paused, seeming to enjoy remembering those days when he could work around the place. "Those two women would sit up in that bedroom, Marial sewing quilt pieces and White Wolf stitching beads. I can still picture them singing and talking and laughing. White Wolf taught my sister and me the legends of the Le-nah-pe, and Marial and I told her family stories from the Bible. I am still amazed by how many beliefs our faiths seem to have in common."

Laura listened intently, fascinated by the bond between those women and its influence on her mother's life and faith.

Lawrence grew quiet. "I remember one time," he continued in a soft voice, "when your mom was little. She got very sick. There was something going around in the school, and she got a really bad case of it. Old Doc Hollings did his best, but the poor dear just lay there feverish and whimpering. White Wolf heard Marial praying, so she went right up there to the bedroom and spent all night chanting and burning sage to cleanse the air. When the sun came up, Christina's fever had broken. We never did figure out if it was the doc's medicine or the smoke and feathers. We didn't care, really. But Christina told us later about the dreams she had that night. The creatures from the forest came and gathered around her bed and sang to her. Then a white raven flew down, spread its wings, and invited the spirit of the sickness to leave. And she watched the two of them fly away together, out the window, and into the moonlight." Laura had no difficulty believing what she was hearing.

"And I know you have visions, Uncle Lawrence!" Before he could answer, Liz appeared in the downstairs doorway. Laura watched admiringly as the dark-skinned woman walk into the room. Her movements were graceful, considering her age and the fact that she was carrying a breakfast tray.

"You must be so hungry," she remarked to Laura as she set the plate of eggs and bacon on the table. Laura helped herself to the mug of coffee immediately.

"I need to wake up first," she exclaimed. "The lines between dreams and reality are still a little blurry." Liz sat down on the sofa, across from Laura. The late-morning sun filled the room, and tiny motes were visible floating in the air.

"When I lived here as a little girl," she recalled, "I thought those flecks of dust were fairies coming to bless my day." Lawrence smiled and chuckled.

"You and Christina had such vivid imaginations."

CHAPTER 20

It wasn't long after Liz's entrance that Simon appeared at the doorway to the great room. His demeanor was that of someone on a mission, but it softened in the presence of Laura.

"Good day to you, Simon. Come in, come in, and thank you for a fine breakfast," complimented the old man.

"Yes, thank you," both women chimed in.

"I seem to be interrupting," Simon apologized.

"Not really," Liz offered. "We were just talking while Laura finished eating. Did you want to tell us something?"

"Just wanted to let you know what I was planning for today and to see if I had forgotten anything."

Lawrence's smile was a mix of pride in this young man and relief that he was willing to continue taking on the daily responsibilities. Laura wiped her mouth with the napkin. It was Monday. She only had a few days left here. *What do I want to do today?*

"I have got to do some laundry," she announced. "And I want to call Cal and fill him in on everything. But that won't take all day. What were you planning, Simon?"

"Well, it's already ten o'clock. The kitchen is cleaned up, almost." His glance fell on Laura's plate. "So a trip to town to the grocery store, a haircut for me, and then I promised Randy I would help work on the tribe's Big House this afternoon. Oh, and I am going to call Dad to see when he wants me to come over to see him this week." The mention of Simon's dad caused Laura's stomach to clench. A flood of emotions overwhelmed her as he continued.

"Laura, I want to tell him about you. Is that okay?"

140

She hesitated. What would he say about her? What kind of introduction did she want him to give? "Let's talk before you make that call," she offered.

"Sure! That's fine." At that moment Lawrence reached over, touched Laura's arm, and said that he really wanted to get those papers in the parlor sorted.

"Since I am not able to move about much with this bum ankle," he suggested, "just park me in there while you go gallivanting about today. I'll be fine."

Liz got up to take away the remaining breakfast dishes. Simon indicated he'd help Lawrence into the parlor while Laura started her laundry.

"Wait," Laura interrupted. "There is one more thing. I really want to learn more about the chemical dumping and soil contamination, you know, what I read about yesterday."

"How about this afternoon when were out on the porch," Lawrence suggested. "If Elizabeth can join us."

"Okay," the older women hollered over her shoulder as she left the room. "I'll come by about four."

Laura took a brief shower, enough to wake her up, and then donned her last clean outfit—olive cargo pants, a beige tank top, and tennis shoes. Carrying her laundry downstairs, she hesitated at the place where she had heard voices before. Sure enough, she recognized Lawrence and Simon discussing something, probably the condition of the old man's ankle and if more pain medicine would be required. She shook her head. *There are mysteries, and then there are just things in life we don't yet understand.*

Continuing down the stairs and then passing through the kitchen, she found the washing machine and dropped in her garments along with a scoop of laundry powder. Had it only been six days since she arrived? How rich and full each one had been. She was struggling to absorb all the information and to keep track of all the relationships, both present and past. As a youngster, she had kept a diary filled with details of her daily events and thoughts. In retrospect, much of it was probably frivolous. But perhaps she should start writing down an account of this visit. It might help clear her mind.

Patterns might begin to emerge, and like the falcon, she could gain some perspective. She decided to ask Simon to stop somewhere in town and pick up a notebook for her.

Lawrence was already settled in his chair in the parlor when she walked in there from the kitchen. The stack of boxes and books were just as the two had left them. "We need to get serious about this," Lawrence chided, "or I'll be dead, and they'll still be here. When I was in the hospital, I kept regretting not getting through all this with you." He was joking, Laura knew, but there was some truth to his words.

"We both have plenty of time." Laura wanted to reassure him. She hoped she was right. They set to organizing the documents, deciding what Laura might take home with her and what should stay in a safe place there at the farm. Simon popped his head in to say he was leaving to go into town.

"Would you pick up a notebook for me?" Laura asked. "I want to start writing…"

"Capturing Lawrence's witticisms and my wisdom? Sure!" Simon laughed. He waved and headed to the car.

"Speaking of diaries," Lawrence said as they heard the car door slam and the engine of the Volvo revving, "I think I remember where Aaron's book is. Do you know how to get to the attic?" Laura nodded. "As girls, Christina and Elizabeth took the other children up in the attic on rainy days to play school. In addition to reading stories and writing the alphabet and numbers on the slate board, those two created nature lessons using Aaron's old journals." For a moment the old man was lost in his memories. Then he sighed. "When Christina finally moved away, Marial packed up all the books and papers from the little 'school' and put them in the attic in a basket Liz had woven. That's where you'll find Aaron's diary, I'll bet."

Up above in a basket, like the medicine doll! Laura got up excitedly and headed for the stairs. She thought she had seen a basket when she was looking around for the dollhouse the other day. Then she stopped. "You still have a good memory, Uncle Lawrence." The old man listened with pleasure to her footfalls on the stairs, then the creaking of the attic door opening, and finally her distant voice.

"Found it!" She returned a few minutes later carrying the basket in her arms as if it were a sacred relic. She placed it on the coffee table and scooted a chair right next to her great-uncle.

Inside the basket was the most intriguing collection of items: notebooks with plants and flowers pressed in them and sketch-books with animal tracks and amazingly lifelike drawings of fish and turtles. Underneath them all was a threadbare book with *Aaron Gardner* burned into the leather cover. As Laura turned each page, she glimpsed the work of this man dedicated to saving the planet from the negative impact of the human industry of his day. Here were his careful drawings of garden plots showing how to guarantee the renewal of the soil. Recipes for natural pesticides and wild animal deterrents were included. Ingredients for herbal remedies that could be cultivated at home were in a separate section. There was even a list of animals that Aaron was concerned might become endangered if they were overhunted. At the back of the little booklet was a roster of those participating in the gatherings at Bittersweet Acres. Some of the names Laura recognized as still represented at the Quaker meeting. The Le-nah-pe families were more difficult for her to iden-tify, and she wondered which of them were Liz's forbears. Lawrence seemed energized as if imbued with the spirit of his own ancestor. Hours passed, but the two did not notice the time until they heard the Volvo returning.

Simon unloaded the groceries before coming into the parlor.

"I'm going to make us some lunch," he told them as he handed Laura a small white paper bag. She pulled out a leather-bound journal.

"Oh, Simon, thank you. It's beautiful." Laura opened the book and noticed the nameplate inside the front cover. Her breath caught. Above the line for the owner's name was an artist's imprint—a pen and ink sketch of a peregrine falcon!

He smiled shyly and walked back to the kitchen.

Once the three had eaten their gazpacho and corn and green bean salad, Simon excused himself to go join Randy Cox. Laura and her great-uncle returned to the parlor. Even with the addition of materials from the attic, it did seem they had made some progress on their task. Laura placed several picture albums and books, including Aaron's diary, on the shelves next to the fireplace. "They belong here where everyone can access them," she told Lawrence. The family Bible from England was then wrapped in acid-free paper and put in a box she retrieved from the linen closet. They decided to hang the framed deed from William Penn on the wall in the dining room. The passenger list from *The Shield* would need to be preserved, so they slipped it in one of the albums for now.

Laura picked up a pack of letters tied in a burgundy ribbon. "What's this?"

Lawrence leaned forward to see. "Ah, there they are!" He seemed delighted and reached for them. "These, my dear, are the letters your grandmother wrote to me when I was away in college." His gnarled fingers stroked them tenderly, as if they were the very hand of the woman who wrote them. "Marial was such a faithful sister, writing me every week with news and goings-on. At the time, I only cared to know that she was well. Later when I reread them, I realized how much of her soul was captured in each line. I want to keep them here with me for now, but later on, I hope you will take them." Laura knew he meant *after I die*. She was willing to wait. She watched as he placed them carefully beside him in the chair.

There was a knock at the side door. Liz hollered hello, and Laura told her to come in. "I know I'm early, but I wondered if Laura wanted to walk over to the ceremonial grounds with me." Laura looked at her great-uncle for a response.

"First, take me back to the great room if you will," Lawrence requested. "I'd like to rest a bit right now."

"Are you all right?" Liz inquired.

"Yes, yes, just weary from answering all Laura's questions," he joked. "And it's time for a pain pill." Both women got up, Laura moving the boxes out of the way while Liz pushed Lawrence's wheelchair across the hall. They helped him get into his bed and arranged his pillows in case he decided to read. Laura brought him a glass of water and his medicine. When they were confident he had all he needed to be comfortable, they each gave him a kiss, stepped out on the porch of the addition, and closed the door.

"He is doing well," commented Liz. "Randy and I were not sure he'd be able to recover from this. I think the fact that you are here and that he has had a mission to accomplish has boosted his will to live." Laura was sad to think that this sweet man might become depressed or lonely, but it wasn't unheard of in people his age. She told Liz of her idea to have Cal and the girls come to visit in the fall.

"You must come for our ga-mwing then!" Liz's response was so immediate and heartfelt that Laura could not imagine refusing. "The celebration would be so much fun for the girls, don't you think?" The image of Noel and Marial dressed in buckskin and dancing around a fire brought a smile to Laura's face.

"When I call home later today, I'll see if I can arrange it."

The afternoon sun was warm, filling the air with the sweet scents of wild flowers mingling with pine. Laura realized they were following the path through the orchard and into the pine forest where she had seen the lights appear at dusk. Even though another mysterious occurrence had a rational explanation, she was unable to let go of the feeling that there were spiritual forces here at Bittersweet Acres that she might never fully comprehend.

CHAPTER 21

When the two women came to the stream and started across the bridge, Laura thought about the newspaper article again. "Liz, can you give me some background on the pollution in the pine barrens now?" The older woman's stride slowed; her shoulders slumped a bit. Any pleasure she had thinking of ga-mwing seemed to dissipate. She walked over to a fallen tree trunk on the bank beside the water, sat down, and beckoned for Laura to join her.

"This is such a sad story. I will tell you some of the history. Later, Lawrence and I will explain what we are doing about it." In the voice of an ancient storyteller, Liz began.

"In the first season of the world, this land was given to humans as a gift from the Creator, and the people lived with a prayer of thanksgiving on their lips. The laws of the Creator put the sun and moon, earth and stars in place; ruled the wind and water and fire and rocks; and designed the circle of life: birth, growth, death, and rebirth. Everything in the world is connected to every other thing, and the blessings of Mother Earth can never be owned and must never be abused. When we honor these laws, everything flourishes."

Liz bowed her head and held her hands out in front of her in an act of both surrendering and receiving. After a moment, she opened her eyes and looked at Laura. "When the Gardner family and other Europeans arrived here, they found luscious jade-green forests filled with an astonishing array of wildlife, as well as waterways crammed with schools of fish so thick that ponds and rivers seemed to be boiling with life. There were flowering meadows and colorful flocks of birds soaring through the skies. And in that pristine wilderness lived the Lenni-Le-nah-pe. Our people taught the newcomers to take from the earth only what they needed. We showed them how to protect the resources we depended on for our survival."

Laura listened intently as Liz described how over time the values of the Le-nah-pe began to change. The settlers brought with them iron pots, metal tools, woven blankets, mirrors, liquor, and guns. They began trading all these things for beads, baskets, animal hides, and luxurious beaver pelts, valued in Europe for making fashionable hats. "We forgot the words of the Creator. Overhunting decimated the beaver population, for example, and caused the destruction of their dams and our wetland habitats. Our economy was destroyed, and our culture declined."

Laura closed her eyes to picture it all: settlers building houses, fencing off fields, cutting down timber, unwittingly destroying habitat for birds and animals. It was too easy to forget that humans don't own land, just hold it in trust.

Liz was standing in the path again, and Laura opened her eyes, stood up and joined her.

"The earth is to be shared, just as air and water are for all of us." Liz spoke again. "The Gardners were more open than some others. They listened to us and adopted many of our traditional ways of living. They shared this land with us, even though they had a paper that said it belonged to them."

"Liz, our Mother Earth is suffering now. I can feel it."

"Yes, and we are obligated to find a way to heal her and protect this land for the future. That is our instruction from the One who gave us this gift. We have been told that we must live so that seven generations of our children will survive in this place." As the two women continued walking single file, following the narrow trail, Laura began to count back: Christina, Marial and Lawrence, Sarah, Aaron…all faithful stewards of Bittersweet Acres. She vowed not to be the generation of her family that failed to honor the will of the Creator.

It was just a bit farther down the path of leaves and pine needles to the clearing. Materials to be used in constructing the tipis and wigwams for families were arranged in neat stacks. Laura watched as Simon, Randy, and the other men struggled to move some of the long, slim wooden poles from a pile and drive them into the ground, forming a circle. Once all the poles were in place, they would be bent in one over the other and lashed together to make the dome of the roof. Liz explained that sheets of bark and woven rush mats would be fastened over them for protection from the elements. Some smaller structures might be covered with skins or cloth. Laura noticed there were shorter, thicker poles to make platforms inside the houses for seats or beds.

She and Liz approached the door of the Big House. Workers were filling the chinks in the logs with mortar. Others were digging the firepits inside the meeting space under the openings in the roof. Some women came in carrying armfuls of grasses, to be spread on the packed earthen floor for seating.

"Two pure fires inside provide light for the ceremonies. There is another fire outside where we will be preparing meals for the people," one of the workers explained.

"How many will be coming?" asked Laura. She counted ten wigwams surrounding the Big House and guessed that families would share space or bring their own tents. Liz said there were very few elders still alive who honored the ancient ways, but all Le-nah-pe were invited, so as many as fifty tribe members might be at the gathering. This year any neighbors wishing to pray with them for the health of the environment were also welcome.

"Once the living spaces are completed, those of us who live close by will stock them with supplies: blankets, utensils for cooking and eating, sleeping mats, and some food stuffs like corn and herbs. We will spend the entire year before ga-mwing making our sleeping mats, sewing festival clothing, and preparing traditional food."

"It sounds like a lot of work," Laura observed.

"We have learned to pace ourselves," Liz replied, "and everyone contributes something." As they walked around the clearing, the older woman seemed to be inspecting the preparations but continued to speak to Laura. Her voice was soft, the tone she used when telling old stories. "All our celebrations were designed to strengthen community. Building wigwams reminds us that we once lived in temporary shelters, moving our camps to the ocean or the forest, depending on the seasons. We had ceremonies throughout the year to mark the births of new babies, the marriages, the rites of passage for young people, and the grieving for those who had died. Ga-mwing is the time when we say thank you—*wa-ni-shi*—to the Creator. Songs and stories, dances and prayers show our gratitude for the gifts we have been given."

Satisfied with the progress of the work, Liz took Laura back to the farmhouse. Although it was still daylight, the path through the pines was in deep shadow. Laura could imagine wood sprites and even the Jersey Devil lurking in the underbrush. She was glad when they reached the stream and the orchard where she could see the house again. As the two women approached the front porch, Liz indicated she would check on Lawrence. Perhaps Laura would like to make that call to her family. "Take all the time you need. I'll fix your uncle something to drink, and when you're done, join us."

Laura was grateful for the solitude of the hall upstairs as she picked up the phone and dialed her home number. Where would she begin? The invitation to ga-mwing? Uncle Lawrence's condition? Simon?

"Hello?"

"Cal, hi. It's Laura."

"Well, stranger, how are you? If you tried to call last night, I'm sorry we didn't answer. It was late when we finally got here."

"Actually, I didn't call. It was a long day, and we all went to bed early too."

"I know how that feels. The girls and I have been on the go every minute since you left, and we went to sleep the minute we finish prayers and kisses."

"Cal, honey"—Laura paused as she gathered her thoughts—"remember how after Mom died you told me you hoped that one day I might locate my father?"

"Yeah," he recalled. "It always seemed to me there was a part of your life story that you needed to fill in." After a silent moment, he added, "Wait! Don't tell me your dad lives in Laurel Hill!"

"Not quite," Laura responded. "But his son does."

"He has another child? Besides you?"

"Well, yes." She took a breath. "His name is Simon Andrews."

"Not the same Simon…" Laura heard Cal make a noise that was something between a gasp and a giggle. "Well, what are the chances of that?" he remarked with more than a little disbelief.

"I know," Laura answered gently. "I am as flabbergasted as you are. My half brother lives here and works for my great-uncle." Cal struggled to regain his composure.

"Um, is your dad still alive?"

"Yep. Lives in Philadelphia. Simon wants to take me there to meet him."

"And?"

"We're going to talk about it later today, before Simon calls to discuss it with him."

"Seriously, Laura, are you okay?" Cal was genuine in his concern for his wife. "This is a really important moment for you." Then he added, "Gosh, I wish I were there." Laura smiled at the sound of caring in his voice.

"Cal, I am still trying to process everything. Right now, I think Simon and I can deal with this. And I'll do better if you stay put and take care of the girls."

"I guess you are right. Sounds like you two and your dad will have a lot to talk through and sort out. You don't need me muddying the waters."

"Thanks for understanding." Laura truly meant that. "And I will tell you the entire bizarre and wonderful story when we are face-to-face. Right now, I have something *else* I want to talk about."

"Okay." It was clear that Cal had more questions, but he yielded to Laura's wishes.

"Remember when I asked you if we could all come visit Uncle Lawrence later this fall?"

"Uh huh. It sounds like an even better idea now. By the way, how is your uncle feeling?"

"He's doing very well. His ankle is in a splint, his ribs only hurt when he laughs, and we are keeping him confined to the first floor. But that doesn't stop us from working through the stack of family papers. In fact, we located a diary that was kept by Aaron, one of the early Gardners, with details about the farm, notes on soil renewal, plants and animals… Oh, Cal, it's a treasure!"

"I'd like to have a look at that."

"I knew you'd be interested! And Aaron kept records of his meetings with the Le-nah-pe tribe members too. He was determined to learn how to maintain the land from the people who lived here before him. Isn't that amazing?"

"Laura, you are sounding, well, excited. Where are you going with this?"

"Well, that's the other thing. At first, I just wanted us to spend time with Lawrence so he could know us and the girls better. Now I am feeling that we should be getting to know this place better. Not just because my mom grew up here. We are to be the caretakers of this land, for another seven generations, as the Le-nah-pe say!"

"Laura?"

"Yes, Cal?"

"Are you thinking of more than just one visit?" There was a touch of alarm in his question.

"Maybe. These few days have been intense for me." *That is putting it mildly*, she thought. "I have been absorbing so much new information that my brain is swirling. What I want to do is finish up here in a couple more days and, then come home and get back to our normal routine, you know, to put it all in perspective. I will tell you everything that has happened. Then we'll work out together what it all means…for the future. But before I leave here, I want to assure Uncle Lawrence that we'll be coming back. In the meantime, you and I will have discussed what our next steps should be. Does that make any sense?"

"What I hear you asking is that all of us return to Laurel Hill with you so that we can explore our role in the legacy of the farm. Am I right?"

"Oh, Cal, that is one of the things I love about you. You take all my ramblings and pull them into a coherent thought. Yes. That is it, exactly. I realize now that the stewardship of this place called Bittersweet Acres is up to me, with some assistance from Simon."

"This could mean significant changes in our life, you realize."

"I know, and it's all fascinating and a bit frightening. Cal, our future is here on this farm. I can almost see it but details are still fuzzy. It just seems to be something we have to consider."

"Just like always, Laura. You are three steps ahead of everyone else."

"It's my falcon spirit telling me to be fearless," she said with a laugh.

"What?" Laura's reference was lost on Cal.

"Oh, one more thing. Remember the lotion I found in the bedroom here? It's a mixture Mom created years ago, something herbal that induces visions and dreams."

"Really? Oh, my! I can see why you will need some time to decompress. Come home, then, as soon as you can. The girls and I have really missed you, and they want to tell you all about Pittsburgh."

"Cal?"

"And, yes, we'll make plans for a family trip to Laurel Hill in the fall. How does that sound?"

"Wonderful!" Laura was silently thankful for such an understanding husband. "I think I'll be able to leave here sometime Wednesday. I want to be sure Lawrence and Simon don't need my help with anything else. If we aren't able to arrange to visit his dad tomorrow, we'll try for the next day and I'll be home Thursday at the latest."

"I hope only the best for your meeting with Jude Andrews. Oh, and inform Lawrence that we'll all be with you next time."

"Thanks, my love. I'll phone you again when I'm ready to head home. Give our sweet girls my love."

As she hung up the phone, Laura looked again at the cluster of family photographs on the hall table. She smiled, confident that she'd be returning with pictures of her own to add to the display.

CHAPTER 22

By the time Laura entered the great room, Liz and Lawrence were in deep conversation. They looked up and motioned for her to come sit with them. There was cold lemonade in a pitcher on the table, and she poured herself a glass before taking a seat. Lawrence began.

"Laura, we want to ask you to help us with something. Elizabeth and I are part of a group of concerned residents in the area working on environmental issues. We wouldn't have involved you if you hadn't reacted with such interest to the newspaper article. Here's the thing, dear. The situation with chemical waste dumping has been going on for a long time. But about ten years ago, the Environmental Protection Agency finally took notice. It has been slow going as you can imagine. We think they will have better luck fixing the whole mess if local folks communicate our suggestions to them. So, we are building a coalition of governments, health departments, and research scientists to come up with short- and long-term solutions." Liz nodded and joined in.

"We want to find answers," she added, "solutions to the issues of cleaning up past spills and of preventing any future disasters. There have to be cost-effective ways for these industries to be responsible citizens of the earth." Laura was astounded at her friend's and her great-uncle's passion. At a point in their lives when they could sit back in their rocking chairs and fold their arms, the two of them were rallying resources for change. Lawrence handed her a brochure their group had put together, highlighting the history of the situation.

The entire problem had started innocuously enough, Laura read.

During the industrial boom just after World War II, the chemical industry grew rapidly in the north-central part of the state. At first, companies stored waste in their own warehouses, but soon they were searching for more disposal sites. They turned to municipal landfills and contracted with trucking companies to dump the materials. In time, it came to light that much of the contents of the storage drums being discarded was volatile and hazardous. So the landfill owners raised their rates for receiving such shipments. Haulers began to look for other less costly ways to dispose of their cargo. Once the Garden State Parkway was completed, convoys of trucks were soon heading south and dumping their loads in remote, unregulated locations in the Pine Barrens.

Lawrence interrupted her reading. "The thing is," he said, "the cleanup processes are expensive and not always based on good science. And while government funding is flowing to the counties along the coast, no one is paying attention to the Delaware River and its tributaries."

"The Ancocas?" Laura asked.

"I am afraid all the waterways will end up polluted if we don't keep people aware of the situation. It will be our farmers' crops that fail and our children developing cancers too." Lawrence's face showed such concern that Laura was deeply moved.

Liz picked up a folder from the table beside her. "We were getting the group together tomorrow at the Meeting House, but now we think we'll hold it here. That way it will be easy for Lawrence to participate. Laura, we want you to join us. Here are our notes and information concerning legal strategies, public education, state and local policy recommendations… We want you to come and sit in on the conversations."

Laura agreed to attend, but only to determine what, if anything, she might contribute to the work of the citizens' group from her office in Harrisburg. Lawrence's face relaxed, and Liz handed the documents to Laura. They both seemed pleased that she was agreeable to their request.

"So did you talk to your husband?" asked Liz, changing the subject.

"Oh, I almost forgot. Yes, they are safely home from their visit to Pittsburgh. I told Cal some of what's been happening but saved a lot of it for when we're face-to-face. He did say that he and the girls would love to come visit this fall. If that's okay with you, Uncle Lawrence."

His face brightened.

"Why, yes, for a Le-nah-pe thanksgiving!" Liz said as she gave a wink. "We'll have to alert Simon, of course. Where is he, by the way?"

Right on cue, the young man appeared in the doorway, announcing that dinner was being served. He had showered and shaved after working on the Big House and somehow had managed to put together a scrumptious vegetable lasagna. Liz and Randy joined them around the dining room table, and during the silent grace before eating, Laura's heart was full of gratitude for life's gifts.

Once the meal ended, the Coxes helped Lawrence back to the great room and sat chatting with him about the plans for tomorrow's group meeting. Laura worked with Simon to get the table cleared and leftovers put away. While they were straightening up the kitchen, Simon brought up their plans to visit Jude Andrews.

"When I call him in a few minutes, do you want to be here with me? He may want to speak to you." Laura had not even considered that possibility, but perhaps a phone conversation might be a good way to break the ice before their visit.

"Okay." She agreed hesitantly. "But if you think he is upset or needs to speak privately to you, I will go to another room."

"Actually, I was running scenarios in my head at the worksite today. I think that after the initial surprise, he will jump at the chance to get acquainted with you. Dad has always been a kind man and a good father to me. I consider your arrival here as a blessing, and I think he will too."

"I hope so." Laura was not sure.

"Well, our talks always start with the usual chatter about his health and mine. Then he asks about Lawrence and the farm. That will be my cue to mention that we've had a visitor, and I'll be sure to tell him to sit down." Simon smiled, and Laura imagined her eighty-some-year-old father falling down in a dead faint at the mention of her name.

"Simon, be sure to let him know that none of this was planned—that you and I are as shocked as he may be. I am more curious about meeting him than angry about his leaving all those years ago." Laura hoped she really meant that.

"Well, shall we give him a call now?" Laura took a deep breath.

"Give me a minute to compose myself. Go ahead and dial the number. I'll come back in just a little while."

Simon gave her a kiss on the cheek, and Laura scurried out of the kitchen.

CHAPTER 23

The phone rang in Jude Andrews's apartment. It rang a second time, and finally someone picked up the receiver and said hello with a familiar pleasant tone.

"It's Simon, Dad. Hi."

"Well, hello, son. It's nice of you to call tonight." The conversation unfolded just as Simon had predicted with accounts of his dad's doctor visits, the quality of the meals in the dining room, and the latest news from the lives of the other octogenarians in the retirement complex.

"How's Lawrence doing?" his dad inquired. Simon described the accidental fall and resulting injuries to the man's ankle. His dad chided him for not being more careful and for leaving temptations around to lure old people to their doom. They both knew the comments were meant in a good-hearted way.

"Dad, we have had a visitor at the farm this week. Uncle Lawrence's great-niece from Harrisburg is here with us."

"How nice. Harrisburg, you say. What's she like, son?"

"Well, she's a lawyer, married with two little girls." Simon looked up and saw Laura in the doorway. He waved for her to come into the kitchen. "Lawrence wanted her to come help him sort out some family memorabilia we came across in the attic."

"That's nice. Company for both of you," offered Jude. Simon looked at Laura and crossed his fingers.

"Dad, she's Christina's daughter, Laura."

Silence. Simon and Laura stood side by side in the dimly lit kitchen, each remembering how they had felt just a few days ago when the reality of their relationship dawned on them. They were more than willing to give Jude the time he needed to react to Simon's words.

"Her name is Laura?" The voice on the phone was soft and thick with emotion. If he had known what Christina named their baby, he seemed to have forgotten it.

"Yeah, Dad, Laura Marshall."

"Christina's daughter," he repeated, and there was a touch of astonishment in his voice.

"Dad, we think Lawrence wanted to resolve all the unfinished business in this family while he was still alive. So he invited her here, to meet me perhaps. I think eventually he hoped she would get to know *you*. Neither Laura nor I had a clue about any of this until she was looking at old pictures the other day. We compared her mother's wedding picture with that one of you and Mom that was taken here… Dad, are you there?"

When the older man spoke again, it was clear that he had been crying. "Simon, I would have told you about all this, but it didn't seem necessary. Her mother and I agreed when we separated that we would not stay in touch. I was to forget my life with her and move on. So I relocated, married your mother, and you know the rest of that story. It was years later when a mutual friend told me Christina had a baby girl, but didn't tell me her name."

"Did anyone contact you when Christina died?"

"No, not at the time. I think I found out in a note from Lawrence some months after her death."

There was another pause. Neither son nor father spoke for a long time.

"Dad, I'll come over to visit you tomorrow, if that's okay. And I want to bring Laura along to meet you. What do you think?"

Again silence. Then the sounds of the older man blowing his nose and sniffling.

"Oh, Simon. Do you think she wants to meet me?"

Simon looked over at Laura and then handed her the phone. She took it and slowly put it to her ear.

"Hello?"

"Laura?" For the first time in her life, she was hearing her father's voice.

"Yes."

"Hello. This is Simon's dad."

What followed was an awkward conversation between two people who had been lost to each other by circumstances and then reunited in a most unlikely way. Laura answered a few questions about herself, her husband, and the children. Simon pulled up one of the kitchen chairs and helped Laura sit down in it. He propped himself up on a stool at the counter, watching Laura's eyes, gauging her mood, smiling as she turned toward him and gave a thumbs-up signal. Laura listened as Jude responded to her questions about the place he was living now. Keeping it light and somewhat superficial, the two shared information, laughing at times, growing a bit more serious as time went on.

"Here, I'll give you back to Simon now." Laura ended their talk. "You two can figure out what we're doing tomorrow." Laura held out her arm and handed over the receiver to her brother. While he wrapped up the call, she grabbed a tissue, wiping her eyes and nose.

"Bye, Dad." Simon hung up. He looked at Laura. "I think that went pretty well."

Laura got up and gave him a bear hug. The two stood there in an embrace as Laura shared some of what their father had said to her.

"I can't wait to see your baby pictures!" she teased. It was going to be interesting having a little brother, she decided.

When Simon and Laura walked over into the great room, Lawrence, Randy, and Liz stopped talking. Their faces were expressionless as they looked up at the two young people. While they prayed for a good outcome from the phone call, one could never predict human nature.

"Dad said he'd love to see us tomorrow," announced Simon. The group exhaled and smiled.

"Good," was all Lawrence said, but he looked relieved.

"What time are you going into the city?" asked Randy. "Remember we need you both back here for the citizens' action group meeting."

"We'll leave here after the morning rush hour, have lunch with Dad, and be back home for dinner." Simon had the trip down to a routine. He knew his father's preference was for a short visit and a meal.

Liz offered to fix lunch for Lawrence. "I'll also have something in the oven for our supper, too, just in case you run a little late."

"Thanks, that's really thoughtful," Laura responded. "I am still nervous about it, but if the man is as easy to be with in person as he is to talk to on the phone, we'll be okay."

"Jude is a fine man, Laura," put in Lawrence. "He loved your mother, and he loved Simon's mom too. I have known him a long time now. He'll open up to you the minute he sees you."

Randy stood and announced it was getting close to his bedtime. Everyone agreed to call it a night, and Simon rushed folks out so he could get Lawrence into bed. "There are scones for you on the kitchen counter," he called to Liz. "Take them home for your breakfast."

She called back a thank-you and took Laura's arm as they walked down the hallway. "Are you going to be all right?"

"I really think so, Liz," Laura answered. "How blessed I am to have this opportunity. And Simon will be there."

"I remember meeting Jude once when he came here to visit," the older woman recalled. "There was a troubled place in his spirit, even though he was content with his life. Perhaps your visit will help heal those deep wounds."

Laura saw her friends off and then returned to say good night to her uncle. The moonlight shone through the great room windows, and the evening breeze was cool. Lawrence was in bed, and Simon was standing beside him holding his hands. The old man was close to sleep already, so Laura just blew him a kiss and went up the stairs to bed. She fell into a fitful slumber.

Who are all these people? I recognize some as members of the Quaker meeting.

There are others I don't know, settlers from a neighboring village, perhaps. And of course several of the Le-nah-pe tribe. They are motioning for me to join them, so I go over to where they are seated. They seem to want me to settle a question for them, and I listen as each side speaks.

One person claims that when they traded blankets with the Le-nah-pe, the fabric was filled with diseases and their children died. Another claims that when workers are hired by local farmers, not everyone is paid a fair wage. There is a disagreement about whether the fertile bottom lands along the river were part of the area allotted for hunting. Another dispute involves some land with rich soil that was claimed by the native people but abandoned in the summer when they migrated to the ocean. When they returned, a Quaker family was living there.

I talk to them about the idea of a peaceable kingdom, a place ruled by tolerance and cooperation. But they laugh and think I am not being realistic. They show me a map and ask me to draw lines to show where they can farm and hunt and live. I tell them I am not qualified to do that. I want them to work it out together. But they seem impatient. Everyone talks at once. Tempers begin to flare up. I am frightened.

Oh, good. Here is Elsa. She will help me sort this out. But when she approaches, she is only carrying the little pot of hand cream. It's the one I keep by my bed. She opens it, and immediately the air is filled with the fragrance of crushed yarrow, so pleasant and spicy. Then the scent of rosemary, oregano, and other herbs rises like a thin cloud from the tiny jar, encircling my head, and floating over the others. It has a calming effect on all of them. They stop shouting and quietly take seats on blankets on the ground. They look at each other and smile, reaching out to hold each other's hands. They begin to sing. I recognize the song. It is the one I heard at the Meeting House on Sunday, the one Simon whistles when he works in the kitchen, the one I hear in my dreams.

As the melody fades, the people stand and face the east. They are praying to the Creator together. Quaker and Le-nah-pe and neighbors all asking for help to keep the land beautiful and productive. I watch as the words they say become visible, swirling together overhead, rising into the sky like smoke from a campfire. Words sparkle and dance overhead as daylight disappears, and the night sky turns deep blue. The prayer words float higher and higher until they become the stars.

Elsa closes the jar and hands it to me. I now have the power to bring people together to save Mother Earth. Mother Earth. Mother. Mother.

CHAPTER 24

Laura awoke to a room filled with morning sunshine. Today she would meet her father for the first time, face-to-face. She remembered the words of the shadowy priest in the church: *Honor your father. Honor your mother.* Then came the words from a long ago dream: *You will find your father someday, and he will be proud of you.* She wondered how well she would do at being Jude's daughter today. *What do daughters say to their dads?* But Laura's main concern at the moment was what to wear.

Fortunately, she had done laundry the day before and had her full wardrobe from which to choose. As she showered, she mentally pictured herself in each possible outfit, looking for just the right image, and finally decided on the blue sundress and her flowered neck scarf. How odd that she cared what her father thought about her clothing. In the mirror, she could always pick out the ways she resembled her mom. Today she had a different question. "What looks did I inherit from you, Jude Andrews?" she asked her reflection. For once, her hair and makeup seemed to be perfect. The outfit she chose was casual but classic. She finished dressing and took one last glance at herself before leaving the bedroom. Yes, she was Laura Marshall at her best, ready to meet the stranger in Philadelphia.

Simon was already in the kitchen making French toast and slicing fresh peaches. He was wearing a pale blue short-sleeved dress shirt, khakis, and dock shoes without socks. After inquiring how they each slept, the conversation turned to the visit. Simon reminded Laura that, although his dad had arthritis, he was able to get around with a cane, like Lawrence. They would meet him at his apartment and have time to talk there. Then Simon would drive them to his dad's favorite restaurant: Old Bookbinders on Walnut Street. Laura admitted being nervous, but Simon indicated that he would do whatever he could to make it a good experience for all of them. While they ate, he entertained her with some of his favorite childhood memories and one or two embarrassing stories that he was sure his dad would bring up.

It was their laughter that Lawrence heard as he slowly made his way to the kitchen, leaning heavily on his cane.

"What's all this racket?" he called out from the hallway.

Looking guiltily at each other, they responded in unison. "Nothing!"

Then Simon got up quickly and went to help the old man into one of the kitchen chairs.

"You two still here? I thought you'd be long gone by now." Lawrence was trying to be gruff, but it wasn't working. Laura put down her fork, wiped her hands on the napkin, and went over to her great-uncle.

"We wouldn't leave without telling you." She hugged his shoulders warmly.

Simon scowled. "And what are you doing out of your wheelchair?"

Lawrence explained how much he missed his morning walks and decided that at least he could start hobbling around in the house a bit. "I don't want to lose the strength in my good leg," he added, patting the side of his thigh.

"Well, promise me you won't do any gimpy limping when I'm not here, please. We can't have you taking another spill."

"Yes, you're right. I shouldn't have ventured out of my room without letting you know. I just heard your voices…" Lawrence stopped. "Laura, your laugh sounds so much like your mother's. For just a moment this morning, I thought I'd find Christina here in the kitchen."

"Do you think Jude will notice the resemblance?" Laura asked.

"If he doesn't, he's daft!" Lawrence answered.

Simon was quiet. Laura realized that as important as today would be for her, something would change for Simon as well. His place as Jude's only child was being supplanted. She would need to be mindful of her interactions with his father.

"Simon, remember when I arrived and didn't know you would be here?" Laura hoped she could disarm any jealously he might be feeling. "You already had a close relationship with my uncle, and I had to begin to build one. It probably felt intrusive at times to you, but I never meant it that way." She paused. "So the same thing may happen today. I hope you know me well enough to understand that I will never do anything intentionally to come between you and your dad."

Simon reached over and took her hand. "I'm not sure how you knew what I was feeling just then."

"It's her falcon spirit!" The voice came from the side porch. Liz Cox had arrived to care for Lawrence, and that was the signal for Simon and Laura to go.

"Just leave it all," the older woman insisted, waving her hands toward the table. "I'll clean up once I get this old man back to his room." She escorted Lawrence out of the kitchen, calling over her shoulder. "You two, be back in time for dinner."

Simon went to start the car. Laura grabbed her handbag, checking to be sure she had the pictures of Calvin and the girls with her. Another quick look in the hall mirror and a fresh application of lipstick. Taking a deep breath she stepped onto the porch and closed the screen door behind her.

The ride from the farm to the city was pleasant, and Simon whistled "Beautiful Dreamer" as he drove. Laura shaded her eyes as they crossed the Ben Franklin Bridge. The morning sun reflected brilliantly off the windows of offices and apartment buildings that made up the Philadelphia skyline. She turned to look out the side window and down to the Delaware River below her. Instantly the dream with the swaying bridge came back to mind, and with it the feelings of helplessness and dread. She saw the old man in the shadows again, heard the flute, saw sparks of light. Slamming her eyes closed, she uttered one word.

"Na-che-si-mus!"

"What? Don't you like my whistling?" Simon feigned a hurt look and then smiled.

"Sorry. It was just something I…" Laura didn't finish her sentence.

Simon reached over, took her hand, and squeezed it gently.

"I'm right here. We're together. Just follow my lead." *The very words he had spoken in her dream!* She let her shoulders relax.

Simon guided the car through the city following the Schuylkill Expressway. They caught a glimpse of the iconic Museum of Art and then Fairmont Park with its charming boat houses, as they drove along the river to City Avenue. Turning onto Lancaster Avenue, they traveled several more blocks, then pulled into the parking area in front of an impressive restored historic building. This was Anderson House, where Jude Andrews lived.

"Well, here we are," Simon announced.

"What an interesting place," Laura commented.

"Yeah, Dad loves that it is close to where we used to live and that it has 'a story.' No doubt he'll tell you all about it."

They got out of the Volvo and made their way to the desk in the foyer. A young man whose name tag read *Julian* greeted Simon by name. He informed him that his father was on the patio having coffee. With a wave of thanks, Simon led Laura across the well-appointed community room and through a set of French doors. Sturdy wrought iron tables and chairs were scattered among decorative planters filled with maiden grass, day lilies, and phlox. Two elderly women were sipping coffee and chatting with an older man at the next table. When they looked up and saw Simon they burst into a titter of greetings. Leaving Laura for the moment, he went over and gave them both air kisses. The man next to them got up and, walking with some difficulty, came over to where Laura was standing.

"Laura."

"Yes… Are you Simon's dad?" As soon as she said it, she realized she had not thought about how to address this man. But apparently, he was prepared for that and simply replied with a nod. Together they went back over to his table. He stood behind her chair until she was seated and then took his own place, leaving a chair across from him for his son.

"You look so much like the way I remember your mother," he remarked. Laura smiled as she fished around in her brain for an appropriate response.

"Thanks. You've changed a bit since your wedding picture," she tried. Then she added quickly, "But Simon has a lovely photo of you and his mom, and you're just a bit thinner now." *Get over here, Simon,* she begged in her head.

Changing the subject, Jude Andrews asked, "Isn't this an interesting place to live? It was built in the 1900s as the Old Man's Home of Philadelphia. Seriously, it was created to care for the aging male population who had no means of support. Years later, they built the addition, began admitting woman, and finally sold it in 1975 to a corporation which runs senior living communities. They made significant upgrades to all the facilities and added programs and staff. There are special rooms for assisted living when you need them. I have a regular apartment on the fifth floor."

Taking his cue, Laura asked about where he lived before coming to Anderson House. Jude described the place he and his wife had owned, the one where Simon was raised. "I expect he'll drive us by there on the way to lunch. He usually does."

"I think we all like to remember our roots," Laura added with cautious warmth. "That's kind of what brought me to New Jersey this week."

Just then Simon arrived at their table with coffees and sat down. He picked up the conversation, and Laura sat back and relaxed for a moment.

"Dad, do you know Mrs. Halsey is having heart surgery next week? She's really worried about it."

"I didn't know that. I'll talk to her later. If it's the same thing I had done, I can ease her mind a bit."

"She'd love that. Now, have you two gotten past the awkward stage yet?" Laura bristled at how direct Simon was at times.

His father replied first, "No, I don't think quite yet." Turning to Laura, he asked, "Where do you want to start, my dear?"

Laura took a sip of coffee since there was not water handy. Then she reached in her wallet and pulled out the plastic folder with her family pictures.

"Let's begin with now and work backward." She looked at Jude, and he nodded in agreement. "This is my husband, Calvin Marshall. We met in grad school."

"And I understand you are a lawyer! That is some accomplishment. Congratulations. Do you have a practice somewhere? Oh, Harrisburg, right?"

"Yes, we've lived in Harrisburg all our married life. Cal is in economic development for Dauphin County, and I am with a firm located near the state capitol complex."

"And who are these sweet angels?" Jude's tone was genuine.

Laura regaled the two men for several minutes with descriptions of her daughters and stories of their growing up years.

"I hope I get to meet them someday," said the old man.

Simon jumped in. "Laura and her family are planning to come to the farm again in a few months. I am sure we can arrange for them to spend some time with you."

Jude looked pleased. "Let's go up to my place now. After we talked last night, I got out some pictures of my family to show you." Laura felt a momentary sting from those words. It registered with her that she was not part of "his family." He had no pictures of her. But the wave of anger quickly softened to sadness, and then a quiet understanding that this kind of healing takes time. Simon helped his dad up, and Laura followed the two men inside to the elevator in the lobby. Again, Laura noted how tasteful the facility renovation were. She was relieved not to find what she had imagined: the residents secured in wheelchairs and positioned in an antiseptic hallway.

As the elevator door opened on the fifth floor, Jude pointed out that the halls on each level were painted a different pastel color. That was done to help residents identify visually whether they were getting off at the correct floor. "My wife Linda loved telling friends that we lived on the Eucalyptus level, but it's really just green."

Linda. His wife. Simon's mother. Something jarred again inside Laura's heart, and she struggled to keep her equilibrium. Jude unlocked his apartment door, and the three went inside. Sunlight filled the living room and a shelf of healthy house plants sat just below the picture window overlooking the parking area. *My mother never had much luck with indoor specimens,* Laura noted. Jude invited them both to sit down while he carefully gave each flowerpot a quarter turn. "Got to keep these from getting lopsided."

Once they were comfortable, Jude took the chair next to Laura. He pulled a shoe box from under the coffee table. Laura was struck by the same feelings she had experienced when she and Lawrence first started going through his papers. *Ambivalence.* There. She named it. Wanting to find out something and yet perhaps not really wanting to know. Simon saw her expression and went into his dad's kitchen, returning with a glass of water for her. She mouthed, "Thank you," and braced herself for what would come next.

"This is going to be quite a process, us getting to know each other, Laura." Jude was trying his best to be casual and businesslike. Laura knew he was struggling. One doesn't meet abandoned daughters every day. "Let me show you a few pictures of my life here in Philadelphia."

Laura nodded. Jude opened the box and handed her a photo of him in a suit and tie at what appeared to be his retirement party. The woman she recognized now as Linda stood beside him, obviously proud, and Simon was next to her. There was a distinct family resemblance: the blonde hair, genuine smiles, and happy eyes. Simon had gotten good genes from each of his parents. Jude then produced several pictures of Linda and Simon taken at their Long Beach Island cottage, one or two more from vacations in the Pocono Mountains, and then one of Simon and his mother standing in front of a beautiful stone colonial home on a tree-lined street. Simon looked to be about fifteen years old. Laura slipped the photo over to him. "This is the house?"

Simon grinned. "Gosh, this was taken in my awkward stage. Yeah, that's the old homestead."

Jude and Simon took turns describing the interior of their family home: a cozy living room with the original wood-burning fireplace, an eat-in kitchen, and a Great Room across the back of the place.

"My bedroom was overlooking the park," Simon added. "And the entire basement was finished, so that's where I hung out with my friends."

"We had kids over all the time to watch sports or movies or shoot pool. Linda and I entertained on the patio a lot or just sat on the porch on a summer evening and watched the cars go by."

"No wonder you liked going to Lawrence's place. He practically lives on his front porch," Laura commented. At that moment, the wedding picture of her mother and Jude came into her mind. She blushed.

"It's okay, honey," Jude replied to her show of emotion. "We are going to bump into awkward memories a lot, I bet, and we'll just have to breathe and move on as best we can."

Simon was thinking of the photograph of his mother and father at Bittersweet Acres.

He wanted to say more about his mother but sensed it was not the time to do it. When Laura asked her next question, he was glad he had kept silent.

"I don't know what to call you," Laura announced, and there was something in her voice that was more demanding than she intended. "I mean, you are my biological father, but honestly I'm not comfortable with Dad." Could something so simple as how to address each other hinder their ability to become friends? This was a conversation that needed to happen at some point. Jude made a stab at giving an answer.

"Laura, I don't have any right to claim to be your dad, even though I am. But I'd like to think I could become somebody you, well, contact now and then, maybe ask for some advice? Oh, I don't know. How about you address me as Jude for now? Simon, what do you think?"

"It's not my call," the younger man replied, leaning far back in his chair as if to remove himself from the discussion.

"What did my mother call you?" Laura asked.

Jude smiled. "Not all of her names for me are repeatable in mixed company." The perfect response. The tension in the room lightened considerably as Laura and Simon pictured Christina and this man scrapping with each other. "She liked Jude best, I think."

"Okay, let's go with that."

CHAPTER 25

For the next half hour, Laura listened intently as the man who had once loved her mother recounted some events from their life together: how they met, where they went on dates, and their wedding at Bittersweet Acres. "It was a long time ago, but we had a really good life," Jude admitted. "Christina was a superb teacher with a kind heart. She went overboard to see that each of the kids in her classes grasped the material in their lessons and could apply them to life." Then he leaned forward, clasping his hands and resting his elbows on his knees. "I was wrapped up in my own work, of course, traveling out of town, staying late at the office to finish up reports. Your mom was such a strong woman that I guess I took for granted that she was content with how things were."

Simon had never been curious about these years in his father's life, the time in Pittsburgh. It puzzled him now that his dad would have given up on his first marriage. So he pressed his father to explain what happened.

"Oh, Christina had all the right skills and gifts to be a pastor. Seminary was a perfect choice for her, and I saw that her passion for ministry was just as strong as her love of teaching." Jude leaned back and closed his eyes momentarily, as if to picture those days. "I have to admit," he continued, "so much that happened was my fault. I was selfish back then. I needed to feel like I was in charge and making all the decisions. I was the one with the big paycheck, after all." His tone grew uneasy.

"So I had to go to business dinners and social events by myself because Christina was involved in a congregational meeting or a hospital visit or a funeral. She preferred not to travel with me to industry conferences and golf outings. I didn't like it and my company executive officers considered it unprofessional for a man to make decisions about work based on his wife's wishes." Jude's voice grew quiet. "Laura, your mother wanted to do what Jesus would have her do. I couldn't compete with God. When she told me we were having a baby, I just refused to accept it. Instead of anticipating all the blessings of being a dad, I saw it as more pressure, more problems in my life." His eyes filled with tears. "I was so, so wrong—about Christina, about God, about my own ambitious dreams…" His voice trailed off.

Laura sat still. She could only watch as the man across from her faced the consequences of his life choices. *What would his life have been like if he had stayed with us?* she wondered. Surely she and her mother could have loved him enough to make him happy and his life fulfilling. But here he was, telling her that at the time he wasn't capable of having that kind of bond with them. Jude looked up. His wet eyes met Laura's.

"You probably think your mother and I cheated you out of something. The fact is that she and I were robbed of being able to enjoy raising you together. I left, and she had to do it alone. I take responsibility for that." He dropped his head and closed his eyes.

Without thinking, Laura reached for Jude's hands. "It's okay, Dad," she whispered. The words came so spontaneously that they surprised her. "Mom always said there is plenty of forgiveness to go around." After several moments, Simon glanced at his wristwatch and broke in.

"This is terrible timing," he apologized, "but we've got lunch reservations." He winced, hoping he had not upset either of his companions. He need not have worried. They were quite willing to regain their composure and comply with his request. Gathering up her purse and Jude's cane, Laura and her dad made their way to the elevator. It seemed that the two of them were coming to an understanding more quickly than either Simon or Laura could have imagined. She recalled her dream words: *It's all a dance, really. Just a dance. But once you begin, you have to keep going.* Laura really did want to discover more about her father and to reveal herself to him at the same time. She would keep going, even if sometimes she felt afraid.

Simon drove them into downtown Philadelphia and parked the Volvo into the garage on South Second Street. It was less than a block from the Old Original Bookbinder's. As they made their way slowly up Walnut Street, Jude explained that this restaurant had quite a past. It was established in 1893 as an oyster saloon on Fifth Street, but old Samuel Bookbinder moved it to its current location to be closer to the docks. It became famous for its raw bar, the crab cake entree, seafood platters, and snapper soup with sherry.

"I loved coming into town for lunches with Mom," Simon commented. "The lobby used to have the world's largest lobster tank!" The party of three pulled open the door, and Laura found the interior of the restaurant inviting with its dark woodwork, brass fixtures, and red leather upholstery on the bar stools. The window panes were leaded glass; the floor appeared to be cobblestone. The young man who greeted them looked dapper in a crisp white shirt, black trousers, and a red apron swashed around his waist. He led them down the length of the bar to a booth in the back, also with seats of red leather and a discreet "reserved for Andrews" card. Jude ordered a Side Car, Laura a glass of chardonnay. Simon claimed designated driver status and asked for iced tea. As they waited for their drinks, Laura realized the setting was intimate enough for them to continue their conversation from the apartment.

"I never thought much about the fact that I didn't have a dad. Mom did a great job of making me feel normal, including me in her life when it was appropriate and giving me space as I needed it to develop my own style."

"That was always one of Christina's gifts," Jude observed. "She knew how to be a good friend, not overly possessive but incredibly caring. I realized later that she had both the good sense and the compassion to give me an opportunity to follow my own path, even though it would not include her...or you."

"We had a good life in Pittsburgh, Dad." There, she said it again, and it felt, well, okay. "And after she died, I discovered she had many close friendships there that sustained her."

"Did Christina ever date anyone...? I mean, was she involved...?" Jude was searching for a way to word his question delicately.

Laura chuckled. "You want to know if she ever loved anyone besides you?"

Jude blushed a bit. "I just wanted Christina to be happy, I guess, once I found Linda. Somehow, I could not bear to picture her sitting alone, filled with regrets." Laura smiled.

"Well, there was no one special in her life that I knew about. But I don't remember her ever seeming *lonely*. She had such spiritual depth that she could go to her room and pray for an hour or take a retreat day, and she'd be renewed and centered again. And as I said, she had good friends."

"Her death…" Jude hesitated. "I didn't know. I could have been there." He was stumbling for the words again.

"My mom was critically ill then," Simon recalled. "I can't imagine you leaving her for any reason."

"Yes, son, you're right." The older man agreed and fell into a silent reverie.

"I wish I had known Christina," said Simon. "She sounds self-aware and grounded, just like you, Laura." Then turning to his dad, he added, "Laura is one of the most 'together' women I have ever met. Of course I've only known her for a week."

Laura sat back from the table and took a good look at these two men with her. One was the father she had never met until today. The other was a half brother she had not known existed a week ago. In a short time, she not only had extended her family to include them, but she had actually grown to like these people. Smiling in amazement, she said a silent "wa-ni-shi" to the Creator and to Mother Earth and to her falcon guide for making all this possible. The waiter arrived with food, and the conversation turned to plans for the rest of the day.

"When we're done here," Simon announced between bites of his lunch, "I'll drive us through a bit of the historic district of Philadelphia—Betsy Ross House, Liberty Bell, and Elfreth's Alley. When you come back in the fall, maybe you and Cal will want to bring the girls here for a tour. We'll also scoot by our old house and get you back home, Dad, before you nod off." Simon turned to Laura. "What is it with old men and their afternoon naps?" Laura pictured

Jude and Lawrence sipping drinks on the front porch together and dozing in the afternoon sun. *Such a peaceful scene.*

Jude asked if Laura had met any of the Lenni-Le-nah-pe folks around the farm. She confirmed that, yes, she had. In fact, some of them would be at the house that evening. "We're discussing New Jersey's pollution and chemical waste issues." Jude listened intently as she shared what she had learned about the group's concerns.

"Keep me informed," he requested of both of them. "I have some friends in Jersey—business contacts, government officials—who may want to join the discussion or offer help somewhere down the road."

Another connection with my dad, Laura mused. *It's a dance. Keep going.*

The drive back to Anderson House seemed too quick. When they stopped at the front door, Jude told them they need not come in with him. He was going to stop by Mrs. Halsey's room for a chat about her heart. He shook hands warmly with Laura and patted Simon on the back. "Come see me again, you two!" he called cheerfully. As they headed home, Laura thanked Simon for lunch, but he informed her that their dad had paid the bill. He added that he was pleased there had been no fisticuffs or shouting matches between the once-abandoned Laura and his headstrong father. *Their* father. In many ways, Simon was delighted that they all were able to become friends so quickly.

"Laura, your mother must have been one special lady. She raised you on her own to be a beautiful person."

"Aw, thanks, Simon. I have my moments. But if I can be half as kind and good as my mom, I'll be doing well." She sat quietly for a moment and then added, "Meeting my dad was something she must have wished for me. The fact that it finally happened makes me believe her spirit has guided the entire course of events."

They crossed the Delaware River and made their way down the highway to Laurel Hills. Simon asked again how Laura was feeling about today and about everything. She gave it some thought before responding.

"Simon, I don't know how long we will have our dad with us, so there's no time for bitterness or recriminations. I can't recapture what we missed, but we can create some good memories from now on. Here!" Laura shouted as she pointed out the track through the meadow to Simon. He whipped the steering wheel around, and the Volvo bounced off the highway and slipped between the fence posts.

"A little more warning, please." He gasped. And they both laughed. *This is just what brothers and sisters do, I bet*, Laura told herself.

Winding along the same dirt path she had driven just one week earlier, she rolled down the car window and breathed in the scent of the meadow as the cricket songs tickled her ears. Serenity overwhelmed her, the same sense of home she had experienced on that first drive. Simon followed the track around the pond and through the orchard to the farmhouse. He parked and turned off the engine. Such stillness, as the sun rested on the tops of the pine trees. Any minute it would disappear into the darkness. Laura had asked to see this place with her mother's eyes, her mother's heart. In that moment, she knew that prayer was being answered.

The two travelers climbed the porch steps together. The screen door creaked open and then slammed shut behind them. "You're back!" Liz's relieved comment came from the dining room along with the aroma of the promised fried chicken, not doubt accompanied by vegetables and gravy, and a pile of warm buttery cornbread. "We've started to eat. Sorry."

Simon and Laura followed the voice and found the Coxes sitting at the table with Lawrence, plates loaded with entree and salad, sweating glasses of iced tea at each place.

"The food's still hot." Lawrence assured the late arrivals. "We figured you might get stuck in traffic."

Simon looked apologetic. "Actually lunch took longer than I thought. Laura and dad just would *not* stop talking." Laura pretended to punch his arm, but they both revealed the good nature of it all in their faces. The two young people sat down across from each other and began to eat while Lawrence quizzed them on their day. It was clear that the three older people had been concerned that all might have been for naught: that Laura and Jude might not get along, that Simon might not accept his role in the Gardner legacy, and that the farm would be lost. They need not have been concerned.

CHAPTER 26

Laura refused any dessert that evening. She wanted to do more reading before the start of the community meeting. She excused herself and made her way up the familiar staircase to her bedroom. Slipping out of her shoes, she plopped down in the rocker beside the window. Liz had placed a stack of manila folders on her dressing table while she was out. Each contained part of the story of the pollution scandal that had rocked Toms River in the 1970s. The tabs read *Industry Data, Chemical Research, Municipal Landfills, Medical Findings*... all information that would be part of any legal action. She wondered just how involved her great-uncle's group was willing to become in resolving what seemed to be a monumental environmental wrongdoing.

As she finished perusing the last file, she caught a glimpse of a light, no, several lights moving among the pine trees. They flickered and disappeared behind tree trunks and branches and then reappeared. It was clear they were moving toward the house. At the same time, Laura heard the crunch of tires on gravel as several vehicles came up the farm driveway and stopped beside the house. The committee members were arriving. She slipped back into her shoes, freshened up in the bathroom, and picked up the folders. She decided to take the shortcut. Opening the hidden door from her room to the addition, she was greeted by the chatter of neighbors gathered in the great room below. Taking a deep breath, she went down the stairs.

"Laura!" It was Wayne Peters. "You're still here. Good!"

"Yes, but I'm planning to head back home tomorrow." Laura noticed Julia Peters engrossed in conversation with a tall man standing beside the door.

"Well, do you at least have time to drop by our place in the morning? For coffee, perhaps?" Wayne's voice had a pleading tone to it.

"Let's see how this evening goes," she hedged. Laura was curious to know more about the Peters but wasn't sure she had the energy to be engaged in one more "bonding" activity. Wayne seemed to accept her response and wandered over to where his wife was standing.

Liz and Randy appeared to be the greeters for the evening event. They were stopping to talk to each person, making introductions as necessary, and pointing out the refreshment table laden with pitchers of lemonade and sassafras tea. There was also a large tray with a selection of cookies from Johnny's German Bakery. When Liz saw Laura, she made her way across the room and slipped an arm around her waist. Guiding her over to the sofa, she sat down with her and whispered some instructions. Laura nodded that she understood. Just then, Simon brought in Lawrence, positioning his wheelchair by the front window. The others in the room all greeted him cordially and then found their places. Liz remained beside Laura. Julia sat down on the other end of the sofa. Randy stood behind them while Wayne pulled up a stool and perched beside Simon.

Lawrence welcomed everyone and introduced Laura. The committee had several small groups for the purpose of gathering information related to subtopics: industrial dumping, health impacts, water safety, land development, governmental policies, etc.

So, Liz invited each person to tell their name and the topic of their study group. Laura was surprised when it was Simon's turn to speak. He was the one person in the meeting who interfaced on their behalf with other neighborhood citizen groups like theirs, and those more well-known organizations like the *Childhood Cancer Cluster* and *Greenpeace*.

After the round of introductions, the tall man who had been talking to Julia before the meeting offered to say a prayer. Laura noticed then his distinctive profile, that of the Le-nah-pe tribe. She watched as all those present in the room opened their arms, placed their hands palms up on their knees, and closed their eyes. She did the same, and in a deep rich voice, the man began to speak.

Oh, Great Spirit, whose voice we hear in the
wind, whose breath gives life to all the world.
Hear us.
We need your strength and wisdom to walk in
beauty.
May our hands always respect the things you
have made.
May our ears stay sharp to hear your instruction.
May our hearts be wise to understand your
teachings.

Laura heard Liz stirring next to her but did not open her eyes.
The scent of pine and sage filled the room. It was warm and sweet.
Taking a deep breath, Laura inhaled the fragrant smoke that drifted
up from the incense burner on the coffee table in front of her. The
prayer continued.

Keep us calm and strong in the face of all that
comes toward us.
We do not seek to be stronger than our brothers
and sisters
but to be brave to fight the Great Enemy:
Selfishness.
May we together be caretakers of Mother Earth.

Without any obvious signal, people opened their eyes and
moved slightly in their seats. Liz and Julia each squeezed Laura's hand
gently, a sign of welcome that she understood. The discussion was
then directed by Randy, who remained standing behind the sofa,
making it awkward for Laura to see his face. But his tone, while calm,
contained an urgency not usually noticeable in his voice. He asked
Julia to read the most up-to-date list of contaminated sites in the
area. She stood, cleared her throat, and began.

"Spring Hill, 15. Forest Grove, 16. Holly Hills, 20. Shady
Maples, 26." With the naming of each location came sighs and mur-

murs from the group. Finally, she reached the last two names on the list. "Chester Town, 31. Laurel Hill, 47." The room fell silent.

Randy thanked Julia for her dogged tracking of these statistics, as disheartening as they were. Then he called on Wayne to present one of the case studies for the evening.

"The Landry Development in Chester Town owns two hundred acres and has it sectioned off into two areas. You all know it used to be a sand-and-gravel pit from the forties to 1968. That's when it became a convenient place to dispose of demolition debris by a local contractor. One area has five sedimentation ponds as part of the closed plant. The other has a leachate collection system. It filters rainfall and liquid from decomposing waste and pumps it out for proper disposal. At present, there's a ten-foot thick layer of refuse which has been proven to contain industrial and commercial solid waste and sewage sludge." The room echoed with murmurs of dismay, but Wayne pressed on. "The New Jersey Department of Environmental Protection has just completed the first round of groundwater investigations. Hold on to your hats, folks. Laurel Hill's shallow aquifers contain volatile organic compounds." He rattled off the names of chemicals Laura did not recognize; but a few, like acetone, benzene, and vinyl chloride, she did. More murmuring. "And the usual culprits: elevated concentrations of metals like arsenic, iron, lead, and thallium."

Lawrence was visibly agitated. He had first joined the group because of his concern for the unique ecosystem of the pine barrens. He learned more about groundwater pollution and was angered by the report that an underground pipeline had been built through Island Beach for dumping chemical waste water several miles offshore. But all this was so close to home for him and his neighbors. He hoped that this group, with assistance from Simon and now Laura, would discover new drive for finding a solution.

Randy asked if anyone had information on cleanup efforts at Landry. A woman who was a bit older than Laura, and a friend of Liz's, spoke up. "The closure plan was approved. Clay covers are in place and residents living down-gradient from the landfill are being supplied by Landry with bottled water."

"But that's not enough," Lawrence added, pounding his fist on the arm of the wheelchair. "What will it take to truly clean it up?"

Simon was ready with some information. "I've talk to the natural resources folks, and they say the best plan of action includes extracting the polluted groundwater and running it through filters and recirculation processes. But the science is still quite new."

"We've got to do more, folks," Randy interjected. "We have to identify sites and quickly close them down. We must monitor the conditions there and take whatever action we need to head off the dangers to plants, wildlife, and humans. We will have to recruit additional scientists and engineers to work with us to develop truly effective reclamation processes."

"And we have to continue the prayers of the people to ask for the Creator's forgiveness and help in making Mother Earth well again." The sweet voice speaking strong words of faith belonged to Elsa, Liz's niece from the farm stand, who was seated next to Simon. Laura had not seen her when the meeting began. She was not one of those included in the introductions so when had she entered the room?

The tall praying man responded, reminding the group they must bring their concerns to the ga-mwing ceremonies. Elsa said several of her friends were going on vision quests to seek dreams that may hold answers to heal the earth. Laura knew at once that she wanted to be back at Bittersweet Acres for those twelve days.

"Now I have an additional case for us to discuss tonight," Randy announced. "And it's a little sensitive. You all remember the old Allison property." Heads nodded.

"Before the Allison's bought it, wasn't it a dairy farm?" Lawrence asked.

"Yep, that's the place, just about a mile due south from here." Randy confirmed. "No one has kept livestock there for years, though." The Allisons owned thirty-six acres of grazing land, with a large two-story building containing washing tanks and troughs. There were sheds scattered across the property, all connected by an unpaved farm road. Randy explained the current situation. "Harston Trucking from Newark approached Sam Allison last year to lease four acres from him. They wanted to use it for storing empty chemical drums while they reconditioned them for resale. The money was good, and the Allison family didn't have any other plans for the place at the time. So they signed the contract."

One of the committee members raised a hand. "Wasn't there a fire over there a couple of weeks ago?"

Randy nodded. "That's what brought this to light. In the process of putting out the blaze in one of those sheds, the fire marshal discovered fifty-plus drums and chemical containers, some of them full." The room became a buzz of expressions of frustration and disbelief. "They took a look around while they were there and found another shed with over one hundred plastic drums filled with liquid. They contacted the police and the EPA right away. All totaled, there were over three hundred containers on the property, many of which had leaked their contents into the ground."

"So the soil is contaminated for sure," Wayne stated. "How about the groundwater?"

"Don't know yet." Laura's thoughts went immediately to their pond and stream and the beautiful turtle, *Chrysemys picta*.

Folks in that room knew Sam Allison and his family. They were not bad people and probably were not aware of the hazards of storage and dumping. They were making choices that would not honor Mother Earth but perhaps not intentionally. Laura listened, distressed by human deception and greed, frustrated by the enormity of the problems, and yet energized to think she might be able to help this group make a difference. Randy's call to order interrupted her thoughts.

"Folks, we've got to call it a night. So here's what I suggest we do. I'm going to make some time to talk to Sam this week. I bet he is sick about all this now that he knows what's going on. Let me know if any of you want to come along. Simon, you'll make your usual contacts and see what you can find out from official sources. Wayne, your group can check on the truckers. See if they have other violations. We'll meet back here in two weeks, sooner if we have any actionable plans. Liz, my love, send us off with your prayers."

The participants stood and easily flowed together to form a circle that included Lawrence. Laura listened to the words from the heart of the woman: "Great Mother Earth, teach us how to trust our heads, our minds, our intuition, our inner knowing, the senses of our flesh, the blessings of our spirits. Teach us to trust these things so that we may enter that sacred space, that we may love beyond our fear, that we may walk the path of caring with the passing of each glorious sun."

A final puff of smoke rose from the incense, trailing after each person as they departed.

Laura stood by the front window, watching what appeared to be lightning bugs weaving through the orchard and into the forest. *They are my friends now,* she mused, remembering the curiosity the lights had stirred up in her the night she arrived at Bittersweet Acres.

Randy came over and stood beside her. "This is a place filled with wonder," he said quietly. Laura turned and looked at him with sadness.

"How can we be so blind, so stubborn, so…"

"Thoughtless and unaware?" Randy sighed. "Laura, we are still those outsiders who do not understand our place in the world."

"This land is such a gift. The Le-nah-pe have always known that. Many of the first Quakers understood. We have to find a balance again, a 'both-and' response to developing as a civilization and preserving the resources we need."

"Liz mentions 'the path of caring' in all her prayers, Laura. Not just words for us. It must be a way of life. We each must find that path, that balance, in order to receive that blessing."

"Randy, I have to do something to help. I am not sure what, but I cannot drive away tomorrow and forget all that I have seen and heard and experienced." A smile formed on her companion's face.

"That was all Lawrence really hoped for, Laura. He knew you could become a gift to this place. But you had to choose it for yourself."

My thoughts keep swirling about, randomly filling with images of lights and drops of water, then deep ravines with rushing, cascading rivers. Faces appear and disappear. A brown and leathery brow morphs into the smooth pink face of my own child. The golden curls I recognize as Simon's hair, but then they straighten and darken until I am looking into a native face with painted cheeks and fierce eyes. Next, I am on the porch, watching my old uncle sleeping, the afternoon sun kissing his lined eyes so that tears edge out from under the lids.

The deerskin drums begin, softly and then with increasing intensity. I see a glow in the pine forest, and like a moth to flame, I rush to reach it. Ducking under limbs, turning to follow the path, I hear the faint reedy chirp of a flute. It plays the melody I have come to recognize, the one from the cave, the one I sang to my medicine doll, the same one hummed by the dark woman.

I burst into a clearing and skid to a halt. Overhead, I see stars, hundreds of stars, and a pale moon which lights the open space in the forest. The Big House stands just in the shadow of the pine trees. Sounds of drums and flute come from inside the house. Voices murmur words I do not know how to speak, but I understand them. I have been invited here. I have been summoned here to share my story and my song.

I walk up the hard-packed earthen path which I know was swept clean with turkey feathers. The doorway to the house is draped in a colorful blanket. I wrap my shawl close around me and touch the shell beads of my necklace I am wearing. Pushing the cloth flap to one side, I step through the opening. The scent of pine, sage, and cedar fill my lungs. As I take my seat, some of the men are dancing in a circle around the center pole of the Big House. The combined sounds of people's voices chanting, dancers' feet shuffling, and drums beating are making me dizzy. I shut my eyes, closing out the light from the two fires but feeling the warmth of the coals reaching my skin.

Just when I begin to doze and dream, someone puts the turtle shell in my hand. I know what I must do. I rattle it, and the room becomes quiet. I stand and begin to sing my story.

"Many black bears from the north were hungry and came to eat our fish and rob our corn cribs. I heard them in our woods as I painted my face and picked up my birch bow and loaded my quiver full of arrows." Those seated around me mumble their encouragement and I continue. "Dressed as a warrior, I offered a prayer to the Creator and walked to the edge of the stream. As I let my first arrow fly toward the bears, I heard rustling leaves behind me." People seem eager to hear my vision and whisper, 'Hoo! Yee!' "I turned to find turtles, hundreds of them,

gathered behind me. They too were prepared by the Creator for battle. As I launched more arrows, they moved forward together like an army, overwhelming some bears and frightening off the rest. We carried the dead bears back to camp where they were skinned and their meat cooked for stew. Although we are heartbroken to have killed brother Bear, we know that together we had saved our land."

I begin to dance as other singers take turns repeating parts of my vision song. The sa-chem tosses tobacco into the fires, a gift of thanksgiving to the Creator. Then women dancers rise and join me as we circle in the opposite direction around the center post with its red and black mask. They are carrying sage wands, and the entire room is filled with the aroma of herbs.

CHAPTER 27

Her eyes still closed, Laura knew someone was in her bedroom, but she was not alarmed. She thought she recognized the quiet padding of moccasins across the hardwood floor but was pleasantly surprised to see Elsa standing over by the window. She was holding an armful of wildflowers and seemed to be searching for something. A container, perhaps.

"Good morning," Laura greeted her.

"Oh, I am so sorry if I woke you," the young girl apologized. "On my way here this morning, I picked these and thought you would like them."

"I do, Elsa! They are beautiful and fragrant. Here, let's put them in this." Laura climbed out of bed and walked over to one of the wardrobes. Opening the doors, she found the antique bowl and pitcher she had seen earlier in the week.

"That's Marial's!" uttered Elsa, clearly delighted to see it again. "We wondered where it was." Laura noted that, after all these years, Liz's family still felt attached to this house and its residents. She liked that. Together the women filled the ewer with water, arranged the bouquet, and placed it on the dressing table. The morning breeze ruffled the blooms and leaves just enough to lightly fragrance the entire room.

"Is everybody up but me?" Laura inquired. She had slept so deeply these past few days that it was a bit of an embarrassment to her.

"No need to worry. Simon has taken Mr. Lawrence to his doctor's appointment in town, but he fixed you something for breakfast. Granny is straightening up the great room, and I am here with you."

There was an air of respect in the way she spoke, something not always present in young people. Laura thought her own girls would be blessed to know Elsa. Her girls! Laura remembered that she was going home today, back to Harrisburg. Noel. Marial. She closed her eyes to picture them clearly and then wrapped her arms around herself as if to hug them close.

"Laura? Are you all right?"

"Oh yes. Thanks. I just remembered I have to pack up and leave this afternoon."

"That's why I'm here, to help you. Just tell me what you want."

"Well, first, I want to eat. Come on, let's see what Simon has left in the kitchen for us."

As they made their way downstairs, Elsa asked several questions about where Laura lived, and about the girls and Cal. Laura thought again of how sheltered Christina must have been growing up on the farm. She guessed Elsa's family was protective of their daughter and would be shocked if she decided to move away from Laurel Hill. The conversation between the two women continued as Laura served herself the omelet, sausages, and fresh tomato slices that Simon had prepared earlier. Elsa poured them each a mug of steaming coffee, adding a pinch of cinnamon.

"I taught that to Simon," she announced proudly. "He used to make the worst coffee, so bitter and strong. So one day, I sat him down and explained how spices and herbs can make food and drink more enjoyable. Now he can't wait to try out new combinations, and he makes much better coffee."

They both smiled. Simon was loved by this community. He had lost his mother. His father, *their father*, would not be alive forever. This was now his home, and he considered these people his family.

Elsa was just placing their dishes in the sink when the telephone rang. Neither of them moved to answer it right away. Then Laura remembered Simon was out, so she dried her hands and grabbed the receiver.

"Laura, hi. It's Julia. I'm so glad you haven't left yet."

"No, I just finished eating. There is something about his country air that makes me lazy."

187

"You just need a few more days here to catch up. City girls are sleep deprived, don't you think?" Laura knew Julia well enough now not to take her comments as criticism.

"Well, I'm afraid I have to go back to being a city girl this afternoon," Laura retorted in a friendly tone.

"Can you stop by here before you do?" Julia sounded almost insistent.

"Sure. Simon has taken Lawrence into town, and I've got to get things packed up here."

"Yes, yes, that's exactly why I want you to come over."

"Okay." Laura was curious.

"Come for lunch, then. The men will have eaten in town. They always do. We'll see you around noon?"

"All right. You've given me just the incentive I need get moving."

"Wonderful. See you then. Bye." Julia hung up. Laura stood looking at the receiver.

"That was strange," she commented.

"Yeah, Julia is like that. She plans things out and lets you know later what she wants you to do. Her heart is right, though."

"Well, I, or rather, we, better get to work."

Liz poked her head into the kitchen.

"I hope you won't mind delaying your activities a bit longer."

Laura was curious and amused. This day was completely out of control, and it was only nine fifteen in the morning! The old woman took Laura by the hand and led her into the parlor. Elsa followed along, and when Laura looked back at her, she was grinning. Something was up between those two.

"Here," Liz announced. In the center of the room sat a small antique trunk. Laura walked over and ran her hands over the weathered wood and worn leather straps. In spite of obvious rough use at some point, it was in rather good condition. Puzzled, she turned to Liz.

"It's the sea chest," the old woman explained.

"It is a lovely old thing," Laura responded, still baffled.

"No, it's *the* sea chest." Liz was adamant.

Racking her brain for any references to a sea chest in the past week, she finally grasped what she was seeing.

"No! You have got to be kidding! Uncle Lawrence didn't tell me he had this!"

"Because *he* didn't know what it was."

Laura dropped into the chair beside the object under discussion. She remembered reading the account of Elizabeth Gardner's arrival in what was then West Jersey. They disembarked with two children, a purse containing five pounds sterling, and all their belongings *in one sea chest*. Could the trunk she was touching be the same one that had belonged to that family over three hundred years ago?

With her fingers, she traced the skillfully dovetailed joints closest to her. The oakwood sides still had bits of waxed leather clinging here and there, apparently an early attempt at waterproofing. Laura looked at her companions for permission to lift the trunk lid. Their body language signaled "Go on!" She gently pushed it up until its hinges locked open. The inside of the lid was fitted out with several compartments, probably designed for holding money and important papers. The tray would have been packed with toiletries and intimate garments while other clothing, household linens, shoes, and coats would fill the remaining space below. Laura imagined that neatly folded blankets or hand-knitted socks for the boys would have been tucked in there for the voyage to America. Her eyes teared up as she pictured the few belongings Elizabeth Gardner might have packed for herself. A linen bonnet, an apron, or leather gloves, perhaps. The slight aroma of lavender accompanied her daydream. Then Laura noticed some papers had been slipped into the lid. Removing them, she discovered several sketchbooks.

"Those are some of your mother's drawings," Liz informed Laura. "She'd go sit beside the creek with her pencils and paper. Christina wanted to make a book of all the plants and wildlife on the farm." Laura turned each page with tenderness, noting the initials "CM" in the lower left-hand corner. "One of those books has her sketches of the spirit guides of each of her friends," Liz added as Laura put the drawing books back in the compartment.

"Now, Laura, there are some things in the bottom of that trunk that I want you to take home to your girls." Liz lifted the tray out of the chest and set it on the floor beside her. She explained each item as she handed it to Laura.

"Here are two turtle shell rattles. Christina and I made them as girls and used them during our ceremonies. And this is a leather drum my brother used to play."

Laura smiled. "I'll have them practice before we come back."

Elsa nodded and promised to teach them the ceremonial dances.

"We are the Turtle Clan," Liz reminded Laura. "We are strong caretakers of Mother Earth. You and your husband and your children have a deep spiritual connection to this place. Oh, and here is a story to read to your family so they can learn who they are." She gave Laura a book with an Eastern painted turtle on the cover. As she turned each page, Laura found a colorful drawing of Le-nah-pe life accompanied by characteristics of members of the clan.

"'The Turtle Clan is methodical in everything they do,'" Laura read aloud with fascination. "'They can always depend on others of their clan for support and protection in times of need.'" She turned a page. "'They are patient and do not like to be rushed. Only when a turtle is certain of its surroundings will it stick out its neck.'" With each statement, the belief grew stronger that she was destined to return to Bittersweet Acres.

"We have hard shells for a reason," Elsa commented. "We are survivors and can live in strange surroundings if we have to, but it feels so good when we slide back into the water which is our home." The simple words of this young woman resonated with what Laura was feeling. She was on the verge of making a decision, of choosing to be where she belonged.

"What's this?" Laura was about to reassemble the trunk when she noticed a bundle about twelve inches long remaining in the bottom. It was tan, like deer hide, wrapped into a pouch shape. Her heart began to beat rapidly as she reached down to retrieve it. It was smooth to her touch. Placing it on her lap, she loosened the ties and opened the wrappings. The medicine doll. *Ow-tas.* Carved from a single piece of wood in the shape of a Le-nah-pe woman. Her hair was dark and straight; and she was dressed in deer skin tunic, leggings, and moccasins. Around her neck were tiny shell beads on a necklace.

"Your family must stay well. Keep her with you always." Liz's tone was filled with love.

Laura nodded. "I will."

CHAPTER 28

While Laura took a warm shower, Elsa changed the linens from the four-poster bed and pulled Laura's clean clothes from the wardrobes. She placed them in neatly folded piles on top of the quilt. The day was already warm, and that meant there would be a good chance for late-afternoon storms. Clean and dressed, Laura brought her toiletries from the bathroom, depositing them in a small makeup bag. She transferred the stacks of clothes into her suitcase, placing the few dirty garments in a zippered side pouch. Elsa had already removed the towels and carried them, along with the bedding downstairs to the laundry room.

It was almost noon, and Laura had to keep her date with the Peters. She found Liz still in the parlor, boxing up the gifts for the girls and some papers and books.

"These are things Lawrence asked me to give you. He said you'd know what they were." Laura felt no need to examine each item with Liz. She trusted her great-uncle to remember what they had decided would be hers.

"I'll be back after lunch," Laura announced.

"That's fine. We'll be here to give you a send-off around two."

Elsa came in the room and suggested that Laura might want to walk over to Peters instead of driving out to the highway and then back up their long farm road. "Go across the bridge. Then follow the fence to the gate. You'll see their house."

It sounded simple enough. Laura was convinced she would remember it when she got there.

Letting the screen door slam behind her, she hopped down the porch steps and headed for the trail she and Simon had taken on their first afternoon walk. She paused when she reached the bridge. There he was, the same Eastern painted turtle looking ever so much like a bump on the log. And yet Laura knew he had been busy swimming and eating since she last saw him. *We've both had productive days, haven't we?* she told him. Just then, he poked out his colorful head and turned it in her direction. For a moment, their eyes met. Then he disappeared inside his shell again.

Laura followed Elsa's directions. The fence edged what had been a pasture for horses, sheep, or cows at one time. She strolled along beside it, recalling some of the dreams that had come to her this past week. Images of the dark woman, the stile, the creek, the cave—it all flooded back. She imagined seeing her mother in the meadow. She knew she would have that scent of wildflowers in her memory forever.

When she arrived at the gate, it was covered with sturdy bittersweet vines, of course, but swung open easily. Julia and Wayne walked this way often, she assumed. That was yet another explanation for those mysterious lights in the evening. The trail beyond the gate had a slight upgrade which tugged at the muscles in Laura's legs. Then it leveled out, and she could glimpse her destination.

The Peters home was similar in style to the Gardner farmhouse—a three-story rectangle. However, it was a wood-frame dwelling with tongue-and-groove siding and a wide porch which surrounded the house on three sides. There were also several tumbledown outbuildings beyond the well-maintained barn. While it once stabled horses, now it only served as shelter for a tractor and Wayne's truck. Julia was waiting at the door, watching Laura climb up the porch steps. She knew the trek through the meadow would work up a thirst, so as she ushered Laura in, she handed her a chilled glass of tea.

"It's lovely here," Laura commented after her initial cooling sip.

"I am amazed these buildings are still standing," was Julia's curt response. What was she referring to? Their age, perhaps, or the workmanship. The cost of the upkeep. Once again, Laura exhaled and decided Julia truly loved just making comments.

Wayne joined them as they found seats in the large well-lit kitchen. The appliances here were updated, of course, just as the ones had been in Lawrence's house. But somehow while the room at Bittersweet Acres remained cozy, this one seemed sterile and unwelcoming. *Efficient would be a better word.* Laura corrected her own thoughts. As her body temperature cooled down, she appreciated the tasty pasta salad Julia had tossed while Wayne had been grilling chicken. She recognized the flavors of fresh basil and parsley.

"This is delicious. Thank you." Laura's gratitude was genuine, but she was still uncertain why Julia's tone that morning had been so insistent.

"Well, we couldn't send you away hungry, could we?"

As the meal ended, Julia's demeanor became uncharacteristically giddy, and Wayne seemed to be enjoying himself as well.

"All right, you two. What is going on here?" Laura knew she was sticking her neck out with her questioning. At that moment she realized she was comfortable enough with this couple to take the risk.

"You just stay right here," Julia ordered with a smile. "Wayne, clear off the table."

Laura sat quite still, unsure what was happening. She thought of the time Cal had planned a surprise birthday party for her, and she walked unaware into a room full of school friends. That was what she was feeling at that moment. Julia returned, just as Wayne finished wiping and drying the table top. She was carrying a large pasteboard box, pale pink with a tiny ivory flower design on it. It took up most of the area of the table. The woman was trying to look serious, but a smile kept creeping onto her face.

"Laura, we all loved Christina and wanted her to be happy. When she and Jude came back here to be married, I could see that they were very much in love. Then when we heard about their divorce, I was just sick. I know people grow apart, but Christina had so much going for her." Her voice was turning solemn. Wayne was clearly impatient with the time Julia was taking. So when she stopped for a breath, he jumped in.

"Christina came here for a visit some time after you were born, Laura. Marial had died, so it was just Lawrence living in the farmhouse then. She brought you over here and asked us to watch you one afternoon so she could do some cleaning out and throwing away. We said sure. You were a good baby and slept most of the time.

"When she came to get you," Julia continued, "she asked me to do her a favor and handed me a bundle wrapped in a bedsheet. 'Do something with this,' was all she said. And then she thanked us, picked you up, and left. Well, I just carried the package up into the spare room for the time being." Laura listened, not moving, her mind racing to figure out what could possibly be in the box.

"It was a week later when I finally got around to opening the bundle. I called Wayne to come up right away. After a few minutes, we agreed what we would do. Laura, we want you have this." With great tenderness, Wayne lifted the lid from the box. Laura stood, looked, and then gasped in unbelief. There lay a white lace dress, pressed and perfectly preserved in ivory tissue paper. A small plastic box held a ring of dried flowers. Laura recognized it all from the photograph. This was Christina's wedding gown, still beautiful after all this time. Her first urge was to pick it up and hug it to her body. Instead, she looked at Wayne and then Julia and began to sob.

"Are you surprised?" Julie asked with expectancy.

"Honey, I think she is just a bit overwhelmed." Wayne was correct.

Finding her voice, Laura stated the obvious. "My mother's dress. The one in the picture. Oh, it is so lovely." She took a breath. "You kept this for me?"

Now the couple began to tear up. "Of course we did," Julia answered. "We both knew it was the right thing to do. Christina never asked about it again. I guess she thought we gave it away. After we had it cleaned and boxed up, we just kept it here and hoped you'd come get it one day."

"I'm kind of sorry she never got to give it to you herself," offered Wayne. "But now you can show it to your little girls. Maybe one of them will want to wear it." At that, Laura sobbed again, and Julia went over and held her until she quit.

"I don't think I'll be fit to drive home after this," Laura squeaked out between her tears.

"Let's have some more of your tea, Julia," suggested Wayne. He helped Laura close up the dress box, and then he carried it out of the room. "I'll bring it over to your place in the truck before you leave."

When Laura checked her watch again, it was almost two o'clock. She had to go.

"There are no words to thank you for the gift you've given me today."

"I'm so glad it made you happy," Julia responded, first wiping her own tears, and then taking a fresh tissue and tenderly blotting Laura's cheek.

"Happy doesn't begin to describe how I feel."

She hugged each of them again warmly and headed down the porch steps, explaining how the walk might help her regain composure before all the goodbyes yet to come. They watched her leave and then Wayne carried the wedding dress in its box to the truck where he placed it gently on a soft blanket in the back.

CHAPTER 29

Clouds were gathering on the horizon, and as she walked toward the farmhouse, Laura could notice a change in the air and a variation in the insect songs. There would be storms before she reached Harrisburg, she was sure. She also could feel her two distinct worlds now merging almost completely. Although she would drive away from the farm in another hour, it would never be far from her mind. She may sit in her office again; but she would see this trail, the meadow fence, the bridge, and *Chrysemys picta*. The thought of the pollution that was bringing harm to Mother Earth and the Turtle Clan was still painful, strengthening her resolve to remain involved in finding solutions. She had a life so rich and full that her heart was ready to burst.

When she reached the farmhouse, the Volvo was parked beside the side porch. Simon and Lawrence were back. Good. Liz and Randy's truck was pulled in beside the other cars. Laura's luggage was in the hallway, along with the box Liz had packed that morning. She found Lawrence sitting in the parlor in his favorite chair.

"What do you think of the sea chest?" she asked him excitedly. Her great-uncle's eyes were bright.

"Liz told me that members of her family found it a long time ago when they lived in the addition. They had it all this time. Then when I started talking to her about getting you to come visit, she remembered it and contacted them. They brought it over, and put it in the shed for the time being. Isn't it a treasure?"

"Today has been full of discoveries," Laura added as she proceeded to tell her great-uncle about the medicine doll, Christina's sketches, and the wedding dress. "Do you want to see it all?" she asked.

"No, that's fine. Liz already has it packed up.

Simon came in just then and sat down. His eyes were filled with concern, and Laura's stomach did its nervous lurch.

"Laura, did Lawrence tell you what the doctor said?"

"Now, Simon, don't get her all upset."

Oh, dear Lord, please no.

"What?" Laura was on high alert.

"Laura, all his vital signs are good," Simon began. "However, the ankle ligament is not healing quickly. For someone his age, it's a difficult process. Dr. Serene wants him to consult a surgeon. They can insert a screw between the tibia and fibula to hold the bones together, relieving pressure on the ligaments. That will make it easier to heal."

Laura reached over and took her great-uncle's hand.

"I don't want any surgery." Lawrence voice was strong.

Laura turned to Simon. "What other choice does he have?"

"Well, if he chooses not to have the operation, his ankle may heal eventually, but he probably will never be able to do those stairs again."

Laura sagged back in her chair. She thought of his charming second-floor bedroom with afternoon sun brightening the faded colors of his braided rug, and of the simple cherry bed and dresser, the overalls hanging on the clothes tree. She liked his space with the ladder-back rocker and night table. That was where he should be, at the end, with his belongings and his memories. But he was ninety-five, and surgery would carry more than the normal risks.

"Don't think about that. We can make do the way we are now." Lawrence sounded determined, and Simon seemed to have argued his point as much as he was willing. Laura kept her opinions out of the discussion. Although she hated to leave without resolving the issue, she was sure it would take a day or two for the prognosis to settle in. Then the decision would be made by the two men she trusted to do the best thing. She would call on the weekend to see what had been decided.

A truck made its way up the drive and parked. It was Julia and Wayne. The Coxes went out to greet them.

"I want to talk about Thanksgiving," Lawrence said loudly, bringing attention back to his concerns.

Simon sighed. "What do you want to know?"

"Laura, are you still coming here for ga-mwing? Bring your husband and the girls, of course."

Laura turned to Simon. "Yes, and we discussed having a chance to visit your dad."

"*Our* dad. Sorry. I keep tripping over that too," Simon confessed.

Lawrence suggested that maybe Jude would be willing to spend a few days with them at the farm. "It would be good to get him out of the city for a bit."

"I'll ask him!" Simon liked the idea, even though it would mean more work for him. When they drove to Philadelphia, either to pick him up or take him back home, Cal and the girls might take the historical tour of the city that they had talked about yesterday.

Simon went outside to find Liz and confirmed the date for the fall Big House Ceremony. Then he came back in and put it on the Chester Hardware calendar in the kitchen. He wrote it on a notepad for Laura, also adding addresses and phone numbers for the Peters, Liz and Randy, and Jude.

"Any other contacts you want?" he asked Laura as he joined everyone who by this time had gathered with Laura and Lawrence in the parlor.

"How about the number for that delightful German bakery in town?" she teased.

It was past time for Laura to leave. Her luggage and the box of treasures Liz had packed for her were already stowed in the Bronco. Laura brought in Christina's wedding dress to show Simon and Lawrence. The old man's eyes filled with tears. He made Julia promise to tell them the whole story over a glass of wine later. Then someone carried the box back outside and slipped it in the backseat of Laura's vehicle.

Simon had prepared some snacks for the road: hard-boiled eggs, celery sticks, grapes, cheese, and dark chocolate bites. Liz brought a thermos of coffee along with a cold bag containing cans of soda.

"I'm only going to Harrisburg," Laura admonished with a laugh.

"Your gas tank's full too," Randy informed her. He had driven her car to a filling station while she was visiting the Peters. "Didn't want you to have to stop once you got on the road."

A lump was forming in Laura's throat. She had come to love these people. Kneeling beside Lawrence's chair, she let her head rest on his shoulder for just a minute.

"I love you, Uncle Lawrence."

"I love you, too, Laura." He patted her head, and she seemed to recall another time long ago when he had done that same thing. "Don't forget to come back."

"I won't," Laura whispered.

She hugged Liz and Randy and then followed Julia and Wayne to the side porch.

"You are such a blessing to this family," Julia commented as she took both of Laura's hands. "Now don't mess it up!" Wayne just shook his head and gave Laura's shoulders a squeeze, and then he and his wife went back inside. Simon brought the food and drinks out and set them in a convenient spot on the front seat of the vehicle. He closed the passenger door and tested it to see that it was locked. Then he walked around to Laura.

"Laura."

"Simon."

They both spoke at once and then laughed at the awkwardness of the moment.

Simon went first. "Please drive carefully, and call us when you get home."

"I will. And you let me know what's going on with that great-uncle of mine."

They hugged, and then she climbed up in the driver's seat, buckling her belt and checking the mirrors. She rolled down the window and smiled.

"See yah!" she called as she drove away.

"See yah, sis!" he called back to her, but the Bronco was already around the bend in the dirt road and out of sight.

CHAPTER 30

September in Laurel Hill was a mix of warm Indian summer days and cool nippy evenings. The porch at Bittersweet Acres still welcomed afternoon conversations and napping, but once the sun went down, most human activities moved inside.

Lawrence did not have surgery on his ankle, opting instead to move permanently into the first floor of the house addition. Simon designed a tasteful way to partition off one section of the great room for private sleeping space and added a shower to the first-floor powder room. Then with the help of Randy and Wayne, he took apart the old cedar bed and reassembled it again in the upstairs bedroom of the addition, with Wayne still complaining about being too old for that sort of thing. Finally they carried down the cherry bed and the rest of contents of Lawrence's second-floor bedroom. When all the construction and moving dust settled, Lawrence was pleased with the result and comfortable with the accommodations made for him. His ankle would heal at its own pace, and he could enjoy walking with his handsome cane again.

In Harrisburg, Laura had shared with her family most of what transpired during her week in New Jersey. The girls were enchanted by the Le-nah-pe lore and played with their drum and rattles. Noel fell in love with the medicine doll and promised to keep it safely in her room. When little Marial heard about the box turtles that live in the streams, she wanted to see one. The whole family found reasons to be excited by the prospect of visiting Uncle Lawrence and meeting Uncle Simon as well.

Each evening, after the girls were tucked in bed, Laura and Cal picked up their own conversation about the future of the farm and the possibilities open to them. They agreed that no firm decision would be made until after the trip in November, but both were exploring options in case they decided to relocate to Laurel Hill.

Eventually the leaves had turned to crimson and gold, and Lawrence phoned Laura to let her know that people were starting to gather for the Le-nah-pe ga-mwing. He was thrilled that so many families were returning, people who had been dear friends of the Gardners for years. "Liz made sure that folks who knew your mom were aware that you were going to be attending. Seems you are a big draw." He chuckled. Laura was delighted, but also recognized that there was a serious side to this celebration and some difficult decisions to be made about the care of the land. She was counting on Lawrence to be a calming presence at those times.

And so on a bright fall morning, Laura and Cal loaded their luggage in the Bronco, buckled the girls in the backseat, and they all headed east, retracing the journey Laura had made back in August. The girls loved to have their mom describe the place they were going, the old farmhouse with secret passageways, and the sweet man she called Uncle Lawrence.

"Tell us some more," or "Say that story again," was a call from the backseat all the way across the turnpike. When they drove through the Amish farmlands, Laura encouraged the girls to look for horses or cows and to identify barns and silos. When the two became restless, Laura hummed the tune they had come to recognize as the Le-nah-pe lullaby, and they settled back to listen and then nodded off.

Laura realized how foreign farm life was to her family. She hoped they could appreciate the history of the area. What if in the end, her husband resisted any notion of moving to Bittersweet Acres? What if she faced a choice like her mother had made between one's love and one's calling? That worrying thought persisted but Laura had faith that they would come to a decision that was best for everyone. As they crossed the Delaware River later that afternoon, she gazed down into the water and then took a deep breath, exhaled, and closed her eyes as she leaned back against the seat.

Cal steered the Bronco into the highway lanes marked with the green overhead signs: Jersey Shore. Noel and Marial woke from their nap, gazing out the windows at the wooded hills and fenced pastures. Noel asked her mother to point out the Red Top Market where the Le-nah-pe lady lived. Laura laughed and promised she would, although the market would be closed at this time of year. Cal hoped he would be able to locate the back road into the farm that Laura had described to him.

The peaceful greeting that Laura had experienced in August was not to be repeated. As they pulled up beside the house, Cal and Laura were swarmed by well-wishers. Liz and Randy came right up to the car, said hello, and whisked the girls out of the backseat. Wayne and several young men Laura did not recognize grabbed the luggage and disappeared into the house. Lawrence was wearing a flannel jacket and sitting in his wicker rocking chair on the front porch conversing with a group of men and women with the beautiful copper skin and black hair. He looked up as Laura approached and beckoned to her.

"Come here, Laura. Come meet some old friends of ours." And the introductions ensued.

Cal seemed completely at ease, which made Laura smile, and Lawrence seemed strong and alert. In a few minutes, Liz opened the front screen door and ushered Noel and Marial onto the porch. They each had a baskets of gingersnap cookies which they offered to the adults while Liz poured cups of cider from an earthen ware jug.

"So these are my great-great-nieces!" Lawrence announced with pride. "How do you do, girls?" He formally shook each of their tiny hands, and they grinned back at him. Then Liz escorted them back into the house. "They will add some sunshine to this old place," he commented as he watched them disappear. Laura excused herself and followed the girls. She found them sitting on stools in the kitchen helping Simon sort cranberries. Noel was telling him about her school, and Marial was asking him when she could go see the turtles. He looked up.

"Laura, I am in love," he crooned, and Marial giggled.

"Please don't let them distract you," Laura offered. "Girls, Uncle Simon is in charge of cooking our dinner," she reminded them.

"It's all under control," he replied. "Miss Marial will be going with me to the bridge in just a few minutes. Noel, do you want to come?"

"I want to see my room now," the little girl announced.

"We've put them both in Lawrence's old room upstairs," Simon instructed.

Laura helped her daughter down from the stool. "Let's go. I'll show you the way," she instructed. They walked out of the kitchen and through the hallway, stopping at the bottom of the staircase. Laura's heart was full as she took each step with Noel by her side. When they reached the top, Laura pointed to the left.

"This is where Daddy and I will sleep. Your room is just over there."

"Who are the people in these pictures?" Noel asked.

Laura squatted down in front of the table on the landing so that she and her daughter were both at eye level with the array of grainy photographs. She pointed to the people, one by one, and named them. "This is your family, sweetie. They lived right here a long time ago."

"Can we live here, Mommy?"

"Would you like that?" Laura asked hesitantly.

"I think so, but first I want to see my room."

Someone had found a set of oak bunk beds and set them up in Lawrence's former bedroom. The other furniture consisted of the ladder back rocking chair from the master bedroom and a wooden chest of drawers that Laura thought may have been kept in the attic. Noel climbed right up the sturdy ladder and sat on the top bunk.

Liz came in just then and clapped her hands with delight.

"I told Randy those beds would work."

"It's perfect, Liz. Thank you," Laura responded.

"Thank you, Granny," echoed Noel.

"All the luggage is in your bedroom. I wasn't sure if Marial would stay in here or sleep with you."

"She'll be fine here with me, Mommy," Noel replied. "If she cries, I'll come and get you."

"All right. I'll bring over all your things, and you can put them away."

Liz stayed with Noel while Laura went to retrieve the girls' belongings. As she opened the door to the master suite, Laura was not prepared for the rush of emotion that overwhelmed her. Her grandmother's room was just as she had left it, minus the rocking chair. She went over and stood by the window, hoping to steady her heart. The smell of smoke from a campfire reminded her that there were people living in the shelters around the Big House. She strained to see where the wigwams had been constructed, but her view was blocked by the tall pines.

Turning from the window, she picked up the small case holding the children's clothing and carried it back to their room. Liz was sitting in the ladder-back rocker, and Noel was in her lap. They were talking about the ga-mwing festival, and Liz was teaching her the words to some songs. Laura set the luggage just inside the door, waved, and went back downstairs. She joined the folks on the front porch again, and Cal asked about the girls.

"It's all good," Laura responded.

As the sun slipped below the horizon, people said their good-byes to Lawrence and walked off toward the pine forest and the location of the Big House. Cal helped Lawrence go inside, and they settled in the parlor until dinnertime. Lawrence invited Cal to peruse the library shelves while he chatted with Laura. She wanted to know how his ankle was healing. Then she inquired what if any progress had been made by the citizen's group on the Landry Development issues and the Allison farm. Her great-uncle finished his update just as Cal joined them, holding in his hand the diary belonging to Aaron Gardner.

"This is incredible!" Cal was clearly amazed at the information captured in the document. "Have you shared this with an historical group or museum?"

"No," admitted Lawrence. "I don't know who might be interested other than family."

"Well, it is a window into life here a long time ago. I think that many people would love to read it. Perhaps we can find a publisher for it."

Just then, Noel and Marial tumbled into the parlor. Marial ran to her mother and jumped in her lap. "I saw a crissy picture!"

Laura laughed. "*Chrysemys picta*," she corrected.

"Oh my!" added Cal. "Noel has been learning Le-nah-pe, and my baby is being taught the scientific name for turtles by Uncle Simon."

As if on cue, Simon appeared at the door to the parlor announcing dinner. "It's a bit casual tonight: Philly cheesesteak sandwiches, french fries, and a salad."

"Wonderful!" Lawrence pronounced as he stood and carefully balanced with his cane. "Let's go, kids!" Noel and Marial bounced to a stand, and Laura herded them into the dining room while Cal escorted her great-uncle. She was happy that her husband seemed to feel comfortable here. After their moment of silent Quaker grace, Cal quizzed Simon and Lawrence about Aaron Gardner. By the time the sandwiches were consumed and dessert was being served, they had made plans to visit Chester Town's historical society the next morning. Of course Laura wanted to go with them, but she could not leave the girls unattended. Simon suggested they ask Elsa to come be with Noel and Marial for the morning. She had been helping in the preparations for ga-mwing, but now all that was done and the festival would begin the next evening. Simon excused himself, made the quick phone call, and returned with confirmation of the arrangements. Noel and Marial were delighted and went willingly with their mother to prepare for bedtime. While Simon cleaned up the kitchen, Cal accompanied Lawrence to the great room, where they continued their conversation about the Gardner property. Eventually, they heard happy footsteps romping down the stairs, and Noel and Marial appeared at the doorway. They were adorable in their matching flannel nightgowns with tiny pink rosebuds and pink slipper socks.

"We want to kiss you good night, Uncle Lawrence," Noel said. The old man opened his arms, and they both ran over to him. Then they hugged their dad and gave him kisses. Laura was beaming as she walked them back out of the room.

"Don't let the bedbugs bite," called Lawrence with a soft laugh.

CHAPTER 31

Early the next morning, after finishing a delicious farm breakfast of scrambled eggs, fried potatoes, and crisp bacon, Laura, Cal, and Lawrence donned jackets and joined Simon in the silver Volvo to head into town. Elsa had arrived in time to see them off. She helped the girls finish their breakfast, brush their teeth, and get dressed. She planned to take a hike around the farm and then let them rake up leaves and play in them. Liz would stop by later to talk about the festival and teach them more songs and dances.

Noel wanted to see the Big House, so Elsa had both girls slip into sweaters and then took them on the path through the pine forest. When they reached the clearing and saw the large log structure, their eyes shone with wonder. She led them into the dark building. Attached to the poles that held up the roof were the masks, carved faces painted half red and half black. Elsa explained they represented the spirits of the world that cared for plants and animals and people. She assured them that there was nothing to be afraid of. They were like angels or guardians. She also explained that there were three clans, the wolf, the turkey, and the turtle, and they would be sitting together during the festival. Marial announced that she wanted to be a turtle. Noel asked about the holes dug in the floor. Elsa said that there would be fires built inside the Big House each evening, to provide light. When the fires were lit, it was the signal for the people to enter and begin the ceremonies.

As they walked out through the blanketed door of the Big House, several children emerged from one of the wigwams. When they saw the girls with Elsa, they ran right over to them. Soon a parade like the pied piper's made its way down the path through the woods and into the yard beside the farmhouse, where Liz was waiting to lead them in games until it was time for their noon meal. After a bit, Simon pulled the Volvo into its usual parking space, and his three passengers emerged. They all found seats on the front porch where they watched the children at play while Elsa joined Simon in setting out lunch. When Noel and Marial came inside, Liz walked the other children back to the clearing and then returned by herself.

While they all ate, Liz related more stories about the ga-mwing festival. She talked about the symbolism of numbers: three was a holy number; four referred to the four corners of the earth and the four elements of earth, water, wind, and fire; and twelve was the interval of time for the cycle of ceremonial events. She explained how the hunt for deer had once been a significant ritual in the fall, and there would be venison served at the feasts. Lawrence suggested that Simon prepare some venison chili so the girls could taste deer meat, but Marial scrunched up her face, and Noel indicated she would never eat Bambi. When both girls went back to consuming their macaroni and cheese, the adults discussed the information from the people at the historical society. The publishing of Aaron's diary was indeed possible. They were also quite interested in examining the sea chest and perhaps adding it to their display. Then Cal turned to Liz and asked a few more questions about the schedule for ga-mwing.

"This year, the first three days of our gatherings will be filled with thanksgiving prayers and telling the stories from our families. We have to become reacquainted if we are going to discover a shared vision," Liz responded. Laura asked what would be happening instead of the three days of hunting, and Liz said she was not sure, but some had suggested holding vision-quests or sweat lodge ceremonies in order to clear minds and hearts.

"You may not wish to participate in everything we do, but after sundown each evening, we will dance and sing and pray. All three clans—wolf, turkey, and turtle—have distinctive rituals and costumes. It's interesting to watch." Liz addressed the girls again. "I will bring you special dresses to wear."

"I want feathers," said Noel.

"I want to be a turtle," demanded Marial.

Laura knew that, in spite of their excitement about the ceremonies, her daughters would not be able to stay awake for the entire evening. Cal suggested that they take turns putting the girls to bed and staying at the farmhouse with them. Elsa volunteered to help organize babysitters, folks she knew who were reliable and who would enjoy spending time with the girls.

That evening, just at sunset, Simon and Lawrence made their way through the crisp night air to the Big House, followed by Laura and her family. They found seats inside with the Turtle Clan near one of the fires. The sa-chem greeted everyone.

"All life is sacred, and everything is connected. Because we all draw our life from the same earth, because we all drink from the same waters, we are one people, we are one world, we are one creation." Then he called on the next person to speak. It was Lawrence! Liz tapped Laura's arm. Simon was standing beside Lawrence as he addressed the gathering.

"This is a special moment," she whispered.

In a clear but shaky voice, Lawrence recited a Quaker call to worship.

> Breathe in the purpose of this place; seek a calm within.
> Here we find forgiveness and forgive; feel the healing miracle begin.
> Breathe out the busy world, the failures of the week;
> Let go of pettiness and pride; wait for God to speak.
> Breathe in communion, friend to friend in this timeless hour;
> Different gifts are drawn to the Source of love and power.
> Breathe out the heart's full thanks for vision and for grace.
> Let Love extend through all our life beyond this place.

As Lawrence was helped to his seat, one of the elders from each clan in turn called on its members to share stories. Some were accounts of recent accomplishments or family celebrations. Others were remembrances of events from years past or stories of the lives of significant people from their group. In between each speech, the turtle rattles were sounded. At the signal of the sa-chem, the drummers would begin, and groups of men or women would get up and begin to do their circle dances. Liz took Noel's hand and led her into one of the women's circles where she followed their steps perfectly. Marial stood beside Laura, hopping up and down in time to the drumming. After almost a full hour of stories and dancing, the girls waved good night, and Laura guided them back to the farmhouse. Upstairs, the aroma of cedar smoke wafted through an open window somewhere. Noel and Marial fell sound asleep listening to the muffled melody of a distant flute.

Laura learned that those from the Quaker meeting who wished to come were welcomed at ga-mwing and that each evening there would be words from both the sa-chem and one of the *friends*. It had been a special honor for Lawrence to be the first, and when she found him seated in the kitchen with his coffee the next morning, she offered congratulations.

"Laura, it has always been that way with us, listening and learning from each other." She remembered the slip of paper in the Bible upstairs. How similar were the thoughts of the Quaker and the Le-nah-pe! For the next eleven days, she and her family would immerse themselves in the ga-mwing activities each evening and explored Laurel Hill and Chester Town during the days.

"Lawrence, you have to guard your energy," Simon had warned. "I'm going to try to get you home by midnight and let you sleep until nine in the mornings."

"That sounds like a good schedule for me, too," Laura offered. "Without a nap, I won't be able to keep up the pace either." Then they asked Lawrence to help them make a list of anything else Cal might do to give him a better idea of what living here might be like for them. Simon suggested contacting Kevin Perkins to schedule lunch at the golf club. Laura thought another visit to the historical society would be in order. Lawrence wanted to introduce Cal to Johnny Bruchhausan or take him for a beer at the Cuckoo Clock!

"On Sunday, we may browse the library at the Meeting House," Laura mentioned as Cal entered the room. "Uncle Lawrence said there are volumes of local history there."

"She's planning my life, isn't she?" Cal said, feigning dismay.

"She's her mother's daughter!" Lawrence replied, followed by a hearty laugh.

CHAPTER 32

The final evening of ga-mwing came and with it a new chill in the air that signaled the approach of winter weather. The ceremony began with all the elders gathered in the Big House to smoke tobacco. Laura and Cal watched as the pipe was shared in silence. Then women brought baskets filled with shell beads to the center of the room. They handed a certain amount to the sa-chem and then to each of the elders and the musicians and anyone who helped with the preparations for the festival. They also placed bead wampum and tobacco in a large bowl, a gift to the Creator.

The speech by the sa-chem had a somber tone. He summarized the discussions during the past twelve days. But in the end, the message was one of hopefulness that as a people they could take action to heal Mother Earth. Then as he looked around the Big House, his eyes fell on Laura. Walking over to her, he held out his hand. Elsa was seated beside her and nudged her. "Stand up," she whispered.

As Laura got to her feet, she understood that he was inviting her to bring the word from those who were not Le-nah-pe. Nervously, she looked to Liz for help. The old woman's eyes shone with pride. "Go with him," she mouthed. Simon was seated beside Lawrence, and both of them were nodding to her to speak. Laura turned to the sa-chem.

"You have something in your heart to share," he advised. "So you must speak it to us."

Laura should have been completely undone by what was happening. But as she looked into the fire closest to her, she saw the image of a falcon. She watched as it rose from the flames and flew up through the opening in the roof and into the sky. She turned her attention to the gathering and began to speak.

"Our planet is seriously ill, and we can feel her pain. We have been reminded of the many ways that the future health of Mother Earth is threatened by our human selfishness, ignorance, and greed. Our Mother needs attention, respect, love, care, and prayer." *Honor your mother. The words of the priest.* "In our comfortable homes, it is easy to remain untouched by the crisis. The poor of the world have suffered first. But soon *our* soil will be poisoned, *our* streams will die, *our* children will become sick." Her audience was quiet and attentive, and Laura felt a spirit guiding her words. "We were called here tonight to look again at our purpose for being in this world: to care for our Mother. That is an awesome task, and the path ahead is stony and filled with obstacles. It is our faith that will strengthen us to continue to walk the road to life. It is the Great Spirit's power that will work through us to restore what was made in the beginning. We must give and receive support one to the other. We must listen to the sounds of the world. We can change the tune we sing to one of peace and joy." As she finished, she seemed dazed, so Elsa went to her and guided her back to her place to shouts of "hoo" and "yee" from those in the room.

As in previous evenings, the clans shared their stories, interspersed with drums and dancing. This time, people shared their visions. Some spoke of the tragic conditions of the earth and others of actions they would take to improve the environment. A member of the citizens' group told about their work and invited others to join them. Lawrence encouraged them to hold gatherings at Bittersweet Acres whenever they needed to discuss the next steps to take. The elders agreed to lead their clan, keeping the issues and activities before their members. It was after ten o'clock when the closing prayer was offered by the sa-chem, each line repeated responsively by all the ga-mwing participants.

> May we walk as brothers and sisters on the same paths
> our grandfathers and grandmothers walked.

May we cross the same streams, watch the deer
leap in the forests
listen for the wolves that call from the hillsides,
look up to see the turkeys roosting in tree
branches
and the hawks circle overhead.
May we honor the frogs that splash, the fish that
swim,
and the turtles that sun on the log.
May the Great Spirit forever dwell in and among us.

The dancing and singing then moved outside and continued long into the night while people filled their plates from the bountiful feast of venison and turkey, corn, squash and other vegetables, bread freshly baked in stone ovens, apples from Lawrence's orchard, and other preserved fruits. Sassafras tea was ladled from a large kettle. When Laura returned to the farmhouse at dawn, she checked on the girls and then changed into her nightgown. Cal was already asleep and contentedly snoring. As she sat on the edge of the four-poster bed and opened the Bible, there was the paper she had tucked inside it.

May the stars carry your sadness away,
May the flowers fill your heart with beauty,
May hope forever wipe away your tears,
And, above all, may the silence make you strong.

Then opening the pot of hand cream, she smoothed it into her skin. Ga-mwing had been an incredible experience for her. *Had Cal been touched by any of the ceremonies?* As she crawled under the covers, she felt exhaustion overwhelm her body. She was thankful that she had no plans for the next day.

I am hot. It is sweltering in this place. When I first entered the wigwam, the warmth enveloped me like a woolen shawl. But the longer I sit here, the more intense the heat becomes. The aroma of tobacco and herbs fills the air. It almost suffocates me. I see stones piled at the doorway. I count them. There are twelve. Waves of heat radiate from them. I watch as the stones shimmer. They seem to float in the air.

Someone is ladling water onto the stones. Steam rises and saturates the tent and the air around me. It fills my lungs. I am trying to say a prayer in Le-nah-pe, words of thanksgiving for this ritual of purification and for the vision I have been given. Someone is singing outside the wigwam. I recognize that voice. I think it is my mother. Then again, it seems to sound like the voice of a young girl!

My eyes had been closed, and when I open them, I see my husband sitting beside me. He is covered with beads of sweat and praying as well. He looks at me and mouths the words to the song we both hear. When did he learn this language? When did I? We are in a strange and wonderful place.

I am comforted by his being here. We are truly together, not just our bodies but also our spirits. I can feel what he is thinking, understand what he is feeling. He must be able to do the same with me. In all our years together, I have never been so at one with him. I imagine if we were able to stand, our dance movements would be seamless, graceful. But it is too hot for me to move.

Are we meant to be so open, so connected to all people? I think of my mother. She was able to sense the inner thoughts of others. Our daughters. Would they grow up in tune with nature? I picture a gray fox with Noel's face, a Painted Turtle who looks like Marial. Cal is laughing at my thoughts.

Someone opens the top of the tent, and the steam rises quickly, straight up to the heavens. Shout of approval "hoo" and "yee" come from the people outside the sweat lodge. A falcon circles overhead—my spirit guide! Its cries offer blessing and assurance to me. Then some creature small and dark makes its way up from the stream and toward our tent. It is a beaver. The animal enters the tent and sits at the feet of my husband, who then reaches down with an open hand. I notice that the beaver carries a twig in its mouth. It drops the twig gently into Cal's open hand and then scurries off toward the stream again. The crowd murmurs as we exit the wigwam together. My husband is holding the gift twig over his heart with one hand. He reaches over and takes hold of my hand with the other.

CHAPTER 33

Laura realized her hand was gently resting in Cal's. They were lying side by side in the big four-poster bed, both lingering in that state between sleep and wakefulness. Opening their eyes at the same moment, they turned, smiled, and kissed. Laura sat up, her dream still vivid. What did it mean? Should she tell Cal about it?

Cal released her hand, rolled back over, sat on the edge of the bed, stretched, and yawned.

"You love it here, don't you?" he asked. "I see it in your eyes and hear it in your voice. You've never been so, well, at peace."

Laura thought back to the previous days and realized Cal was correct. She had been at ease, even with all that was going on. The girls, too, refrained from their usual fussing. She grinned. "I told you this place was magical!" she said, a reminder of her phone call to him back in August.

"And, now that the native festival had ended, we have to get ready for a traditional Thanksgiving," Cal commented, patting his stomach. "I need to fast a few days to prepare for that."

Laura reached over and put her hand on her husband's arm. She had to ask him an important question, the one that had been sitting in her heart for months now. "Cal, could *you* be happy here?" His silence was unsettling but not a surprise. Laura knew he always thought things through before giving an answer. "Well?"

Cal gently coaxed her over beside him. "Laura, I have never experienced the serenity I feel here. Even though the farm is close to Philadelphia and Chester Town, when we come up the driveway to this place, everything else melts away." He paused and turned his head away from Laura, looking out the window. Was he crying? "I love your uncle and want to make the years he has left good. If that requires you're being here with him, *our* being here, I think we have to consider it."

He turned back and looked at Laura. His eyes were wet. She wrapped her arms around him and sobbed in relief and joy. She was sure that they were meant to come to Bittersweet Acres. Cal spoke next.

"Let's get dressed. There is something I found yesterday that I want to show you and the girls!" The energy in his voice startled Laura. He headed into the bathroom, talking over his shoulder. "It's down by the stream. A beaver dam."

Noel and Marial were already perched on their stools in the kitchen when Cal and Laura came down for breakfast. Simon had placed hot Belgian waffles in front of them on the bright-orange pottery plates Laura remembered from her very first breakfast in this house. Noel was depositing a blueberry in each of the sections of her waffle while Marial had sprinkled as much confectioner's sugar on the counter as on her plate.

"Oh, Simon, you should have called us to feed the children," protested Laura.

"Nonsense. Everything is under control, right, girls?"

Their mouths were full of pastry and syrup, so they just nodded.

Simon walked over to the wall calendar as he spoke to Laura. "I was planning to go get Dad and bring him here for Thanksgiving. Would you mind picking him up tomorrow? That would give us Tuesday and Wednesday with him, and then he'll already be here for the Chester Town parade and our dinner. I could drive him back on Friday."

That was one piece of Laura's life that remained unresolved. She wanted to introduce her family to Jude Andrews. Perhaps doing it in this restful setting made the most sense. Laura looked at Cal.

"I would be happy to have some time to get to know this 'mystery man,'" he responded to her glance. The way he spoke was lighthearted, she noted, without a trace of bitterness. He continued, addressing Simon. "We'll make the trip, and you can focus on food preparation, not that we ever need to eat again!"

Laura was just wondering where Jude would sleep when Simon answered her question. "I think he'll be happy over in the addition with Lawrence. That upstairs room is vacant, at least for now." Cal asked again, "Laura, is all this okay with you?"

"Yes," she affirmed. "I want him to have time to play with his granddaughters and also to meet with some of the folks in our citizen's group. He has offered to put us in touch with people who can help us."

The girls had finished their breakfast, so they ran off to find Uncle Lawrence. He had promised to show them a photo of their grandmother on her pony and other old pictures of the farm, back when they kept animals. Laura and Cal sat across from each other at the kitchen table, sipping sweet cinnamon coffee and munching on toast and homemade apple butter. From his post by the sink, Simon shared with Cal the idea of taking the girls to tour Philadelphia when they went to pick up Jude. "You can leave after breakfast, walk around the historic district, and have lunch at the Automat downtown."

"I'd like that," responded Cal. "It sounds like just enough for the girls at this age. We'll save the art museum and the zoo for the spring." Laura's eyes widened. Her husband *was* making a long-term commitment to this place!

A knock on the screen door announced the arrival of Liz and Randy. They explained they had finished helping the ga-mwing campers load their vehicles and clean up the grounds. Most of them had positive reactions to the gathering and expressed the desire to teach Le-nah-pe traditions in their families and to practice the old ways whenever possible.

"Liz," Laura ventured, "I had a dream about my spirit guide, the falcon, again last night."

"Good," the old woman responded. "Whenever our guides appear, we are blessed. They let us know we are on the correct path."

"Well, I also dreamed about another animal. A beaver."

Laura noticed that Liz and Randy gave each other a knowing glance.

Then the old woman spoke, and her voice became that of a storyteller once again.

"When the beaver comes into your life, it is a sign for you to begin the work on your project. The size of the project does not matter. What is important is that you follow through on your plans." Both Laura and Cal listened intently. "The beaver is a sign for getting organized. They build their home and maintain it, even if it may not seem ideal. So perhaps you are being reminded to start getting your tools together. You may not know which ones you will need, but when the time comes, you must be ready, for then you will need to move quickly."

"That's really interesting," Cal responded. "I found a beaver dam just yesterday, down beside the stream. I think it was empty, but I'm not sure."

Liz smiled. "Or it is just waiting for her entire family to move in."

"Where are your girls?" asked Randy.

Laura had to think for a moment. It was such a luxury to have so many adults keeping watch over her children. "Ah, they're with Uncle Lawrence," she remembered.

"We told Elsa to come over. She wants to show Noel how to embroider, and she has a Le-nah-pe doll for Marial."

"I have to go to town, a quick grocery run," Simon announced. "Laura, want to come along?"

"Sure. What about you, Cal?"

"I want to spend some time reading up on the water quality issues you all have been trying to address. Liz, can I pick your brain about it too?"

"Yes, of course. First, let's go find out what's going on with your great-uncle."

Liz, Cal, and Randy strolled out of the kitchen and across the hall to the farmhouse addition. Simon and Laura reviewed the meal plans for Thanksgiving Day, as well as other food they might want to have on hand. Simon telephoned his father and confirmed that, yes, he would love to come the next day and stay through Friday lunch. "But we will be decorating for Christmas on the weekend, and it's quite a big party. I have to be back for that!" Simon smiled, pleased that his dad was so engaged in his community.

The next day, Simon took Lawrence for his routine doctor's visit. He had helped Cal map out their tour of Philadelphia and sent him off with Laura and the girls. After exploring historic Philadelphia and eating their lunch selections at Horn & Hardart, the four of them swung by Anderson House to pick up Laura's dad. By the time they returned to the farm, Noel and Marial were asleep on each side of their mom in the backseat while Jude, seated up front, was still regaling Cal with the benefits of living and working in the area. Elsa came out the side door and helped Laura get the girls inside. It was chilly, and the clouds were building in the west. Snow was expected that evening, she informed them.

Meanwhile, Liz and Elsa had prepared Jude's room with clean linens, and Randy carried his overnight case upstairs. Lawrence was delighted to greet his holiday visitor. The two sat in front of the fireplace in the great room, and Simon brought in a bottle of sherry and two crystal glasses. The whole house filled with the aroma of the garlic marinara sauce simmering on the stove and homemade bread baking in the oven. Cal and Laura settled down in the parlor, where someone had also lit a crackling fire. The girls were on the floor in front of them, working together to solve a wooden jigsaw puzzle of farm animals, a gift from their great-great-uncle.

Cal spoke first. "Laura, I can see how much your family means to you. Even you and Jude are meant to be together now. I keep thinking that there must be a way for us to make a living here." He paused and then smiled. "You have already figured it out, haven't you, Falcon Woman?"

"Well," Laura began, "isn't it interesting that after law school, I took the multijurisdictional bar exam so I can practice in Pennsylvania, New York, and New Jersey?" Cal had forgotten that. "And don't you have some connections in environmental engineering circles that might just be useful here? We could explore it." Cal agreed with his wife and listened as she continued to make her case. "The school district is great for the girls. I know we'd be giving up a lot. And we'd have to sell our house in Harrisburg. So be honest, now. Would you be content living here?"

Cal turned his body slightly in order to face his wife. Then he took her hand. "There are a lot of details we'd have to work out, but, honey, you have convinced me that we ought to begin planning to move to Bittersweet Acres."

Laura's eyes were shining. "Like Liz says, when the beaver appears to you, get organized. We need to get our tools together." Laura snuggled closer to Cal. The girls finished their puzzle and climbed up on the sofa between them.

Laura hugged them and smiled. "When the time comes, we want to be ready!"

CHAPTER 34

The "time" came the following spring. Simon had relocated to the farmhouse addition once Cal and Laura announced their plans to live in Laurel Hill. He settled comfortably in its upstairs bedroom and was finishing up renovation of the kitchen in that part of the house. Cal and Laura sold their home in suburban Harrisburg and made the move to the farm. Laura's family had the original part of the home completely to themselves, although they all ate dinner together most evenings. Noel was content to be in the bedroom that had belonged to Lawrence. After a few months, however, Marial moved into what had been Simon's room. Both girls enjoyed helping transform the airy space in the attic into a playroom much as it had been for their grandmother when she was a child.

Laura was welcomed into a law firm in nearby Plum Hill. She was assigned right away to work on litigation related to Superfund sites. Cal's credentials eventually landed him a position with Rutgers University Cooperative Extension in their water resources program. He set to work designing and implementing storm water infrastructure. A number of companies retained him as a consultant, helping them address community water resource issues in the Delaware Estuary. Together he and Laura formed *Laurel Hill Citizens for Clean Water*—an advocacy group for stricter water testing and treatment.

Jude Andrews became a frequent visitor to the farm over the years. He seemed to thrive on having long conversations with Lawrence about old times and watching his granddaughters grow. Being with his children, Simon and Laura, was also a blessing.

On one late-summer afternoon in 1993, when the sun was still warm and the farmhouse bathed in gold, many of the folks of

Chester Town and Laurel Hill gathered at Bittersweet Acres to cel-
ebrate Lawrence Gardner's one hundredth birthday. In spite of his
frail body, his mind was as sharp as ever. He never seemed to tire of
sharing stories about the Gardner family with his friends and neighbors and listening to them recounting their own tales from life in the
olden days.

After the guest departed, Cal and Laura sat with her great-uncle
on the front porch while Marial and Noel were being entertained by
Simon and Elsa in the parlor. The beautiful young Le-nah-pe woman
had won Simon's affections. They shared a deep love for the land
and the farm, and now for each other. Their wedding would be held
in November at the Episcopal Church in town, and the reception
would become part of a ga-mwing celebration.

That afternoon, Lawrence was resting in his favorite wicker
chaise with a plaid blanket tucked around his thin legs. There was a
slight smile on his face. Laura's own anxious feelings had vanished,
she noticed. Lawrence leaned his head back and closed his eyes.

"I still hear the voices, you know." Laura thought of the first
time he had told her that. She looked over at Cal, who seemed to
accept her great-uncle's words without question. She smiled because,
of course, she had heard voices too. "Don't mention it to Simon or
anyone really, because they will ship me off to 'the home' sure as anything." The old man paused. "I never *see* the people, you know. I just
hear their conversations."

"Are they happy?" Laura inquired as she had the first time.

"Most times. My sister Marial is fussing with me or Christina,
or maybe it's our mom calling us all to dinner." Laura nodded her
understanding.

"Now that I live here," Laura admitted, "I feel so close to my
mom that some days I think I can hear her talking to me. I guess
memories are like that." The old man smiled in agreement.

Later that evening, Laura was preparing for bed and remembering fondly her trip to Laurel Hill four years before. She thought of
the first night she spent in her grandmother's bedroom and all the
mysteries she encountered. The pot of herbal hand cream had special
properties, she had discovered. Lights in the forest were neighbors

preparing for ga-mwing. Voices on the stairs were those of women friends. All these had logical explanations. Her longing to bring her daughters here had been fulfilled. Now they were soundly sleeping across the hall. Pictures of her family were on the table on the landing with the rest of the Gardner clan. And on pleasant evenings after the girls went to bed, she enjoyed the night sounds and evening breezes as she sat on the front porch with Cal. It seemed that her quest was finally over. She slipped under the same wedding ring quilt that still adorned the four-poster bed and curled up next to her sleeping husband.

EPILOGUE

I hear a noise, a muffled murmur. I know it is somewhere here in the house. I sit up and get out of bed, all the time wondering, listening. Voices! I open the bedroom door, but the sound is not on the staircase. Turning back into my room, I realize now it is a conversation taking place in the great room.

Uncle Lawrence! Someone is with him. Something is happening. I place my hand on the wall and unlock the hidden panel door. I am greeted by a potent whiff of pine and cedar incense rising from below. As I breathe in the familiar aromas, I recognize the old man's quavering tones.

"I can't go outside. What is that sister of mine thinking?" His muttering makes no sense to me.

Another voice, soft and gentle. A woman.

"Come with me now. We've all been waiting for you."

"My jacket!" Lawrence does not sound angry but urgent. "Please hand me my jacket."

I hear movement, the scuff of soft shoes, the rustle of sheets.

"There. Is that better?" It's the woman.

"Thank you." Lawrence's voice again.

"You smell like all outdoors!" comments the woman.

"Is that a good thing?"

"You bet it is!"

Laura opened her eyes and sat up in bed. She grabbed her robe and hurried down the steps to the great room. When she reached Uncle Lawrence, he was lying in his bed. A contented smile graced his weathered face, the look that Laura had come to love. She touched his hand. It was icy cold. Wrapping her robe around her, she rushed over to the front window. One light, then two, moved through the orchard. Then more sparks gathered around, like fireflies dancing in time with an unheard melody. She watched the twinkling cluster as it moved along the edge of the field and into the pine trees. It became smaller and dimmer, and then suddenly it was gone and the forest was dark again. She let out a sigh but did not cry. Not just then. She turned back to the room and took a seat in the ladder-back rocker beside her great-uncle's body. Quietly she sang,

> 'Tis the gift to be simple, 'tis the gift to be free
> 'tis the gift to come down where you ought to be
> And when we find ourselves in the place just right
> 'Twill be in the valley of love and delight.

Bittersweet Acres had been home to generations of Gardners. It had become sacred space for Lawrence, and a touchstone of joy and peace for Christina. Now this place was gifted to Laura; and the spirits of those she cherished would linger here, just out of sight, in all the places they loved.